dirty truths

BOYS OF BELLEROSE
BOOK 2

JAYMIN EVE

TATE JAMES

Tate James

Jaymin Eve

Dirty Truths: Boys Of Bellerose #2
Copyright © Tate James, Jaymin Eve 2022
All rights reserved
First published in 2023
James, Tate
Eve, Jaymin
Dirty Truths: Boys of Bellerose #2

Cover design: Emily Wittig
Editing: Jax Garren (line).

This book is dedicated to our foolish optimism and chronic overachieving. It's just a match made in heaven, baby! Or maybe the other place, come to think of it. Whatever, it works.

follow us

For book discussions, giveaways, and general shit talking from Tate or Jaymin, please check out their reader groups on Facebook:

Tate James – The Fox Hole
Jaymin Eve – The Nerd Herd

content warning

Boys of Bellerose is a rock star mafia reverse harem
story where the female main character finds her
happily ever after with more than one lover. It's a four
book series, so cliffhangers should be expected
throughout, until they find their happy ending.
This series touches on darker themes and includes both
graphic sex and graphic violence.
Some characters have traumatic pasts, and there is
mention of miscarriage, abuse, drug use, addiction, and
murder.
Should you have concerns, please apply discretion in
deciding if this story is right for you.

- Tate & Jaymin

one

JACE

The blonde chick cried out as I thrust another two times, before the lackluster rush of my release had me blowing my fucking load. She continued to moan and writhe below me, no doubt hoping I'd make her come too, but I was done.

I made no excuses about who I was these days. They wanted the rock star cock, and they got it, but this dick gave zero fucks about them or their pleasure.

Rolling off her, I found my pants in the next seconds, pulled them on, and headed for the door. She called out after me with a breathy *Jace, baby,* but I was already done. Finished. Forgotten her damn name.

Had I even asked her name? Probably not. She was a

bad choice, anyway. From a glance, she looked too much like *her*. Billie *fucking* Bellerose.

Security waited for me outside, one of them handing me a leather jacket, which I shrugged on. I ended up without a shirt more times than not these days, but these guys were well trained. No one said a word as they followed me down to the car that was waiting out front. I'd paid for the whole night, but I never stayed longer than it took me to get off.

I kept my head down as I slid into the backseat of the blacked-out SUV—not wanting to make myself an easy target for the paparazzi constantly following me around—so I didn't realize I had company until the car door closed.

"Don't fucking start," I growled, pulling a rolled joint out of the pocket of my jacket. I'd raided Rhett's stash before he woke up this morning; he was so fucked up these days that he'd never notice.

Grayson gave a long-suffering sigh but said nothing. Yet. He just waited for me to light up, then stole the joint from my lips before I even got a full drag.

"Dick," I muttered, waiting for him to take a puff before he handed it back.

He exhaled heavily, filling the back of the car with thick, musky weed smoke. "Good shit," he grunted. "Rhett's?"

I just tipped my head back, filling my own lungs as my head swirled. I'd been hitting drugs and alcohol harder than usual, but nothing compared to Rhett. Poor bastard was suffering a broken heart. I got it. I'd been there, with the same ruthless bitch.

"Why're you here, Gray?" I drawled, refocusing on the broad-shouldered fuck beside me.

He leveled me with a hard glare. "I need a reason? I thought we were a band, Jace."

I scoffed, an ugly sound. "Don't give me that shit, Gray. Hurricane Billie destroyed us, and you know it."

His mouth twisted with anger. He'd been more into that temptress bitch than he'd ever let on, but I could recognize it in his eyes every time I said her name. I almost wished she would turn up again, just to see Gray rip her a new asshole.

"Billie isn't responsible for this," he said in a low rumble. "Flo is. And Tucker. If they hadn't—"

"Bull*shit*," I spat. "Bullshit. Flo and Tom fucked up by trying to sell her back to the Riccis, but look how it all turned out. She wasn't abducted, she *ran away*. Willingly. No one forced her to go, Gray, she left of her own volition. The sooner you two accept it, the better you'll both be."

Grayson's fist balled in his lap, and I got the feeling he'd happily punch me in the teeth right now. I didn't

3

even care. Maybe it'd be good if he did... make me *feel* something other than numb.

"How can you be so sure?" he asked softly. "You, of all people—"

"Yeah!" I shouted, sitting up to glare daggers. "*Me*, of all people. I know her so much better than you, regardless of what seductive stories she sucked you in with. I know you've worked it up in your head that her video message was coerced, but you're fucking delusional. No one forces Billie Bellerose to do anything she doesn't wanna do."

Grayson said nothing in response, but his silent disagreement was deafening. Even after Billie had sent a video message *specifically* telling him to stop looking for her, he couldn't accept that she wasn't in some kind of danger.

I'd always known Rhett had a crazy hero complex, but Gray took it to a whole other level. That first week after she'd disappeared, he'd turned into a total stranger. A scary, violent stranger. The only thing that had stopped the insanity was Billie's message telling him she was *fine* and to please *respect her choice.*

Fucking whore.

They couldn't say I didn't warn them, though. Either of them. I'd said it from day one—she was toying with them and sooner or later she'd go running back to

Angelo. That smug son of a bitch always came out on top.

"The label has been trying to contact you," Gray said, changing the subject. "Did you call them back?"

I grunted an annoyed sound. "Fuck the label."

Grayson's elbow hit my ribs and knocked the air out of my lungs, making me choke on the inhale of smoke I'd just taken. "Screw you, Adams," he growled. "This band is more than just you. You're fucking with all our careers while you sulk about the girl who broke your heart *eight damn years ago*."

I narrowed my eyes at him. "You're one to talk, asshole."

"Call head office back, Jace. In case you forgot, we signed contracts and we're currently in breach." His expression was impassive. Cold. Closed off. I envied him for that ability.

It irritated me that he was right. Not only had we cut our tour short—right before going international—but we also owed our record label a new album, and right now I had a grand total of fucking *nothing* to submit.

Trouble was, I also had no desire to write new music. Before Billie reappeared, I'd been struggling with writer's block. I couldn't keep writing music about her; it'd been too damn long and I was *tired*. But then

5

she came crashing back into my life, and now every time I picked up a pen, *all* I could think of was *her*.

"I'm too fucking sober for this shit," I grumbled, reaching forward to knock on the privacy glass dividing us from the driver. "Let me out here."

Gray was two seconds away from smashing my head into the window, I could see it written all over him. Better I remove myself than have to deal with a broken nose.

"Jace, you can't just keep *faking* it. Sooner or later, you have to man up and face your damage."

I scoffed. "That's where you're wrong, Gray." I popped my door open as the car rolled to a stop in front of another busy nightclub and climbed out on slightly wobbly legs. "I'm young, rich, famous, *hot*. I'm living my best fucking life with no damage left to face. *She* ran back into the arms of her backstabbing lover, so I'm washing my hands clean."

Not waiting for his response, I slammed the car door shut and cut the line to the entrance of the club. A bouncer put out a hand to stop me, then within seconds realized who I was and let me in. It was nice being famous sometimes.

Ralph, my bodyguard, shadowed me, like he always did, and I ignored him, like I always did. Gray had gotten under my skin, and I was suddenly too worked up to try and go home. Rhett would be there, wallowing in self-pity, and I couldn't face that yet.

I'd never regretted sharing a penthouse apartment with my best friend, but damn, it was growing uncomfortable.

My gaze scanned the crowd as I pushed my way over to the bar. I needed a shot of some hard liquor, then probably something stronger. Glancing over my shoulder, I tipped my head to Ralph. "Find me some coke or something," I ordered him. "Gray fucked my mood right up."

Ralph was a professional. He just dipped a short nod, then melted into the crowd to do as I'd asked. He wouldn't be far away if anything happened. But I wasn't worried.

"Hey, you're Jace Adams, right?" A breathy female voice jerked my attention to the left. My undoubtedly bloodshot eyes scanned the girl from head to toe. She was young, maybe twenty-one at best, and her mousy blonde hair was tied up in two high ponytails. Her whole look screamed *innocent,* but the calculating gleam in her eye said she was more than down to party with a rock star.

"I sure am," I replied with a sly, flirtatious smile.

Her eyes sparkled with excitement, and she wet her lips. "Are you here with the rest of Bellerose?"

That soured my mood. Another girl who'd rather fuck Rhett or Gray over me? Maybe I was losing my good looks.

"Nope," I replied, turning back to the bar and giving her a cold shoulder. It didn't last long, though, as her delicate fingers threaded around my wrist to pull my attention once more. "What?"

Her brows lifted at my harsh tone, then she lowered her eyes in a practiced coy gesture. "Can I suck your dick in the bathroom?"

Christ. It wasn't even a challenge anymore.

"Sure," I agreed with a shrug. She grinned and tightened her grip on my wrist, eagerly pulling me after her as she led the way to the bathrooms. Ralph passed me a small baggy of coke on my way past, and I smirked to let him know where I was headed.

The girl wasted no time, undoing my pants before I even locked the stall door, dropping to her knees on the disgusting floor, and wrapping her lips around my soft cock.

"Fucking hell," I grunted, leaning my shoulders against the door and grabbing her two ponytails in my fists. It was easy enough to close my eyes and picture... *someone else.* That got me hard. I let my eyes open just a crack, just enough to squint at her in the dim light and *pretend.*

I was rough with her, not giving a fuck about her feelings, then blew my load down her throat without even a word of warning. She choked on it, understandably, but I was already pulling my jeans back up over my wet dick.

"Thanks," I muttered, opening the door while she spluttered and coughed. I crossed to the vanity where a girl stared in shock, her hands under a running tap totally forgotten.

Ignoring her, I dried off a patch of the marble counter and dumped out a small pile of coke. From my pocket, I pulled out my black AmEx to cut a couple of lines, then used an already rolled hundred dollar bill to snort one. If you're going to be a cliché, you need to go the whole hog.

"Jace, what—" The girl stumbled out of the stall, still wiping her face from where her eyes had watered and streaked her makeup. She cut off abruptly when she saw the other girl standing there staring at me. Then glared.

"Here," I said, handing blondie my rolled up note. "Help yourself. You earned it." I grabbed her face and kissed her, tasting myself on her tongue and feeling nothing but self-loathing. She was just... some girl. Not my girl.

With a deeply disappointed sigh, I walked away and left her to the remaining lines.

"Fuck," I breathed as I stalked back into the club. There was only one reason I'd gotten hard for that chick, and it was her vague resemblance to Billie goddamn Bellerose. Maybe Gray was right... I needed therapy.

"You good?" Ralph asked as I exited the club once more.

I gave a bitter laugh. "Far from it." Then I groaned and scrubbed my hands over my face. I'd make an appointment with my therapist in the morning. "Let's go home. I need to make sure Rhett's still alive."

That wasn't even an exaggeration. My best friend had been *spiraling,* and I'd done nothing to help. Fuck, worse than that, I'd just left him to deal with his heartbreak alone because deep down I was jealous. I wouldn't want Billie back if she fucking *paid* me... but I was still jealous.

I hated that girl more now than ever before. It wasn't just me she'd hurt, it was Rhett too. And Gray. Billie Bellerose had a lot to fucking answer for, so yeah... maybe it was time for a new album.

two

GRAYSON

The phone rang once before I answered it. I'd been sitting and waiting. Expecting the call to arrive at any time. And in my impatience, I refused to move from the fucking computer until that happened.

"Talk to me," I said shortly.

There was a pause, and a breathy sigh released before Johnson said, "She's still exactly where she's been for the past week: in Siena, holed up in the Ricci main mansion on the other side of the river. She hasn't left the house since her shopping trip last week."

Dark anger was my constant companion, but if I let

myself fall into the swirling pit in my gut, I'd be no better than Jace and Rhett. Broken and fucking useless.

Broken men saved no one. I knew that from experience, and I wasn't quite ready to give up my responsibility toward a certain blonde.

"Stay on her," I told him. "Report in tomorrow, and this time don't be fucking late."

Johnson was a piece of shit, but he was good at his job. Tracking, stalking, sticking his nose into business that wasn't his to know. In this situation, that skillset was exactly what I needed to ensure the situation with Billie wasn't escalating.

Hanging up before he could say another word, I sank back into the plush computer chair, tapping my finger on the table as I breathed through my fury. The urge to storm the Ricci compound and kill every motherfucker there was riding me hard, and even when I dropped my head in my hands and massaged at my temples to relieve some of the tension, that urge didn't fade.

When Billie took off on us two months ago, I'd immediately gone into action, but thanks to the Riccis' money and pull with the local law, it had taken me almost two weeks to find out where she was being kept. Another week to see her with my own eyes, as she trailed listless after Angelo. That piece of shit appeared protective enough as he escorted her to the car, opening the door and buckling her in, but there was no look of joy or happiness on her face.

She was a prisoner. I knew the signs, but I also recognized that there was more than just a physical hold keeping her with the Riccis now. A stronger reason held her there, and until that mystery was unraveled, I couldn't go starting a fucking war to break her out.

Hence why Johnson was keeping a permanent eye on her, to the sweet tune of eight grand a week. I'd pay ten times that to know the second she was in danger. I was too fucking famous these days to linger easily in the shadows, so Johnson was the best option.

Despite what Jace and Rhett believed, I knew that Billie hadn't left us through her own choice. If there was one thing I could do, it was read people, and that girl had been all in with Bellerose. Until she wasn't, and the reason for that was the mystery I still had to unravel.

Pushing back, I climbed to my feet, shutting down my encrypted files that contained everything I knew about the situation so far. I'd had to reach out to members of my old family back in Hawaii for help with hacking into the police system. My skills were there, but I didn't have the right tech setup to keep my identity a secret. In truth, I probably didn't even have the skills any longer. The world of hacking moved fast, with new techniques and skills required to keep up, and I'd grown rusty in my life with Bellerose.

There was one skill set I'd never lose though—cold-blooded killing. If Billie needed me, that skill was far more useful than hacking. Back home, I'd been the muscle. The silent death stalking you in the night. They called me *The Maker*, as in, you'd just met your maker, and I would be the last fucking thing you saw in this world.

The sun had all but set by the time I left my office and wandered back into the main living area of my house. I was debating a shower or food when there was a knock at the door. Since I lived in one of the most secure estates in Naples, there was no fucking reason for anyone to be knocking at my door.

Only Rhett and Jace had free access, and those fuckers would be out of their minds by now, unable to speak, let alone get their asses here. Moving toward the door, I lifted my Glock from the entry drawer and palmed it by my right side. When I reached the door, I sure as fuck didn't peer through the peep hole. Or as I liked to call them, *target holes*. It was one of my favorite ways to blow someone's brains out without even having to see them.

Grabbing the handle, I counted to three, ready to

yank the door open so fast that whoever was on the other side would be taken by surprise. That split second was all I'd need to end them if they were here trying to fuck with me. It had been a long time since I'd had to worry about an assassin on my tail, but after reaching out to my old contacts, there was a risk. I'd no doubt reminded those evil assholes that I'd gotten out and was living my own life.

Then there was the Ricci family. They might have picked up on Johnson and were here to deal with the issue.

Regardless, whoever was on the other side, they were in for a big fucking surprise if they thought I'd go down easily.

Putting my plan into action, I silently twisted the handle and jerked the door open. My gun was in their face in the next second.

When a very feminine gasp registered, I winced and relaxed my grip on the weapon.

"Of all the people I wasn't expecting to turn up on my doorstep..." I tucked my gun into the back of my jeans and folded my arms, glaring down at the girl on my porch. "What do you want, Florence?"

She chewed her lip as she met my gaze, her own eyes scared and uncertain. "Gray... I need your help." There was a whine to her voice that she never used to have. It betrayed weakness and, honestly, didn't give me even a flash of compassion for her situation.

"You made your bed, Flo," I replied, ready to close the door in her face. I was still *pissed* at her for what she and Tom had tried to do. They'd set Billie up. They hadn't given a shit what the Riccis wanted to do with her—*to* her—and hadn't said a damn word until she was long gone.

"Gray, *please*," Flo begged. "I can't... Please don't shut me out. You guys are all I have, and I'm *sorry*, okay? I'm so fucking sorry, but there was no harm done in the end, right? Billie went with them willingly, so she is probably grateful that we called her boyfriend."

My teeth ground together as I bit back the need to tear her head off. She didn't know I'd put a tracker on Billie, and if I showed anyone those surveillance photos, they'd say she looks *fine*.

Fucking *fine*. Such a pile of shit. But without any concrete proof, it was just the suspicions of a paranoid, angry man.

"What do you want, Florence?" I asked again, instead of saying everything I really wanted to say.

She wet her lips, her fingers twisting in the hem of her Bellerose tour t-shirt. "We still owe the label a new record, don't we? I know they aren't happy about us canceling the rest of the tour, so I thought—"

My bitter laughter cut her off, and her hopeful expression drained away. "You thought, what? Get the band back together and make some music?" I shook my head, then ran a hand over my hair. "You're deluded, girl."

"Gray!" she exclaimed, slapping her hand against the door when I tried to close it. "Come on, I'm serious. I can't... *fuck*, I can't afford to pay the label back for our advance, and if they sue..."

I frowned, peering at her harder. "How? Where the fuck is all your money, Flo?" As far as I knew, she didn't own property or cars and always dressed in thrift-store clothes and band merch. Even without our tour—which we were in deep legal shit over cancelling—we still made crap loads from album sales. None of us should have to work again for the rest of our lives.

Her eyes dipped to the ground. "Tom took it all," she whispered. "I'm totally broke, and I'm desperate."

My lips parted in shock as her confession sank in. Then my fist balled up and I punched a hole through my wall while picturing Tom Tuckers face.

"Shit, Gray!" Flo exclaimed, reaching for my hand as I shook drywall dust off my knuckles. "Dude, what the hell?"

I gently extracted my hand from her grip, not

feeling the cuts I'd opened up over old scars. "You're a fucking idiot, Florence, you know that?"

She grimaced. "Yeah, I know."

I gave a heavy sigh and nodded. "It's not up to me, and you know it. If you're going to come back to Bellerose..."

"I know," she whispered, "I need Rhett to forgive me."

"That's gonna be harder than you think," I told her, squinting down at my hand. Shit, it was bleeding on my cream carpet. "I'll get you in to see him; the rest is on you. So I suggest you come up with a fucking impeccable argument because you won't get another shot. Clear?"

Flo bobbed her head frantically in agreement. "Clear."

I cast my eyes to the sky, wishing for not the first time that I had faith in a higher power. Maybe then I could shirk the weight of everyone's problems onto someone more qualified.

"I'll call you," I grunted, making it clear that I wasn't inviting her inside. She didn't need to see my surveillance notes and photographs of Billie scattered all over my coffee table. It'd only make me look obsessive and desperate, when really, I was just *concerned*.

Florence looked like she was going to hug me, so I gave her a little nudge back out of my doorway, then shut the door fully this time. I hated people coming to my house. The next person who showed up unannounced probably would get shot.

"Okay, thanks!" she called through the door, her voice muffled. "I'll just... I'll wait for your call! It was good to see you, Gray!"

Huffing an irritated sigh, I went to clean up my hand. Fucking Flo... we should have known Tom was screwing her over. Hell, we did know, just not that he was *also* stealing from her.

If I got my hands on that slimy shit...

My fist tightened around the bottle of antiseptic I'd just pulled from my bathroom cabinet, crushing the plastic and squirting brown-orange liquid everywhere, picturing Tom's head exploding. If that was the worst that happened to Tom Tucker, he'd be getting off easy.

three

RHETT

"One tequila... two tequila... three tequila..." I sang to myself between shots of amber liquor, barely even feeling the burn anymore. Hell, my veins stopped pumping blood weeks ago; I was pure alcohol and cocaine now.

What was I saying again?

Fuzzy confusion crossed my eyes as I slid from the couch to the carpet, my head swimming too hard to hold me upright.

"Floor." Someone else muttered nearby.

The couch dipped near where my head rested, and I cracked my eyes to squint up at Jace. "Huh?"

He nodded to my empty shot glasses. "One tequila, two tequila, three tequila, *floor.*" He pointed at my position on the carpet. Funny fuck.

I didn't have it in me to laugh, so I just grunted. Then yawned. When was the last time I'd slept?

"Come on, I'll help you get to bed," Jace told me, reading my mind. Or hell, maybe I'd said it out loud. Who knew these days?

Still, I batted his helpful hand away when he tried to pull me up off the carpet. "Fuck off," I mumbled. "I don't need your help."

Jace knew me well enough that he didn't argue, just sat back and watched as I rolled onto all fours like a drunken armadillo, then started crawling my ass out of the living room. I had enough experience being wasted not to try walking upright. Last time, I'd stumbled into a doorframe and given myself a black eye.

By the time I'd dragged myself into my tangled mess of sheets, I'd totally forgotten Jace was following me. I flinched when he dropped a bucket onto the hardwood floor beside my bed, then glared up at him.

"What?" he replied, scowling. "Can't hurt to have it nearby for when you start to sober up."

I scoffed, my eyes rolling back into my head. Fucking hell, when did we move onto a ship? That was

21

the only logical explanation for why I was swaying so much. Right? Or maybe that was the tequila.

"Fuck off with your smug face, Jace," I mumbled. Then snickered. "That rhymes. Smug face Jace. Gimme those." I waved a hand at my bedside table where a pill bottle sat half empty.

Jace picked it up and read the label, nosy prick, then sighed. "Rhett... you're a goddamn mess, bro. You need to clean up."

My only response was to stick my hand out, asking silently for the pills again.

Jace glowered, but he uncapped the bottle and shook two little white pills out into my waiting palm. I didn't bother with water, just dry swallowed them both and snuggled my face into a pillow. They'd work quickly now that I had so much liquor in my system. Would I wake up? Debatable. There was a reason you're not supposed to mix booze and sleeping pills, but it was fucking preferable to the insomnia.

"I'll be here when you wake up," Jace said with a sad voice, probably thinking I had already passed out. "We can talk then."

Not fucking likely. Jace was *never* here when I was even remotely sober. Too busy running from his own past come back to haunt him. Too preoccupied ignoring his own baggage and indulging in his addiction of choice: anonymous pussy.

I wished I could do the same... but the idea of fucking a groupie made me physically ill.

Or maybe that was just the tequila again.

Who knew? Who fucking cared?

"Get up, Silver," someone said *way* too close to my ear.

I winced, covering my head with a pillow to dull the sound. "Screw off, dickhead," I snarled, not giving a shit if they could hear me. It was Jace again. I think. Maybe Gray? Nah, too melodic for Gray, who sounded more like he sang in a thrash metal band. Jace, then. Dick.

Blankets were ripped off me far too abruptly, and my body flailed in reflex.

Jace's unmistakable snicker made me quit thrashing.

"Fuck *off*," I shouted, sitting up to reach for my blanket. It was too damn cold to be chilling in my boxers and nothing else. I was too goddamn hungover. Where was the bottle of tequila?

"Get up, Silver," he repeated, screwing up his face. "And take a fucking shower; you *stink*."

I caught the towel he tossed at me and lifted an arm to sniff my pit. Oh yeah, he wasn't wrong. The fact that my own smell made my stomach roll and twist was the *only* reason I dragged my aching ass off to the bathroom. Jace's bullying had fucking nothing to do with it.

"Why are you so goddamn *bright* this morning?" I drawled as I stripped and climbed into the shower. Jace'd followed me, and I didn't care. We'd been best friends and bandmates long enough that he'd seen my dick a thousand times. We had no qualms about nudity anymore.

"I started writing a song last night," he told me with a sly grin.

My brows shot up as I peered through the glass shower screen. "Seriously?"

He shrugged. "Seemed like it was time."

I scoffed. "Gray got to you, huh? He turned up here yesterday, too."

"Oh yeah? How'd you get him to leave?"

I screwed my eyes shut, trying to remember. "Pretty sure I threw a gin bottle at him and called him an ugly shrew."

Jace spluttered a laugh. "What the fuck? An ugly shrew? Where do you come up with this shit?"

I chuckled, using a liberal amount of soap in my pits and groin. "Fuck if I know. I was trashed and he came in here all nagging like an annoying, big bird... and you know he gets all butthurt when people say he's ugly." Because it was blatantly untrue. Gray was a great looking guy, but he was big and broad, rocking scars and long hair... He wasn't pretty like Jace. So he was often referred to as *less attractive* than the rest of Bellerose.

"I'm so confused," Jace admitted, looking it. "How did you get to *shrew* from big bird? Wasn't Big Bird a chicken?"

I rinsed my soap off and turned off the shower.

"Jace... brother. I love you, but fuck, you're dumb sometimes. Big Bird was a huge-ass canary, and a *shrew* is, like, the lanky bird with the big beak who delivers babies." I took the towel from his hand when he held it out to me and dried off.

Jace chuckled. "That's a *stork*. A shrew is like a rat. Or a mole. Or... some small rodent kinda thing with poisonous saliva. Which is actually funnier, picturing how confused Gray would have been when you said that. Anyway, yeah, he reminded me that we owe the label an album, so I started writing something that I want you to hear."

"Oh, just like that, huh?" The bitterness in my voice cut like acid. I tied the towel around my waist and swiped a hand over my peacock-blue mohawk—not that I'd bothered to gel it in weeks, and the sides were starting to grow out in my natural shade of dirty blond.

Stalking out of the bathroom, I headed for the kitchen. I was too fucking sober for Jace's bullshit, and my hangover was *pounding*. It felt like Grayson was parked up in my frontal lobe, beating the crap out of my brain matter.

Glancing around, I couldn't spot the tequila bottle I'd been working on last night. Or was it this morning? Whatever, it was nowhere to be seen. Maybe I'd finished it and Jace cleaned it up.

Or maybe… "Where the fuck is all the booze?" I demanded, whirling around when I found the kitchen dry.

Jace folded his arms, his expression set in a stubborn look. "I threw it out. It's time you sobered up, Rhett. You're wallowing in self-pity like you were in love with that bitch."

My jaw dropped to the floor. "Excuse me?"

"You fucking heard me. You were hitting it for two weeks, and you're acting like your wife of twelve years just left. Pull yourself together, bro; we have an album to write. If your dick is lonely, there's plenty of other sluts out there who'd crawl over broken glass to get railed by the great Rhett Silver."

I snatched up the closest thing to me, a crystal

tumbler, and hurled it at Jace in a flash of acidic rage. It smashed against the wall behind him, and the bastard barely even flinched.

"Kinda just proving my point, bro," he muttered, giving the shattered mess a long look. Then he sighed and moved closer like he had a death wish. "Rhett... I know this whole shit with Billie has triggered you. I'm not as ignorant as you think. But *you* need to recognize the differences here. She's not your mom. Billie is just an opportunistic, backstabbing bitch. She didn't love you, and *you* didn't love *her*. She's just great pussy and nothing more, but *I get it*. I've been in your shoes. She has that way of making you feel like you were soulmates, right? Like you've known her in a previous life or you're fated mates or some shit, but it's all *bullshit*."

I shook my head, shutting out my best friend's hate-filled words. He didn't know. He had *no* clue.

"You don't fucking get it, Jace," I muttered, scrubbing my hands over my face in frustration. I needed alcohol, or drugs, or *something*. I needed a break from my own mind. "It's never enough. Never e-fucking-nough. What do I have to do, huh? What do I have to do to just make her *choose me* for once?"

As soon as those words left my lips, I paled and my stomach twisted. Fuck, he was right. I was mixing

Billie's betrayal up with my mom's from ten years ago. Jesus Christ, I needed to get high. Maybe it was a good day for an acid trip? Nah, hallucinations sounded like a shitty idea right now.

"Just... leave me alone," I told him with a defeated, somewhat embarrassed groan.

"Can't do that," he replied, shaking his head. "You're my best friend. I can't just watch you self-destruct while I do nothing. So, you're gonna sober up, eat some vegetables, drink some water, then help me with these lyrics I started while you were passed out."

He clapped me on the shoulder, the dude equivalent of a hug, and I shook him off. I wasn't in the mood for his positivity right now; my hangover was way too rough.

"Go to hell, Jace. You can't just fix everything in a snap because you suddenly had a moment of creativity." I yanked open a drawer and fished out a set of car keys. My jacket was nowhere to be seen, but Jace's was hanging by the door and that'd do.

"Rhett, where are you going?" my friend protested as I stuffed my feet into a pair of boots. "We need to—" His protest cut off at the sound of a heavy knock on our door. I scowled at Jace, but he looked just as confused. "Who the fuck is that?"

"You tell me," I muttered, crossing over the

entryway and jerking the door open. I wasn't worried about it being a crazed fan, because they'd had to have cleared security in the foyer of our building already. "Oh seriously? What the *fuck*, Jace? Is this some kind of fucking intervention?"

Grayson just glared back at me, his expression pissy. Possibly he was still upset over the *ugly shrew* thing. "Maybe, if that's what you need. You gonna let us in?"

I curled my lip in disgust. "You? Sure. *Her*? Hell no. You're not welcome here, Florence."

"Jesus, Rhett," Jace snapped, pushing me aside to allow Grayson inside. "You don't have to lash out at us; we're your family."

I scoffed a bitter laugh, shaking my head. "Unbelievable," I muttered. "Suit yourself, entertain the snake in our grass. I'm outta here."

Not waiting for a response, I brushed past Flo—the fucking traitor—and jumped into the elevator before it disappeared back to another floor. Fuck this, fuck them and their fucking intervention, I wasn't putting up with it.

Family meant nothing to me, and Jace damn well knew it.

I needed to get fucked up because all I could think about was how Billie had gone back to an abusive relationship. She'd made that choice, just like my mom had when she left me for dead ten years ago. I *hated* thinking about her, so the only option was to get obliterated on whatever drug I could get my hands on. Maybe this time it would kill me. I couldn't even find it in me to care.

BILLIE

O f all the insane things I'd done in my life just to survive, this had to be the *most* ridiculous. And dangerous, no less. Angelo's father had his metaphorical hand around my throat, and just the slightest misstep could see him tighten his grip, cutting off my air and choking me to death.

That was why I went along with it. I'd had a taste of the Ricci wrath already and never wanted to go back there. So I smiled politely as a staff member of the exclusive Siena Country Club held out my chair for me.

"Try to look slightly less like you have broken glass in your panties, Bella," Angelo muttered in my ear,

31

pretending like we were sharing an intimate moment as he sat beside me. "I thought you were a better actress than this."

Pasting a smile on my lips, I turned my head so I could bat my lashes to my ex. "Eat a dick, Angelo," I whispered without dropping my smile. From a distance, we just looked like lovers speaking quietly. It couldn't be further from the truth.

He smirked, running his tongue over his teeth. "Not my thing, Bella. You know that."

I was saved the need to respond by one of Angelo's aunties approaching us with a wide smile.

Her initial greeting was all in Italian, which only soured my mood further since I couldn't understand her and she damn well knew it. To say I was being received *badly* by Angelo's family would be an understatement. It was *awkward*, especially since I'd known a lot of his family when we were kids.

Then, I'd been Angelo's innocent, schoolboy crush. The harmless little girl next door. Until I was no longer so innocent, or harmless. Then I'd become an enemy to the Ricci family, and *that* was what they all remembered.

"In English, Tia Donna, please. Bella still doesn't speak Italian." Well, that was something. At least Angelo was pretending to care about appearances.

Tia Donna gave me a brittle smile, her head-to-toe glance sharp and disapproving. "Hmm," she huffed. "Well, what's done is done, Angelo. Your father wishes to speak with you."

Angelo gave a short nod, then leaned in to whisper in my ear again. "Stay here, Bella. Don't leave this table until I return." He said it quietly, so I forced myself to smile like he'd said something sweet. Like a man in love with his mistress.

Ugh. *Mistress*. How degrading. But that was the long and short of it since Angelo *was* still married with no intention of divorcing his wife any time soon. The only reason he was permitted to openly take a mistress now was—

"When's it due?" Tia Donna asked, nodding her weathered face at my belly.

I licked my lips, watching Angelo walk away. He glanced back, and our gazes locked for a tense moment. He thought I was going to run, but I wasn't a fucking idiot. I knew what was at stake here, not just for me but for both of us.

"Uh, April," I replied, snapping my gaze back to Donna. "Another five months." My hand smoothed over the swell of my belly, not even slightly disguised by the pastel-blue dress I wore. It felt like such a slap in the face to those who knew Valentina, showing off my *fertility*.

That was why Angelo had been *permitted* a mistress. He and Valentina had been married for nearly eight years, and she had yet to get pregnant. Not even a scare of a missed period to offer the family a sliver of hope. Giovanni Ricci was a man determined to secure his family line of succession. In recent years he had become frustrated enough that he didn't give a shit who the mother was, so long as his son conceived a child with *someone*.

Enter Angelo's *insane* plan. Make me his baby mama. Okay, fine, his mistress. I didn't know which title was more insulting.

"...better hope that's a boy," Tia Donna was saying, her mouth twisted with disapproval. "The family won't accept anything less."

Whatever the fuck that *was meant to mean.*

The old, heavyset woman waddled away again after delivering that little gem of a threat, leaving me alone at the table. I blew out a long sigh, resting my elbows on the table and dropping my head to my hands. Fucking hell. I'd forgotten how judgmental Angelo's relatives were.

Not that he'd exactly gone out of his way to remind me. While I'd recovered from the torture and beating I'd taken at his guys' hands, he'd been there for me twenty-four seven. Then, six weeks ago after I'd gotten the all clear from the well-paid home doctor—all my injuries were healing well and I no longer needed anything stronger than aspirin for pain—he'd just up and disappeared. I could count on *one hand* how often I'd seen him since then, and none of those visits had been about any kind of reconciliation for our past transgressions. Hell, I'd go so far as to say our relationship was more toxic now than ever before.

"Hey, you're Bella, right?" a woman's voice jerked me out of my little silent pity party. I inhaled sharply and sat back up with my fake smile pasted across my lips.

"Billie," I corrected her, "Yeah, that's me." I extended my hand to shake hers, but she just eyed my fingers like they were made of rancid fish.

Her overlined lips twisted with disgust, and her hip popped to the side as she shifted her gaze to my pregnant belly. "So it's true then? He's been cheating on Vee?"

My lips parted but no words exited my mouth. What the actual shit was I supposed to say to that? This was exactly why I had *begged* not to come to this luncheon with the Ricci family.

When I didn't reply, the girl just gave me a

disgusted look. "Angelo could have had his pick of any girl in Siena, and he chose to put a baby in *you*?" It seemed like a rhetorical question, so I just gave a small shrug in response. What else did she want from me? "If you had a shred of decency, you wouldn't be parading that around here. Everyone *loves* Vee, so don't go dreaming of a future as Mrs. Ricci. It'll never happen. You're just an incubator and nothing more."

To emphasize her point, she upended her glass of red wine directly onto my medium-sized bump, soaking my pastel dress in claret.

"Oops," she sneered. "Guess you need to leave now. *Byeeee!*"

I couldn't even find it within myself to be mad about it, because I *wanted* to leave. So I just started laughing and pushed back from my chair. "Thanks. It was nice meeting you..." I trailed off, looking her up and down the same way she'd eyed me. "Whatever your name is." Not that I cared.

"It's Jenna," she snapped at my back as I walked away, but I didn't respond. Seriously, why the fuck would I even care? She clearly thought herself more important than anyone else in the room.

When I reached the country club foyer, I gave a heavy sigh of relief. Just being out of that dining room had eased some of the pressure in my head. I wished more than anything that I could *actually* leave... to crawl back into my bed at Angelo's house where I'd been kept prisoner for more than two months now. But his car had been valeted, and I had no way to pay for a taxi.

"Ma'am, are you okay?" one of the club staff asked cautiously, giving me a concerned look. "Do you need help to clean up? Can we call someone?"

I glanced down at the mess of red wine soaking through my dress, completely covering the swell of my midsection. Great. "Um, no I'll be fine," I mumbled. "I just need the restrooms?"

The woman escorted me down the hall to the ladies' room, then asked again if she could call one of my friends to help. It was with a bitter smile that I shook my head. "No, thanks. I don't have any friends here."

How true *that* was.

I locked myself in the restroom, then just stared at myself in the mirror. The dress was totally ruined; there was no point even attempting to clean it up. All I'd achieve was to soak myself through.

At a loss for what else to do, I just stood there. For ages. Just stood there, staring at my reflection and questioning what the *fuck* I was doing with my life.

Some time later a knock on the door startled me,

and my heart raced with a surge of adrenaline from fright.

"Occupied, sorry!" I called out. Thankfully, the country club was fancy enough to have individual bathrooms, not just stalls in a larger restroom. It meant I could hide out here without having to sit on top of a toilet.

"Bella, it's me," a deep voice replied, "let me in."

Groaning to myself, I crossed over and unlocked the door. "Hi, sweetie, did you miss me?"

Angelo's scowl was dark enough to send fear ricocheting through me. Would he hurt me if I pushed him? I honestly had no idea. He was like a stick of lit dynamite these days.

"Seriously, Bella? I leave you for *five fucking minutes,* and you—"

"Get assaulted by one of your wife's friends and her glass of merlot? Yes. I did. Are you shocked? Because I'm not. Can we leave yet?" I was scared of him and what he was capable of. But I wasn't physically able to hold back my attitude. Not with how deep our history ran.

He was so torn, scrubbing a hand over his freshly cropped hair. "Fucking hell," he growled. Then he looked at my wine-drenched dress again. "Yes, I guess we have to. I've made an appearance, and you've been seen. That'll have to do, for today."

Relief rushed through me so hard my shoulders sagged, and I didn't even protest when Angelo gripped my elbow harder than necessary as he escorted me *quickly* out of the country club. We needed to wait a few minutes at the front door for the valet to fetch Angelo's car, and neither of us seemed to know what to say. It was a deeply uncomfortable silence, even after the car pulled up and we climbed inside.

"So, um, what was it that your father wanted to announce?" I asked, curiosity winning out over awkwardness as we drove back toward the Ricci mansion on the riverside. Thankfully, the elder Riccis, Giovanni and Fiorella, lived in their country estate now, so we had the whole place to ourselves. No doubt that was how Angelo avoided me so effortlessly.

He glanced over at me as he drove, his tattooed hands tightening on the steering wheel like he was picturing strangling me.

"I have no idea," he snapped. "We left before he made the announcement."

I swallowed hard. "Um, will we be in trouble for that?" His family took this shit *dead* seriously.

Angelo heaved a sigh. "Us? No. Me? Yes. But it'll be fine. Just... let me get you home, and I'll go smooth things over. You were probably right about this being a bad idea."

Without meaning to, I laughed. "No shit."

He glanced over at me again; this time a small smile curved his lips. "You're gonna be the death of me, Bella."

I bit the inside of my lip, shifting my gaze out the window to avoid replying. A horrible feeling swirled through my chest as I was too sure he meant that literally. I was in way over my head with Angelo Ricci, and all I wanted to do was run crying back into the arms of Bellerose.

They must all *hate* me by now. Even Rhett...

Fuck, that hurt.

five

BILLIE

Three weeks had passed since that incident, and the only reason I even knew that it was a Friday was tonight's huge fundraiser benefitting Siena Homeless, a charity gala event honoring the Ricci family's position as pillars of this community.

Ironic, considering eighty percent of their income was derived through illegal means, with only twenty percent being legit through their restaurants. They were determined to be seen as upstanding citizens, firmly planted in the upper echelons of Siena, and not a single person could—or would—stand in their way. Especially not their son's trashy mistress.

Giovanni's words, not mine.

"You will ensure she's there, showing off the future heir," he snarled to Angelo after I suggested that it might be better for me not to make an appearance. The head of the Ricci clan made great pains to never address me directly.

"You know that Vee is going to be there," Angelo reminded his father. "Maybe it would be best to save the drama for another night."

His wife. His fucking wife was going to be there for fuck's sake. There hadn't ever been a worse idea than this one, and considering the agreement Angelo and I had entered into, that was saying a lot.

Biting back the urge to speak again, I crossed my arms and sighed, sinking deeper into myself. I'd been slowly losing pieces of who I was over the past two and a half months. Piece by piece. Drop by drop. I'd bled out my pain in tears and heartache, suffered in silence as I screamed and cried into my pillow, and now I was numb.

Some days I kind of wished I'd just stepped out in front of one of those bullets back in the restaurant. Better me than Liz. She hadn't deserved to die and would probably have gone on to live a half-decent life. Not as someone's prisoner with a ticking bomb over her head, anyway.

"Don't fucking question me again," Giovanni snapped at his son and heir. "If you're not there tonight, I promise, there'll be serious consequences. We can never let them know there are cracks in our armor, or they will destroy us."

Apparently, parading your pregnant mistress was fine, not a crack to be seen, but heaven forbid you hid her away in the house when there was an event on. Cracking all over the place.

Giovanni was gone in the next instant, and I didn't feel the tension flee from me like it would have a few weeks ago. I'd moved past feeling relief in any way, shape, or form. Now it was just pain and duty. And if that duty didn't work out, I couldn't find it in myself to care.

The lack of fear over my death was starting to concern me. Or at least it would have if I honestly had any fucks left to give.

"Bella," Angelo said, voice loud enough that I knew it wasn't the first time he'd addressed me. "What's wrong with you?"

Blinking slowly at him, I tried to find my way back into my own body. It was almost as if part of my soul left when shit got intense these days, and it was growing harder to return each time.

"What did you say?"

There was very little fire in my voice, and as he stepped closer, eyebrows bunching together, I swallowed roughly.

"I said, we have no choice about tonight, but I'll make sure to protect you from anyone who might want to hurt you on Vee's behalf." His look of concern remained strongly etched across his features.

"Cool," I said listlessly, hand falling to the swell of my stomach. "I'll find something to wear."

One thing I didn't lack for was clothing, shoes, and accessories. An entire room, as large as my old apartment, was filled to the brim with every designer outfit that you could imagine. All of them with the tags still on, since I was more comfortable in sweats these days.

Turning away, I thought Angelo said something else, but I'd already closed off my mind and senses to him, mentally preparing for whatever horrible shit I would go through tonight at this Ricci event. I'd be dressed like a mafia princess, but they'd all know I was the whore.

"Fucking hell, Bella!"

His growled curse was loud enough that it actually registered, and before I could react, Angelo's firm grip wrapped around my shoulders and he spun me, leaning down at the same time to slam his lips against mine. It was a hard, aggressive move, and it reminded me just a little of how Grayson liked to dominate my mouth.

Of course, this wasn't Grayson. Not even fucking close. Angelo's kiss only filled me with fear and disgust for the abuse of his power over me.

With a cry, I slapped my hands against his chest, attempting to push him away. Only it was like moving a fucking building. I'd never be able to move Angelo when he didn't want to move.

In fact, the strength in the body beneath my palms actually took me by surprise. He'd always been fit, even when we were teens, but now he was solid muscle. Muscle that was refusing to let me go. The firm grip of his hands bit into my biceps, holding me firmly in place.

Terror traced its way down my spine, a truly strong emotion for the first time in a long time. But mingled in that fear was a faint sense of familiarity that had flutters racing across my chest.

Angelo growled again and slowed the aggression of his kiss, easing the pace, as his lips parted and he pressed his tongue forward, demanding entry. I wanted to bite him, but for some reason I couldn't bring myself to do that. If anything, it was harder to not open my mouth and allow him the access he wanted.

My head spun as the taste of scotch and plums

assaulted me, and I knew he'd had a drink before he'd taken this meeting with his father. Probably a good idea considering what had happened after Giovanni arrived.

Beneath the alcohol, though, there was that hint of spice I always associated with Angelo. My Angelo. The one who had loved me and held me together when my life was falling apart. He'd treated me like I was precious, and in a different way than Jace. At one point in time, just before that fateful day I'd destroyed everything, I'd been on top of the world. I'd been loved by these two boys. Loved, fucked, adored, and cherished. They taught me about my heart, soul, and especially the wants and needs of my body.

Until it had all exploded in a ball of flames, literally. Flames that would steal away what remained of my family... and my baby.

A therapist would no doubt tell me I was spiraling with Angelo, due to the triggering of past scars and losses I'd never dealt with. Especially since I was currently firmly entrenched into the role of mafia-heir baby mama. But then again, maybe a therapist would just tell me I was a weak, pathetic mess and to pull myself together.

Both were no doubt true and accurate.

"Angel," I growled, finally jerking my face away from his. He was near bent in half to bring himself to my level, and he showed no surprise when I hauled back and slapped him hard across the face. If anything, when he jerked away, blinking down at me from his normal height, he actually looked pleased. Small fucking smirk and everything.

He took a step closer to me again, and my stomach swirled while I fought the urge to run or... maybe kiss him again. Pathetic. Mess. It was legit.

His eyes were hooded as he leaned in closer, the smirk remaining in place. "If you disappear on me again, Bella," he drawled smoothly, and I shivered at the sudden chill in the air. "I won't hesitate to fuck you back to life, do you understand? I need you to get your head in the game, and I need it now. There's no room for error here, or we're both dead. *Do you fucking understand?*"

I was nodding, but in my mind, all I could hear was *fuck you back to life.* Why did my body tighten at that sentence, and not in fear... How could I feel anything for this man, who was a stranger to me now and part of the very family who was working hard to destroy me.

Fighting the urge to scream, I choked on my next breath before taking off from the room and heading toward my private quarters. Angelo had given me my own room, bathroom, and that huge walk-in closet. It was more than I'd ever had before, and I was craving the security, false as it may be, that I felt inside my prison.

When I stumbled into my room, I slammed the door behind me and leaned back against it. For a second, I thought there was a flash of light from outside my window, but when I crossed to close the curtains, I could see nothing on the other side of the small balcony.

Unsure what to do, my energy roiling inside, I paced back and forth across the room, my feet sinking into the plush gray carpet, as I fought the urge to scream. My skin pulsed, itching, irritating me until I had to resist the urge to scratch away at my own flesh, scouring it from muscle and bone.

What the hell was Angelo thinking, kissing me, stirring up old memories, his hands pressing into my flesh hard enough that I could still feel the touch against my skin? How fucking dare he! How dare he think he had the right to *fuck me back to life*. I didn't need him. I didn't need any of them.

In the end, I only had myself to rely on, and that was never going to change, no matter how many gorgeous, rich, and talented men popped in and out of my life. My uber independence had been learned the hard way, and if anything, the last few months had only reinforced this concept.

I hadn't heard from one member of Bellerose. Not one of them had tried to contact me after Angelo forced me to send a message. At least not that I knew of.

I couldn't blame them since they no doubt believed I had taken off and left them, but they also knew that I'd been threatened with kidnapping. I had actually been kidnapped, and still there was no word of them checking in on me. Had my little video message really been so convincing? Where were the men who fought for their woman? I was a shitty actress and thought for sure they'd see right through my *please don't look for me, I'm happy here* bullshit.

A bitter laugh escaped as I finally slowed, the red marks bright on my forearms where I'd scraped my nails across the skin in the hopes of easing my turmoil. I'd been with Rhett for a few weeks. It was nothing in the scheme of life. Gray and I had barely even been together, and Jace... well, Jace had more reason to hate me than anyone.

Throwing myself a pity party because none of those rockstars ran to my rescue was pathetic, and since I barely had a shred of dignity left to my name, I needed to sort what remained of my self-worth immediately.

I could give up a lot in the name of staying alive, but what would be the point if I lost every part of myself along the way? Might as well confess to the facade now and take the punishment for it. If it wasn't for the fact that I'd implicate Angelo in this as well...

But at least I understood now why he'd kissed me.

I'd been spiraling. I'd been losing myself to the dark fog in my head, and there was no time for that. No time and no chance of surviving this farce with Angelo.

I had to get it together now, and the first step to that was showering and picking out a dress.

It was charity gala night, and I was going to be there.

six

BILLIE

I was starting to think torture by the Ricci goons was preferable to *charity galas.*

"Waitress, I'll take a glass of chardonnay. Get it to me while it's still cold this time."

I eyed the leggy brunette, the twentieth person to attempt to order a drink from me, and shot her a winning smile. "Absolutely, no problem. I'll be right back."

Some funny fucker had arranged for every member of Valentina's family, the Altissimos, who were scattered about liberally, to treat me like a paid server. Not even good enough to be the whorey mistress, I was now the hired help.

Which, actually, didn't offend me at all. I'd been the hired help for most of my life, and it was good, honest work. If anything, I was amused by their little game, which only occurred whenever Angelo had been ferried off by his father to talk shop with some of the VIPs in the room. Despite his words about protecting me from everyone here, he could only do so much when he was *working.*

At least no one had thrown their wine at me this time, so that was a win. Walking away from the chardonnay lady, I arched my back, stretching out the ache developing there. Needing the bathroom, thanks to the multiple waters I'd consumed in my bid to remain awake amidst the glitz and glamor, I headed in the direction of the restrooms, wishing I was anywhere but here.

Not just here, but here and sober. Was there a worse combination?

Everything felt uncomfortable as I stumbled my way through the crowd. My Saint Laurent pumps were only a few inches high, but I wasn't used to heels. Or the slinky black Chanel dress that hugged my small bump, boobs, and butt like a second skin.

If it wasn't for the sleeves to my wrists and high neckline, I'd have felt half naked in this number— despite it being far more conservative than many of the dresses in this room. Apparently, charity events were the fancier version of Halloween: a perfect excuse for a chick to lose as many parts of her clothing as possible and not be called a whore.

That label was saved for me these days. Whore and waitress.

Eh, I'd probably been called worse.

Angelo had kept all social media and news articles from crossing my path since I'd been delivered into his possession, but no doubt the media was having a field day with my sudden departure from Bellerose. I could only imagine the headlines after being the first girl to "date" Rhett Silver in forever.

I was being watched closely as I walked through the large ballroom and managed to enter one of the smaller bathrooms. For the first time tonight, I had a little luck, as it was completely empty.

It took more than a few minutes to maneuver myself into a position to pee without destroying my dress. This pregnancy shit was harder than I'd expected. When I emerged and started to wash my hands at the sink, barely even glancing at the pale shadow of a reflection in the mirror, the door to the room opened. Noise entered briefly with the new occupant, before fading as the door closed behind her.

Finishing up, I dried my hands on the luxurious

hand towels provided, and as I turned to exit, I came face to face with a goddess. She stood a head taller than me, her heels a good six-inches high as she towered over me. She had flaming red hair, a statement piece that made my dirty-blonde curls look positively lame. Her makeup was flawless, and large, emerald eyes examined me as she pursed blood-red lips, a similar shade to her hair.

Her dress was black as well, but it was far more extravagant than mine as it draped down her centerfold body, spilling across the floor. Clearly, far more expensive too.

"Bella, I've been looking everywhere for you," she said, shocking the shit out of me. Blinking rapidly, my stomach started to do some deep churning as I figured out who this was: Valentina. *The wife.* She was the only person who made sense in this situation, and she was the sort of stunning beauty to perfectly match Angelo's tall, dark, and devastatingly handsome. Fucking hell, she was *gorgeous,* and I was the other woman.

"You need a waitress?" I said, acting more blasé than I felt.

My heartbeat slammed against my chest as I went to move around her, praying she wouldn't stop me before I made a beeline for Angelo to get the hell out of here. We'd showed up, he'd talked shop with his dad and the high rollers, and it was time to bail now before *Vee* murdered me.

My prayers were dashed when her hand wrapped around my forearm, blood red nail flashing, but she didn't dig them in as I'd expected. "I've wanted to meet you for a long time," she said suddenly, offering a sheepish smile. "Sorry I was late tonight, but I'm here now, and I think it's time we talked."

A very light breeze could have knocked me on my ass as I stared. "Sorry, what?"

I mean, was I hallucinating? Had someone slipped something in my water?

There was no other reasonable explanation.

While I was still trying to figure out if I'd unintentionally taken some sort of wicked drug that turned everything topsy-turvy, Valentina released me and moved toward the door. A second later there was an ominous click of the lock slotting into place, and I shook myself out of the daze, expecting this was the point her polite facade faded and she tried to slit my throat with her lethal claws. Shit, she was a mafia princess; she probably had a gun tucked up her skirt.

"I don't want any trouble," I said shortly, crossing my arms over my chest like that might protect me. In reality, all it did was emphasize the belly beneath. Valentina's eyes lingered on my mid-section for a beat before she took a deep breath and lifted her gaze to meet mine.

There was no anger in her light brown eyes; if anything, she looked relieved.

"You might want the sort of trouble I'm offering," she said simply, and I was grateful that she stopped a few feet away, giving me a false sense of security. "Because I could be a very good ally for you in this world, and without my guidance, you might fall into one of the many, *many* dark traps littered about."

My eyes narrowed on her as my mouth fell open. "Okay look, call me paranoid but I'm not buying the act." This had to be some sort of prank. Like, *drop a vat of blood on my head at the dance* sort of prank. "What's your angle? What do you want from me exactly?" Even if she was legit with her offer for help, no one did that without expecting something in return. No one. Not even people who gave a shit about me.

Except for maybe Rhett...

My Zeppelin.

Fuck.

This was not the time to fall into that mental headspace. Not when I was face to face with Angelo's *wife.*

"You don't understand," she said with a shake of her head. "I'm sorry; I'm not explaining myself correctly. For some reason, I expected that A would have filled you in on our situation, but I forgot what a gentleman he is. He wouldn't share my secrets."

A had to be Angelo, and for some reason, it riled me right up that she knew he was a gentleman. I mean, not that he actually was, but the familiarity in her tone told me that they were more than just people who'd married to unite their families—like he'd claimed back when his father forced them to get engaged at age seventeen. They were friends. More, no doubt. Lovers for sure, since they'd been trying to get pregnant.

And now I had to wonder if I was the one who was about to commit murder. I was already a homewrecker, might as well add the title of murderer to it.

"Angelo and I don't really talk," I said stiffly, arms starting to ache from how tightly I was holding them against my chest. "Not anymore." Because we used to. We used to talk about *everything*.

Her eyes flitted down to my stomach once more, but she was classy enough not to add any comment like *I can see that talking is the last thing you get up to* or something similar.

"Angelo and I are married in name only," she said quickly as she once again met my gaze. Sincerity bled from her, which was disconcerting. "I hate being part of this mafia family, and he's my shield against the depravity of the world. If I hadn't been married off to him, I would have been to someone else. Someone probably way worse. Men in our world aren't typically *kind*."

Her face implored me to believe her, and despite my better judgment, I did.

"So, you've never been... uh... you know. In love?"

I already knew they didn't live together. I'd been staying at the Ricci compound for months, and not once had Valentina even visited. Angelo had said she was in Italy, and I'd accepted that, but the house didn't hold one of her personal items. I'd been through every damn room, and there was no sign of her presence.

She shook her head, a strangled laugh escaping. "I have a girlfriend who is my whole life. She's a secret though, and I pray that you will take that as seriously as I am taking your safety. If my father finds out that I'm gay, he will murder me *and* her. That's not just a saying, but a fact. I wasn't always the Altissimo heir."

That she'd so willingly shared that with me was a huge indication that she'd approached me tonight with the right intentions. I mean, if I told anyone, no doubt she could have me knocked off in seconds, but it was still a risk.

Or it would be, if I was an asshole like any one of the other women at this stupid fucking party. Lucky for

Valentina, I considered myself to have a shred of decency.

"I'll never breathe a word," I promised, some of the tension releasing from my body. "I'm so sorry you can't be with the person you love, like you deserve. No one should ever have to hide their heart."

Her lips quivered and her eyes watered as she cleared her throat. "My life was predetermined before birth. I'm well used to the role I must play to survive, all the while hoping one day there will be a path to freedom. Maybe with my father's death. Maybe it won't be until my own death. But one day, by some means, I'll be free of this cage."

The urge to cross to her and hug her trembling body was strong, but I resisted. We weren't friends. But maybe one day we could be.

"I'm sorry if I'm making life harder for you," I said, finally letting my arms fall to my sides. I also took a deep breath, filling my lungs properly for the first time since she'd entered the bathroom. "Angelo and I have an arrangement, but I never wanted that to come at a risk to you."

She waved me off before she delicately wiped at the moisture under her eyes. Somehow, she didn't smudge her makeup or look like a hot mess. Sorceress. "There's no risk to me. If there's one thing the Altissimo family understands, it's mistresses and children out of wedlock. It was made clear to me more than a year ago that Angelo had both families' consent to take a mistress, if it meant a baby would be made. And honestly, my father had already written me off as infertile after all these years without me getting pregnant. He has no idea that I've never even *seen* Angelo's dick, let alone touched it." She shuddered like the idea of Angelo's cock made her nauseous.

The surge of relief I felt at that was strong, and I would not be examining why. Nope. Today I lived in denial.

"I honestly had many expectations when it came to meeting you," I told her with a shake of my head. A small laugh escaped. "Many of them ended in bloodshed." Another laugh. "Actually, all of them did. I never for one moment thought this was how it would go."

Valentina let out a chuckle of her own. "I'm just sorry that I can't control the rest of my family. I have to keep playing the game, which includes allowing them to believe I'm heartbroken by your appearance in A's life. But I wanted you to know, in person, that I am so grateful that his one true love is back. He's spoken a lot about you over the years, and even though he's never said anything specific about your time together, it was always clear that he never got over you. I could tell."

She was smiling gently, and at this point I was more uncomfortable than when I'd thought she was going to kill me. "Uh, I mean, we're not even friends, let alone lovers." Despite my pregnant belly between us. Crap. I gestured to the swell under my dress. "This is just a short-term solution to save us all in the long term."

Her smile didn't fade. "It wouldn't matter the danger; Angelo would never make this kind of commitment with just anyone. Only you. Only his Bella. Besides, babies are hardly *short term*." She laughed gently, but I couldn't muster up even a smile in return.

My body burned as my heart pulsed faster, and the very visceral reaction I was having should alarm me. Angelo and I were an act, just like Angelo and Valentina were.

I couldn't forget that, and I couldn't fall into the falsely woven fairytale of us being long-lost loves.

The truth of it all was that I was just a temporary visitor in his life, and as soon as we figured out how to get around his father's bloodthirsty nature, I'd be gone.

In the wind, just like I'd been eight years ago.

seven

GRAYSON

M y fists slammed into the bag over and over without any control. Pure power and anger rode those punches, and I was throwing everything into it. A tearing sound registered a beat later and I saw that I'd smashed right through the cover, rags and sand pouring out around my hits.

Breathing heavily, I pulled back and fought to control the red tinging my vision. As the weeks had passed with very little information, teamed with the lack of movement in returning Billie to our lives, my mood had grown beyond fucked-up. The others were on their way here now so we could talk music, but my head was so far from the rock star game that I wondered if maybe I was done with this life.

If I didn't have contractual obligations that, if unfulfilled, would cause issues for my band, I'd probably just walk away.

When the knock sounded on the front door, I left the small workout room, unwrapping my hands. The wraps were black, which hid the blood from all the new cuts across my knuckles. The boxing bag wasn't the only object I'd broken recently.

Opening the door, I found Rhett, Jace, and Florence standing there. Well, Flo was four steps back while Rhett shot her dark looks, but the three of them were here, at least. This might be the final album we ever made together, and despite everything, I hoped that we found our rhythm.

"Hi," I said, voice rougher thanks to my raging workout. "Come in. I'll shower and change."

As I turned away, Jace called my name. "There's no time," he said.

"Why the fuck not?" I shot back straight away. "We've got all day."

He shook his head sadly, and the *sexiest man alive* for the past five years running looked like a bag of shit as he ran a hand through his hair, more baggage under his eyes than Flo and Tom had in their relationship. "The label is kidnapping us to ensure that this album gets made. You have five minutes to throw clothes in a bag, and then we need to exit to the limo."

Fuck. That only meant one thing when it came to Big Noise Records.

"No," I said bluntly. "I refuse." I had too many things going on here, and how could I get updates on Billie if I was locked up with my bandmates? Not to mention the cameras...

Rhett, wobbling on his feet, glared daggers. "Do you think we'd all be fucking here if refusal was an option? We refuse, we get sued. And I need money for drugs to numb the noise. So pack your shit and get your stubborn fuck of an ass in the car."

He stomped back down toward the street, his steps weaving dangerously. Rhett was far from sober right now, and that was cause for concern.

I arched an accusing brow at Jace, and he had the good grace to look ashamed. Rhett was his responsibility, and one he'd grossly neglected over the last few months.

"Come on, man," our lead singer coaxed. "It's time we all moved on. Forgive and forget and all that shit. We're too good to let some chick tear us apart."

My blood boiled, but I swallowed it back. He didn't see what I had seen in Billie's video all those weeks ago. He didn't see the prisoner being coached on what to say. He just saw his first love, the girl who broke his heart, living down to all his shitty expectations.

"This isn't about her," I replied, glancing away as a trickle of blood splattered the doorframe. I needed to clean it up before it set in. "I can't leave right now. Maybe I can Zoom call in or some shit."

Jace scoffed. "Sure. Whatever, man. Don't say we didn't try this the easy way."

With that cryptic warning, he stalked away, hands stuffed in his pockets. That left me standing there with silent Flo, who looked to be on the verge of tears.

"Sorry," I grunted, feeling anything but. "Jace and Rhett write all the music anyway. They don't need me there for collaboration."

"Gray..." she replied with a pleading look on her face. She wanted me to play middleman. Peacemaker. How could I when I hadn't forgiven her myself?

My phone rang from my living room, and I gripped the front door. "Sorry, Flo. Good luck with them." Then I closed the door in her face and went to look for my phone where I'd left it before my workout.

I found it on my coffee table, beside my folder on Billie Bellerose research. The caller ID showed as *Unknown Number,* and a chill chased down my spine. I stared at the screen, and the call ended without me answering.

"Shit," I breathed, dread flooding my gut. I'd been expecting it for weeks, but it was still a shock.

Tossing my phone back down, I took my ass off to shower and wallow in denial for a little longer. There was no way I'd get away with using my *old* resources and connections without them asking something in return. Stupid me, I'd thought I could just pay cash like any other buyer.

I took my time in the shower, watching my blood mix with the water as it swirled down the drain, then patched up my split knuckles without even bothering to get dressed afterward. It was one of the main reasons I lived alone when we weren't on tour. I liked to be naked.

"Christ, and here I was starting to think maybe I missed working for you degenerates," a woman said when I walked through to my kitchen, making me nearly jump out of my skin. "Then I get an eyeful of *that* and remember what a fucking headache you all are."

I glanced down at my dick, then back up at my manager. "Brenda, you know you missed us." I opened my arms to hug her, and she just gave a vexed sigh as she hugged me back. "I thought you were still on leave."

"I am," she snapped, narrowing her eyes as she leaned back against my counter. "Go put some pants on so I don't have to talk to your trouser snake, babe. Go on, shoo. I'm helping myself to your liquor."

I grinned but went to do as she asked. Brenda was only two years older than me but always treated all of us in Bellerose like her children. I'd missed her bossy ass on this last tour.

When I returned to the kitchen *with pants*, I found her sipping a small glass of Scotch with a blissed-out look on her face.

"Should you be drinking that?" I asked, arching a brow.

Her answering expression was scathing. "Fuck off, Grayson. You try parenting a tiny demon who *never fucking sleeps,* and then let's see how you react when someone questions your choices. Hmm? Wanna trade places? Because my spawn hasn't slept more than two hours in a row since the night he entered this world. Let's swap? I'll *happily* take on Rhett's detox, Flo's crappy choices, and Jace's soul-crushing denial for a full night's sleep."

I raised my hands in surrender. "When you put it like that..."

"Sit down," she ordered me, nodding to a vacant chair at my table. "Talk to me."

I sat but didn't feel particularly forthcoming with information.

After a long silence, Brenda sighed. "Gray… remember when I first met you?"

I grunted. "Like it was yesterday." She'd picked me up in a Starbucks. I'd been searching the job ads in the local newspaper, circling shit I thought maybe I could get hired for without even a GED. One of my favorite rock songs had come on the radio, and I'd drummed along with two pens on the tabletop, not thinking anything of it as I felt the music in my bones. That was how I'd started out as a kid, then I'd been infinitely lucky when I caught the attention of an old retired rocker from the eighties who'd taken me under his wing. Much to my family's irritation.

Brenda had been getting coffee before heading to open auditions at Big Noise Records and coerced me into going with her. The auditions had been for Bellerose, and the rest was history.

"You'd had this… deeply haunted look in your eyes back then," she told me gently, her gaze far too intense and knowing. "You were so lost in your own skin, searching for a *reason*."

I knew exactly what she meant. I'd just cut ties with my uncle's crime syndicate and turned my back on the only profession I'd ever been good at. I had *so* much blood on my hands that the idea of taking a job as a dishwasher or janitor felt so fucking *docile*. So normal. Then Brenda strutted into my life with her sharp power suit and bright ideas for negotiating some diamond crusted pay deals for her musicians. She already had Jace, but he needed a *band*.

"I thought it was such a joke that day," I murmured, smiling at the memory, "like an elaborate set up."

Brenda's answering smile was warm. "And now look where you are. Grayson Taylor, international rock star." She paused, her lips pursed. "But those shadows are back all of a sudden. Is that why you refused to go to the Big Noise content house? Your old life caught up with you again?"

I scrubbed a hand over my beard, making a mental note to trim it tomorrow. "Something like that," I muttered.

Brenda watched me for a long moment, like she was mentally peeling back my layers and looking inside. Then she tilted her head to the side. "And what about this girl that Rhett and Jace seem to be in a disagreement over? Did you have anything to do with her and what happened between them?"

This girl. She made Billie sound like an anonymous groupie.

I laughed bitterly. "This girl," I repeated, shaking my head. "You mean Billie Bellerose?"

There was no physical reaction from our manager, which told me she had already been well aware and was no doubt testing me to see what I'd reveal.

"She's been inspiring the band for almost a decade," she finally said with a shrug. "Hopefully, we get another hit album out of this."

I had to laugh. "Always thinking like a manager. But did you know that she was on the run from the Ricci family, who wanted her dead? And we were the ones standing between her and death... at least up until Flo and Tom sold her out." This was the sort of shit a manager should know, and it was on all of us for not keeping her updated.

"Jesus," Brenda muttered, reaching for the whiskey. I cocked a brow, and she snarled my way. "Shut your mouth, Taylor. I'll pump and dump when we're done here. Alright, shit. Billie Bellerose and the Riccis again. Fuck me. Angelo should have taken up my offer years ago to get out."

"Wait, you knew Angelo Ricci?"

She smirked. "Oh, I surprised you, hmm? Yes, I offered Angel a contract, same as Jace. He couldn't take it because of his family, but..." She shrugged. "Kid had more talent in his big toe than most musicians I get into my office ever achieve."

I blew out a long breath. "Don't ever let Rhett hear you say that. Especially now."

Brenda nodded her agreement. "So. Billie Bellerose and Rhett Silver... I have to say, I didn't see that pairing before it happened." I couldn't help myself—I winced. Brenda scoffed. "Oh, *now* I see. Shit, this girl must be something spectacular to get you lot all bent out of shape. Where is she now?"

Pouring myself a shot of Scotch, I gritted my teeth. Then huffed a frustrated sound. "Back with Angelo. The Riccis were hunting her pretty hard; Jace thinks she stole something from them. She *seemed* to be terrified of them catching up with her and then... *poof*... changed her mind and went skipping back into his arms." I kept my tone as even as possible, trying not to betray my own thoughts on that sequence of events, but it was impossible not to.

"You don't think that's what happened," my manager commented, pursing her lips thoughtfully. "Hmm. Well... as interesting as your love lives are, none of this is helping you fulfill your contracts with Big Noise. And *that*..."

"Is why you're here?" I guessed with a dry voice. "Great."

71

"Listen, Gray. I know you're savvy with your money. You could afford to pay back all the advances and fork out for legal fees, but do you really want to dump that on Flo's plate right now? Or Rhett's?"

"You don't have to guilt me, Brenda. I'm fully prepared to make the new album and satisfy our contract, I just can't move into the fucking *content house*." It wasn't just a house for Big Noise artists to hole up and work on music, it was also wired up with dozens of hidden cameras to gather "behind the scenes" content for the label to use in promotional shit later while marketing the album. I couldn't think of anything worse right now.

"Because of the cameras? Or because of your past catching up with you?" She was too perceptive for her own good.

I shrugged. *Both.* I hated the thought of being *watched* constantly, but more than that, I couldn't risk putting my bandmates in danger if the big bad wolf came knocking. Big Noise content house was famous, too. Hardly hidden away.

Brenda nodded thoughtfully. "Alright. Go pack a bag; I'll work on a compromise."

I wanted to protest, but for what? I needed to make this album with my band, and if anyone could meet all of our unusual needs, it was Brenda. So I just nodded tersely and went to do as I was told. I trusted her to come up with a better alternative. Something we could all be somewhat comfortable with.

The only way she could truly fix us, though, was to bring back the real Bellerose.

Billie.

BILLIE

"**W**hat the fuck do you mean?" I exclaimed. No doubt my expression was comical as I blinked stupidly at Angelo. But he'd just dropped the biggest damn bombshell on me, and I had zero idea how to deal with it.

"The Ricci corporation just acquired a few record labels in a merger deal with Sunrise Enterprises, and one of them was Big Noise Records."

"You own Bellerose?"

I mean, why did the fucking universe hate me? And

Jace, apparently, because this would have to be his worst nightmare come to life.

Angelo shrugged. "The Ricci corporation does. Father has decided to take a more vested effort in diversifying our interests, and it looks like he's heading into the entertainment industry."

The timing of this was suspicious, to say the very least. It wasn't like Giovanni Ricci was unaware of Angelo's and my connection to Bellerose. Fuck, the name had been mine first, and that old asshole knew it. The fact that he was attempting to control the band was a power play, and I couldn't believe Angelo was so... *calm* about it.

"Come on," I said, barely resisting the urge to roll my eyes. "As if he didn't pick up Bellerose's label as another means to control us both." Seriously, there was no way I should have to spell this out to someone of his level of intellect.

Angelo's expression barely shifted, but I knew him well enough to see that tightening skin beside his eyes. The slight thinning of his lips. And the way the deep, rich brown of his eyes appeared to grow even darker. Oh, yeah, Angelo was very aware of what his father was doing, but he'd decided to just go along without questioning Giovanni. We all chose our paths of survival, and Angelo's was to choke down his instinct to lead, allowing his controlling fuck of a father to keep him on a short leash.

"What else did he say?"

It was the day after the charity event, and while I had been meeting his wife in the bathroom, Angelo was being introduced to the bigwigs of the record industry. Including the director of Big Noise. All part of the merger, which was set to be complete by mid next week.

"He said that I would have to take over this new business acquisition until it was all settled, probably for the next six months. I'll be traveling to check out our assets and get everything into line. It's a pain in the ass, but we just need to do the job for now, and eventually he'll lose interest."

Why did I have the sense that this time that asshole would not lose interest? This was personal to Angelo and me, and Giovanni would exploit it for everything.

After I rubbed my face, the stress giving me an instant headache, I finally looked up to see Angelo's expression legitimately darken. "You don't need to stress, Bella. He can't hurt Bellerose. They're famous, rich, and powerful." His anger morphed to annoyance. "They'll ditch Big Noise as soon as they hear of the merger and probably go out on their own under an independent label. That would be the smart thing to do with their power and resources. Jace never did like to be controlled, and I'm honestly surprised he's lasted this long under some asshole's thumb."

Forcing my facial muscles to relax since, clearly, I wasn't as well-versed as Angelo in hiding my emotions, I tried to subtly shake off the tension in my stiff limbs. "Jace isn't the same guy we grew up with," I informed him. "What I did to him... it broke him. I think he's coasted along ever since. He should be grateful that supreme talent and charisma has saved him from what appears to be bad management by Big Noise."

I mean, someone appointed Tom Tucker as a tour manager, and that was all the evidence we needed to know that whoever was making decisions was a fucking moron.

Angelo waved me off as if he was more than done with this conversation. "We'll find out the rock star's thoughts on it soon enough. Father wants me to head straight for Big Noise and get it into line first. The other labels can wait until early into the new year."

Of course they could. And there was absolutely no reason why Bellerose's label was first off the block. No reason at all.

Fuck my life.

"When do you leave?" I asked. It wasn't as if I'd seen

Angelo a lot over the last few weeks, but this time it sounded like I'd be completely alone. .

"*We,*" he said, crossing his arms so the simple white shirt he wore stretched across broad shoulders. "You're coming with me."

If I'd thought I was horrified before, it was nothing on how I felt now.

"No," I breathed, shaking my head. "No! Have you lost your fucking mind."

It was a rhetorical question since it was clear he absolutely had.

"There's no other option, Bella. You're not safe here without me. Bottom line."

"I'm not safe there," I shot back. "Bellerose hates me. Like... *hate* hate. If we run into them, there's no chance you'll get anything dealt with. They'll fight us every step of the way."

"Enough!" he snarled. "Just fucking stop. You don't dictate to me, Billie. I'm the one who controls the narrative here. Bellerose will have an issue even if it's just me, but they get the same fucking choices in life as I do. None. We're all puppets to a higher master, and for now, there's nothing else that can be done. So shut the fuck up, pack a bag, and get your ass downstairs. We are heading for Naples."

Great. Just great. Naples, Illinois, was a few hours

from Siena and home to both Big Noise Records headquarters and all of Bellerose's members.

Shivers traced down my spine at his tone. Angelo was fucking done with this conversation, and he'd let me push him as far as he was willing to go today. If I continued on, there would be consequences. Shitty ones. Not that he'd laid a hand on me since moving me in as his mistress, but the threat was constantly there. Maybe he wouldn't do it himself, but there were plenty of Ricci goons who would.

"Fine," I said shortly, the word rasping over my dry throat. "Give me twenty minutes."

Without waiting for his reply—because *fuck him*—I turned away and stumbled from the sitting room, hating this fucking day. This whole fucking life. When I reached my private quarters, aka the gilded cage, I dragged down a small case that was at the top of my wardrobe and threw in a bunch of random clothes. I gave zero shits what I wore, and since most of the time I was in huge hoodies and coats—thank you winter for helping me hide the baby belly—it didn't matter what went underneath.

By the time I'd added toiletries and shoes, the case was near overflowing, and I had to sit on it to get it closed. I managed with a little effort, huffing since I was an unfit fuck, and then I waited for my *master* to arrive and order me to the car. I'd sold my soul to the devil long ago when I got involved in this family, and the funniest part of it all was that I still had no idea why they'd been trying to kill me in the first place. It wasn't just about me witnessing the murder, since they knew I wasn't about to tell anyone, and the police were in their pocket anyway. It was something more.

I'd asked Angelo, and he'd given me the same vague shit about me waiting on a table and supposedly overhearing an important conversation. I wasn't buying that for a second, especially when no one had tried to question me after Angelo saved me from torture.

From bits and pieces I'd heard during dinners with the Riccis, they were in a quiet criminal war with a new family in Siena. One who had risen quickly, amassing a ton of power in a way that didn't feel natural. Like they were being backed by another older, richer family who wanted to keep their hands clean. Or as clean as possible.

The Wilson family were into shit even shadier than the Riccis, and that was saying something. Maybe Giovanni thought I was working for them, that I'd been working as a waitress that night at the bequest of the Wilsons and was somehow spying on the Riccis. No doubt he assumed my relationship with Angelo was just part of the plan, and everyone was biding their time until they could knock me off in a less obvious way.

After their heir was born, of course.

Or maybe I'd been dismissed as not a threat when compared to the Wilsons? No one told me *shit* in the Ricci house, but I had ears and from the snippets I'd overheard, destroying the Wilson family appeared to be their focus for now. The new player had become too powerful, so they would be wiped out entirely.

Tension rode the Ricci house hard most days, and I felt like we were in this eerie calm before the storm. The interfamily gangland politics were a whole tangled web in this criminal world, and maybe it was for the best that Angelo and I were being given a chance to remove ourselves. At least for now.

Clearly, Angelo sensed the danger too, or possibly, he didn't like the thought of his *prisoner* being outside of his control for weeks or months while he dealt with this new merger. I wasn't going to argue again. The devil I knew was better than the one I didn't, and even if Bellerose iced the fuck out of me, I could deal with it. They weren't killers. Angelo was. Not a hard choice to make.

Shit, we probably wouldn't even see them. I was fairly sure they didn't hang out at the record studio on the regular, even if it was in the same city where they'd all set up their home bases.

Don't ask me how I knew where they all lived; my patheticness recently was better left unrevealed. Besides, Naples was a *huge* city; it's not like we'd just cross paths at Dutch Brothers.

There was a knock on the door, and I pushed myself up to stand, shuffling the heavy bag forward with my foot. "Yeah," I called. "Come in."

In the time it'd taken to pack my shit, I'd resigned myself to this next venture. It helped cool my anger, leaving me calm, if sullen. Angelo might scare the shit out of me, but I truly didn't believe he would hurt me *physically*. At least not without a real reason. With that touch of optimism, I'd try my best to be amicable and get along with him for this next part of our insane plan.

When the door swung open, I lifted my head from where I was nudging the bag forward still, and a near silent gasp escaped before I could stop it. Angelo wasn't on the other side of the doorway. It was Giovanni, his beady eyes narrowed as he stared coldly at me, like I was a rat that had stumbled under his feet. When the fuck had he dropped by this compound?

"All packed, I see," he said, voice without any inflection. He didn't need a tone since his face told me everything. This asshole loathed the very sight of me.

"How's my future grandson coming along? I haven't seen any updated ultrasounds, and at this point, I'd expect confirmation of sex. I'm sure I don't need to remind you we need a boy to carry the Ricci name."

Of course this misogynistic piece of shit required a male heir. What was this, the dark ages?

Swallowing hard to clear the lump in my throat, I forced a friendly smile across my face. It was disconcerting for him to direct conversation my way. Generally, he talked over and around me. But never *to me*. "Everything is coming along great with the baby." I patted my belly to emphasize it. "Angel and I have decided that we're not finding out the sex. I mean, I can't change it now, amiright?"

My forced laugh sounded absolutely ridiculous, but I was midway through my act and couldn't back down now. Giovanni always *hated* me calling his son Angel, so I was making every effort to reuse the old nickname just to piss him off.

"But I can see you're excited to become a Grandpa, so I promise to send you the next ultrasound images," I lied. "We're trying not to have too many taken, in case the sound waves are damaging to the baby. Only the best for the Ricci heir."

Everything from my mouth was pure bullshit, but Giovanni didn't appear to notice. I was banking on him having never bothered to attend one doctor's appointment with Fiorella—Angelo's mom—giving him no real idea of developmental milestones. It was working in our favor at the moment, since the last person I wanted to discuss any pregnancy with was this murdering cocksucker.

I was hoping he would fuck off now that he'd said his piece. He instead stepped into the room, moving close enough to me that my skin prickled, and I had to actively fight the urge to back up.

You never ran from a predator, right? Or was I supposed to run?

Giovanni reached out and placed his hand on my stomach. No asking for permission or even hesitating. If I'd thought my skin was prickling before, it was nothing on how I felt as he touched me. Like he owned me.

Bile rose in my throat, and I wondered what the punishment would be if I let loose and hurled all over him. At least it would get him away from me for now, even if he killed me for it later.

"Has he started to kick?" he asked, eyes narrowed.

I shook my head roughly. "The position of my placenta is stopping us from feeling the kicks yet," I rasped. "But I'll be sure to let you know the moment I do. My OBGYN warned us that it might be hard to feel anything even when *he* is bigger. But I really hope we do."

All new mothers would want to feel their child's kicks, right? It felt like the right thing to say.

One fuckup here, and I'd be dead, so it was critical that I played my part with far more acting skill than I actually possessed. This part of survival I knew for sure.

Giovanni pressed in even closer, staring down at me, his hand sandwiched on my belly between us. "I can see why my son is so obsessed with you," he murmured, his eyes, dark like Angelo's but without the warmth his son's possessed, locked on me. "You were a pretty child, but you've grown into a captivating woman. Maybe there is room for you in the Ricci—"

"Bella!" The snapped word came from the doorway, making me nearly jump out of my skin. "What are you doing?" Angelo strolled in, showing no real sign he was bothered by the way his father was touching me. "We need to get going; hurry up."

No one moved, and I silently counted in my head, needing to stay calm until this creep got away from me. The moment he did, I needed to burn these clothes and scrub my skin within an inch of its life. The prickling across it was near unbearable now.

"Right," Giovanni said. "You're off to Big Noise."

Angelo nodded, and when his father *finally* moved

away, he positioned himself so he was standing as a barrier between me and the head of the Ricci organization. The Don, Godfather, Big Boss. He used many names and titles, but they all meant one thing: He was the one who decided who lived and died here, and we couldn't afford to piss him off. Okay, I might be making those names up after watching too many mafia movies, but I was pretty sure his goons didn't call him Big G or Vanni.

Still, Angelo put his body between us, and that gave me enough time to scrub away the single hot tear that'd escaped my eye and get my game face back on.

"Report in as soon as you arrive," Giovanni said, whatever mood he'd been channeling before, when he assaulted the concept of personal space, disappearing. "And don't disappoint me, Angelo."

"Never, father," Angel said softly but with this lethal undercurrent that I wasn't sure I'd heard from him before. "Always the obedient son."

He was. Always obedient. He'd sacrificed all of his dreams for this family, and part of me wondered if one day, when he took over the reins, he'd be as fucked up and damaged as his father.

From then on, he'd be my Angel no more.

Just Angelo Ricci.

Forever lost to me.

nine

BILLIE

H ot blood splattered my face and chest, and a scream caught in my throat. My whole body froze, utterly locked up as the paunchy man in a suit with a new hole through his head collapsed to the carpet of the conference room floor.

"Bella! What the *fuck?*" Angelo roared, grabbing my arm hard enough to hurt as he dragged me out of the room. I couldn't tear my eyes away from the dead man, though. His sightless eyes stared up at the ceiling, the hole in the center of his forehead almost mocking his death for how neat it was. The mess of blood pooling beneath him betrayed a different story at the exit wound, though.

Holy shit.

Angelo was shaking my arm, talking—no, yelling—and all I could hear was static. White noise. Holy *shit*. He'd just shot that man. In a conference room. Holy *shit!*

Angelo dragged me away from the dead man, hauling me along the corridor of Big Noise Records, and I couldn't seem to make my body work to fight back. I just stumbled over my own feet and let him manhandle me into the ladies' room.

"...know how dangerous that was? You could have been hurt! Christ, Bella, you were supposed to be in the café!"

I swallowed hard, deliberately not looking at the mirror as Angelo used rough paper towels to clean the blood from my face. "You didn't give me any money," I mumbled, feeling numb. Everything was numb. He'd just *killed a man,* and he was here cleaning my face. What the fuck was going on?

Angelo stopped his frantic dabbing and stared at me like I'd just spoken in Klingon.

"You told me to get coffee," I elaborated, reminding him of the conversation we'd had not five minutes ago. "You said to get a coffee, and Trish took me to the café on level four, but—"

Angelo cut me off with a gusty, defeated sigh. "But I hadn't given you any money, and you have nothing of your own. Shit, Bella, I'm so sorry. I forget, sometimes, that you're... you know."

"Your prisoner?" I was slowly regaining my senses. The numbness was fading and leaving chills in its path. "Yeah, well... it is what it is."

I pulled out of his grip, wincing at the ache in my arm where he'd been gripping me, then bravely turned to face the mirror. *Holy shit.*

Swallowing hard, I yanked a paper towel from the dispenser and wet it under the tap. It wasn't a *lot* of blood, but it was enough. Which begged the question: What quantity of someone else's blood would be *not enough* to be concerned about? I guessed Angelo would know the answer to that, but I didn't have the stomach to ask.

"Bella, you know I'm only doing this to keep you safe," Angelo said in a darkly quiet voice. He stood at my back, and I met his gaze in the mirror as I pulled more paper towels from the dispenser.

I cleared my throat before responding, forcing myself to break eye contact and focus on the *blood* on my skin. "You're doing this to buy yourself time, Angel," I said softly. "And Valentina. Which is fine, but don't pretend you're doing me any favors with this." I gestured to my belly, feeling sick.

Angelo's brow creased, and he stepped closer. His arm circled around me, and his hand rested ever so gently on the swell of my bump. "Would it really be so bad? For us to be together? To raise a child just like we planned to all those years ago? We could be happy, Bella..."

For a moment, I slipped. I slipped into the fantasy that I always used to dream of as a stupid teenager in love with two boys. Two best friends. But look how that had all ended, with me standing here eight—nearly nine—years later, heartbroken, trapped, and splattered in blood.

"Why did you kill him?" I asked, changing the subject and trying to ignore my disappointment when Angelo's hand fell away from my body and he moved to give me space.

He pulled another paper towel, handing it to me as I tossed the one I'd been using into the trash.

"Because that's my job," he muttered, stuffing his hands into his pockets. "Giovanni didn't start with Big Noise because of Bellerose; in fact, I think he'd rather I had nothing to do with them. He started here because several execs on the board have ties to the Wilson family."

He watched me carefully as he said this, waiting for

me to ask who the Wilsons were. I just pursed my lips and finished cleaning the blood from my neck.

"So, you just kill them all?" I asked when he said nothing more.

Angelo shrugged. "Pretty much." There was a long pause within which I just stared blankly at my own reflection. Then Angelo sighed and scrubbed a hand over his face. The movement shifted his suit jacket, drawing my attention to the gun holstered at his hip. Fucking hell, when had my Angel become a killer? Or had he always been this way and I'd been too dumb and blind to see it?

"Come on, I'll take you back to the hotel," he said, opening the restroom door for me and waiting expectantly.

I started to exit, then hesitated and frowned. "What about—"

"I have people," he admitted with a grimace. "It'll be handled by a cleaner. We should go."

Nodding, I walked with him down the corridor— away from the blood-soaked conference room—and tried to make peace with my new reality. Like it or not, I was now an accomplice to murder.

A deep shiver ran through me as I got into the elevator, and without meaning to, I moved away from Angelo. He scared me, and that in and of itself broke my heart. Once upon a time, I'd trusted him enough to lean on his support after I told my parents I was pregnant at sixteen. I'd trusted him enough that we'd started planning a future together. Him, me, and the baby.

But then I'd lost my parents, lost the baby, and eventually, I'd lost Angel too... And all this was after losing Jace. Was it really any surprise I'd ended up spiraling to the point I was at when Rhett had saved me?

The Big Noise building was nearly empty since the sun had barely even risen for the day, so there were no familiar musicians lurking around. Thank fuck for small mercies.

"You won't run into them here," Angelo murmured as we crossed the foyer, like he could read my mind. "Bellerose, I mean. I should have told you sooner; I'm not that fucking cruel."

I bit back all the questions clamoring in my mind and played dumb. "Why would that be cruel?" I asked quietly.

Angelo gave a small, cold laugh. "I'm not an idiot, Bella. You and Jace reconnected. I'm shocked it took this long and *these* circumstances, but it wasn't exactly unexpected."

I nearly tripped in my confusion, then started laughing. A lot. So much that I soon began to hiccup.

Okay, there was a good chance that was shock from seeing a guy get shot finally setting in. Regardless, though, Angelo just waited while I dissolved from laughing into crying, then he dragged me into a forceful hug.

"I didn't reconnect with Jace, you deadshit," I mumbled between sobs—because tears were now streaming from my eyes. "I was with Rhett... and Grayson. Jace still hated me, and I can almost guarantee he'd happily run me over with a truck if he saw me now."

Angelo didn't say anything for a while, just rubbed my back while my crying subsided. Then he gave a small chuckle. "Rhett *and* Grayson? You always did love being the meat in a man sandwich, huh?"

His tone was teasing, not judgmental at all, but it reminded me of the past. My cheeks flamed hot, and I pushed out of his embrace. "None of your fucking business, Angel. Can we just go?"

"Sure thing, Bella." He led the way out to our waiting car, driven by one of the *many* Ricci goons.

Neither of us spoke for the whole drive back to our downtown-Naples hotel, and by the time we got to the room, my eyes ached. It was barely eight in the morning, and I was already exhausted.

"Is this how it's going to be?" I asked, glancing

around the impressive suite. "You're just here to kill people that are *suspected* of being Wilson affiliates?"

Angelo didn't respond immediately, taking his time to empty his pockets onto the dining table and unstrap his gun. He didn't take the clip out or anything like normal people might do to make it *safe*, but I guess that was just part of his life. He was never safe, as the Ricci heir.

"No, it won't be," he finally said. "But... things happen. People get shot. I can't apologize for that, Bella. It just is what it is."

I nodded, taking in his honesty and choking back the wave of fear that reminded me he was a stranger now.

"How many people have you killed?" I croaked, somehow *needing* to know.

He arched a brow, then shook his head slowly. "Sweetheart... you don't want me to answer that question. Go take a shower, then take the day to rest. I'll ensure no one disturbs you here so you can relax."

I understood and wet my lips before jerking my head in acknowledgment.

Sensing the conversation was well and truly over, I made my way into the bedroom and closed the door firmly behind myself. Only then did I let my shoulders sag, and my spirits plummeted.

What the fuck am I doing here? This is the worst plan I've ever had. Hands down, dumbest shit ever.

Except it wasn't *my* plan, it was Angelo's. Now it was too late to back out without getting both of us killed, so I was making lemonade.

ten

JACE

We'd been dropped in buttfuck nowhere with nothing but fields and some large patches of forest nearby. It was the sort of fresh-air escape from reality I'd daydreamed about while on tour, but the reality was that there was no booze, no food delivery, and less than no pussy.

It was a farm. There were honest-to-god *animals* on the property.

How the fuck was a musician supposed to music like this? No one could be creative under these circumstances, and we were already two hundred and fifty percent done with Rhett as he came off the cocktail of substances he'd been hammering into his body for the past two months.

Jesus, I needed earplugs to block out his endless complaints.

"Shut the fuck up, you whiny cunt," Brenda snarled, and I found a genuine smile for the first time in days. There was a reason she was so in demand with rock stars. She knew how to baby us, but she also knew when to call us on our shit. Both made us better musicians. Better humans, really.

"I'm going to leave," Rhett growled back, his voice clear, even if his eyes were bloodshot as shit as he paced across the large living space. This might not be a penthouse in the city, but it was far from a dump. "I need booze and weed at minimum, even if you keep all the coke for yourself."

I settled further into the couch, strumming my guitar quietly, while I let those two go at it. We'd arrived late last night, and Brenda was scheduled to leave this morning after we got settled. Grayson and Florence hadn't made it out of their rooms yet, but it was early, so that was understandable.

Even if out of character for our drummer.

Brenda shook her head at him. "Rhett, you know I love the fuck out of you. You four are my kids, and I'm sorry that I let you down by not being here when you needed me, but I promise, I'm here now. I'm also not walking away. I will hold your hand through this bullshit, and we will come out the other side stronger."

Rhett wanted to argue, that flash of anger in his eyes familiar. I'd seen it a lot recently, but as a guy with more than his fair share of mommy issues, he was apparently not willing to rip his adopted "mom" a new asshole. That streak of decency was what got the poor fucker into trouble all the time. It was what Billie had taken advantage of, and many times over the past two months, I'd wondered if she'd destroyed the final slivers of good in him.

But nope. It was still there, deeply ingrained.

Dumb fucker.

"Let's just focus on the music," I finally said, also feeling the impact of this label-enforced *retreat*. "The sooner we get this album made, the sooner we can get the fuck out of here."

Brenda clapped her hands together before she dropped them to her slim hips. There was no sign she'd recently had a baby, and dressed as she was in light denim jeans and a simple white shirt, it was hard to believe she was any older than us. "That's the spirit. We need to use the angst and pain of the past few months and turn that into the record that destroys all others. Show them that no one breaks you and the bullshit news articles aren't dictating your lives."

Rhett stopped pacing and I stopped strumming the strings for a beat as we both stared at her.

"What news articles?"

It wasn't like any of us checked social media or followed up on rumors about Bellerose, but generally, we were kept updated on any major scandals. Had Rhett and I really been so out of it that we'd missed something major...?

Brenda narrowed her eyes at us. "I sent you all multiple emails about a new blog account called *The Dirty Truths*. They've been heavily focused on Bellerose for the past month or so. Big Noise has their PR team dealing with it best they can, but these assholes are very good at covering their tracks."

I caught Rhett's eye, and he looked as confused as I felt. "Show me the account," I snarled, because I was a demanding fuck. She deserved it anyway since she'd taken our phones from us—except from Gray, who'd threatened bodily harm to anyone who touched his shit but promised to leave it in his room at all hours so it didn't interfere with our songwriting.

Brenda didn't argue, pulling out her huge-ass phone that she ran all our lives from. She hit a few buttons before finding what she wanted, and handed the device across the table to me. Rhett strolled over and sat next to me, and for once he didn't smell like he'd rolled out of a bar. Moving the screen so we could both read, I stared at the plain black webpage with a simple neon-blue header.

The Dirty Truths.

That was it. No author note. No date. No indication who this site belonged to, and if Big Noise couldn't figure anything out, then they were good at covering their tracks.

Scrolling along, I came to the most recent headline.

Bellerose goes into hiding. Their addictions hit a new high.

The article under that went into detail about how we'd been living a life of depravity the past two months, but Big Noise had ferried us into hiding in an attempt to sober us up and save our reputation while we worked on the next album.

It was nothing groundbreaking, but there was enough truth in this article for me to know they had some sort of insider feeding them information. We were used to it, from friends to those at Big Noise and even family. Almost everybody had a price, and loyalty was a rare commodity, especially in our world.

Rhett snorted tiredly. "Same old bullshit."

"Keep reading," Brenda pushed.

Billie Bellerose has gained plenty of pounds since leaving the band in disarray, looking festively plump ahead of Thanksgiving.

That article was a typical cunt move of the media, implying that Billie was overweight. Billie might be a lot of things, but her curves were lush and she was hot as fuck. I mean, only if you were into disloyal, backstabbing, untrustworthy chicks.

Rhett made a rumbling sound beside me, and I quickly scrolled past the article with its blurry Billie and Angelo pic–my own rage was buried under my loathing, which made it easier to move onto the third. Its heading was a little more personal.

Billie Bellerose sends the band named after her into a spiral.

This article had a lot of personal information about all our past relationships with Billie... and many intimate details about the brief romances between her, Rhett, and Grayson.

"What the fuck," Rhett growled, leaning forward, some of that fatigue fading from his face. The only reason he was up this early was he never went to sleep. Wasn't sure he'd slept more than a few hours a night since Billie left, even with his concoctions of pharmaceuticals and drugs. "How could they possibly know any of this? I mean, we didn't parade Billie around. We never even mentioned her name, but they know everything."

Brenda nodded as she pursed her lips. "Right, these fuckers have someone on the inside, but I have no idea who it is. They're stirring shit up hard and fast, and it's probably a good idea to let Billie know that she could be targeted by the paps if she heads out in public. Now that they know she's the Bellerose from your band name, life is never going to be the same for her again."

A snort escaped Rhett. "What she deserves."

He wouldn't get an argument from me. "So, this is the real reason behind this secluded fucking prison instead of the Big Noise content house," I said with a sigh. "You don't want any of our sessions leaking early."

Brenda shot me her Grinchiest smile. "Aw, Jace, look at you putting two and two together and getting the correct answer." I flipped her off, and that smile grew. "But yes, if we have a leak, then we're back to not trusting anyone again. Tom would have been keeping Big Noise updated on what you were doing on tour, so this could still be coming from him, but either way, it's not in our best interests to have you in a house strewn with Big Noise surveillance."

"And you let me believe you were placating my need for privacy," Grayson drawled as he entered the room.

She shrugged. "There's a reason I'm the best in the

business. It's all about learning *how to manage* you little assholes without you realizing that's what I'm doing. It's a specific skillset I possess and put to daily use."

Gray just smiled, before dropping a kiss on her cheek. "I'm aware of what you do, but I appreciate it all the same."

He took a seat on the couch across from us, and I leaned over and handed him the phone, while Brenda caught him up on the site. There were dozens of articles on the simply designed page, all of them quite accurately depicting our recent dramas.

Gray read through quietly, expression unchanging. The bastard rarely let anything slip unless he wanted to, including his blind reaction to fucked up news—one of his many skills I envied, since I'd been told often that my emotions were clear across my face.

There had really been no other path in life for me other than a musician, bleeding into my lyrics every night for thousands of Bellerose fans. Rhett was similar, needing the creative outlet for his fucked up, broken soul. Not to mention the adoration that filled holes inside us we'd rather not examine. Gray, on the other hand, could have done anything. He'd easily wander through dozens of careers and excel in each and every single one. Nothing ever touched him soul deep.

Well, except maybe one golden-haired bitch, who

clearly didn't deserve one fucking second of our time and emotional energy.

"This isn't the first mole within our team, and it won't be the last," Brenda said, reminding us that most humans were pieces of shit. "Let's just focus on getting this album made, and when it releases, no one will care about the drama of your past tour."

I had my doubts, but we did need to make the album, and soon. We were pushing our contractual obligations as it was, and if we wanted to break ties with Big Noise, we needed to finish up this shit first.

When Gray handed the phone back to Brenda, it rang almost immediately, and she groaned. "Okay, I need to take this. They're giving us updates on the Sunrise merger. I'll leave you all to it; food is already prepared and ready for the week in the fridge and pantry, and I expect some updates soon."

We'd heard the rumors of a corporate merger, but since we were all ready to fuck off from this label, we honestly didn't care what other asshole had bought out the parent company. Time to focus on what was important.

Rhett's eyes were narrowed to slits as he leaned forward. "Bring us weed at minimum," he reminded her. "We cannot be creative like this."

"I can," Grayson said with a smirk. Sanctimonious motherfucker.

Rhett didn't even bother to look his way, but his expression did soften as he pleaded with Brenda. "It's just weed. It's not even fucking illegal here. I have to get some sleep, or I'll be less than useless."

She stepped closer and brushed a hand across his shoulder before giving his arm a squeeze. "If you deliver on some initial track ideas and sounds for the album, then I promise to bring some top quality weed for you. It's a give-give relationship, but you have to give first."

Rhett shook her hand off, but Brenda wasn't offended as she let out a small laugh. "Thanks for understanding."

If looks could kill… or at least maim, then she'd be in trouble, but before Rhett let loose with any of the vitriol that was no doubt percolating around his head, she left the room, waving over her shoulder as she went. "See you tomorrow."

None of us spoke until the front door slammed shut and the automatic locking system clicked into place. We weren't literal prisoners—we could unlock the house at any time—but with literal wilderness around us, there was no fucking reason to leave, which was the supposed point of us being here, along with keeping *The Dirty Truths* light on updates.

"What if Florence is the mole," Rhett said suddenly, leaning forward to rest his elbows on his knees as he looked between Gray and me. "I mean, it's not like that bitch hasn't sold us out already this year, even if it was for that piece-of-shit boyfriend. She has no money, apparently, so what's to stop her from doing it again for the right paycheck?"

The chick in question walked through the door a minute later, yawning and rubbing at her face. She was still dressed in the oversized Bellerose shirt and tiny shorts she slept in, and at first I thought she didn't hear Rhett, until she said, "I have done a lot of fucked up things recently, but selling out Bellerose to the media is not one of them."

There was no anger or offense in her tone. She didn't care that Rhett suspected her, and I already knew she believed she deserved this treatment. In some ways she did, but in other ways Flo had always been a lost little girl. Without family. Without guidance. She'd raised herself, and at times, she fucked up.

We all fucked up. But I got where Rhett's lack of trust was coming from—it'd take me a hot minute to trust her ass again too. We had to work together, though, which meant keeping shit as amicable as possible under the circumstances.

"We should get breakfast going," I said, pushing

myself to stand. It was odd not being hungover, but at the same time, nice to feel normal. I had energy. I had some creative buzz.

I was ready to get this fucking album done, and then finally we could move on.

Leave this fucked up year behind. Once and for all.

eleven

BILLIE

A soft tap on the bedroom door saw me jerking awake with a gasp. I'd never slept deeply at the best of times, but after being beaten half to death by the Ricci goons and held in a cage, I was lucky to snatch an hour at a time without nightmares.

"Bella?" Angelo called through the closed—and locked—door. "Are you awake?"

I groaned as I pushed up to sitting. How long had I slept? Ugh, forty minutes. Cool.

"Bella?" Angelo asked again.

"I am now," I snapped back, irritated at my lack of rest. "What's wrong?"

"Uh, are you dressed? Someone is here that wants to meet you." His tone was weird. Uncomfortable, even. Was his father here? No, he wouldn't want to *meet me.*

I glanced down at myself. I'd been sleeping in just my undies, so that was a firm *no* on being dressed. "I need like ten minutes," I shouted back. "Can I have that, sir?" My sarcasm was thick, but the whole invisible shackles shit was grating on my nerves.

"Sure thing, *sweetheart,*" he replied, emphasizing the endearment. Oops, he must not be alone out there. Gritting my teeth, I made my way into the en suite bathroom to take a shower. Ten minutes was bullshit; I needed at least half an hour to transform myself back into the polite, obedient mafia mistress that Angelo needed me to be.

By the time I emerged into the living room of our suite, I was fully prepared to find some man irritated at being made to wait. So I was shocked nearly speechless to find a mid-thirties woman sitting on the couch sipping tea and smiling at Angelo.

Angelo... who held a giggling baby like a fucking pro.

"Uh... hi?" My confused gaze snapped between the woman and Angelo, then to the baby and back to Angelo again. "What, um, what...? Who, uh... hi. Sorry,

I'm—" I put my hand out to shake with the woman, suddenly remembering my manners.

"You're Billie Bellerose," she cut me off, placing her cup down and rising to her feet. Then her eyes widened as she took in my pregnant belly. "And you're pregnant. Holy shit. Angelo, you failed to mention this part..."

Angelo shot me a dark look, one that sent a shiver down my spine. "I didn't think it relevant."

"Oh no? Hmm." The woman pursed her lips, giving my bump a narrow-eyed look. "What are you, about four months?"

I hesitated, looking to Angelo for guidance. Who was this woman?

"I know what you're implying, Brenda, but it's *my* baby. Don't go causing unnecessary drama. Fuck knows that blog site is doing enough of that without you adding more scandal." Angelo's words were hard and edged with warning, but his smile was still soft for the baby he held. Then he blew a raspberry on the baby's belly, making peals of laughter bubble out of the small human.

The woman muttered some choice swear words under her breath, then turned back to me with an apologetic smile. "Sorry, gosh, that was rude of me. I'm Brenda Greer. I've heard so much about you, Billie, I

110

need to remind myself that rumor is not truth. Come, sit."

Still confused and weirded out, I made my way over to the couch where Angelo sat with the baby. Why was he holding the baby like that? It was messing me up inside.

"Oh, that's James," Brenda added, smiling in the baby's direction. "He's just five months old, so unfortunately, when his daddy is at work, he's gotta come along with me. Milk machine and all."

"James is no trouble," Angelo said while pulling faces at the infant. "Are you? You're just a happy baby who loves his mama, aren't you?"

Did he just... *baby talk*?

Brenda chuckled, then turned her attention to me. "Well. I definitely wasn't expecting you to be pregnant, Billie, so that complicates what I was planning."

"Spit it out, Brenda. What do you want?" Angelo was terse, to the point, but still snuggling James. It was making my brain short-circuit. At no point in all of this drama did I ever stop and think about Angelo *actually being a fucking father*. He was a natural, and it was freaking me the hell out.

Brenda didn't seem offended by his tone; she just flicked him a cursory glance before returning her gaze to me. "Billie, maybe the boys never mentioned me

since I was off work and adjusting to life as a new mom
—like I still should be if it weren't for this fucking
merger mess—but I'm the manager for Bellerose."

Oh.

I glanced down at my belly, now understanding her
concern. She thought I was carrying a Bellerose baby.

"I see," I murmured.

Brenda tilted her head to the side. "I'm not sure you
do, honey. I came here to ask for your help, but this...
this is not going to go down well." She was talking
about my belly again.

I frowned. "I don't follow. I'm not carrying Rhett's
baby, if that's the concern. It's Angelo's. We have all the
medical records if you want to see them to verify. I can
understand that it'd be a whole PR mess for the band to
have an unplanned pregnancy, but that's not this.
Angelo and I are—"

"That's not what this is about," Brenda cut me off.
She glanced at Angelo, then sighed. "Bellerose is in a
bad way right now. Jace seems to be totally detached
from his emotions, which, given your history and
current state is kind of understandable. Didn't you—"

"Yes," Angelo growled. "Leave it alone, Brenda.
Billie and I were both there; we don't need to revisit
ancient history." Like when I'd told Jace I was leaving
him for his best friend, shattering his heart right after

he'd signed his recording contract. With Brenda. That now made sense why she was familiar with Angelo, since she'd offered him the same contract back then.

She nodded. "Well, anyway. Flo is on the outs; apparently, she orchestrated some kind of abduction of Billie, which, of course, didn't happen. Thank goodness. But the boys are holding her accountable anyway."

It took all my control not to react. As far as Bellerose was concerned, I'd willingly returned to Angelo. But that *wasn't* what had happened. I *had* been abducted that night, stolen away and tortured by Ricci men until Angelo saved me. And now I was finding out that *Florence* was the one responsible.

Holy *shit*. I would kill her. I'd fucking *kill her*.

Angelo must have read my mind again because he placed a hand on my knee and gave me a little squeeze, grounding me and reminding me of the act we had to maintain. Happy couple.

Brenda was still talking, so I swallowed my rage and focused on what she was saying. "...and Rhett is one overdose away from being involuntarily admitted into rehab. That boy is all kinds of messed up, and I have no idea what to do to help him. Actually, that's not true; I *had* an idea but now... not so much." Another pointed look at my belly.

I wet my lips, grasping onto what she was saying.

"Rhett... why is he so bad? I didn't... I mean, we were together but not serious. And not for long. Surely, I didn't..." Was I to blame?

Brenda shook her head. "It's not on you, Billie. It's on him and his long-term refusal to seek professional help. I read the blog post about how you two met, so you already know about his white-knight impulses. That's all baggage from his childhood, and something recently has triggered a spiral."

"If I was to speculate," Angelo murmured, rocking James as the little dude's eyes drifted shut, "I'd say that Billie leaving him to return to, in his opinion, an abusive relationship has triggered his memory of his own mother choosing to stay with her abuser rather than escape with her son."

My jaw dropped, and Brenda sighed. "Really, Angelo?"

The tattoo-covered mafia heir just shrugged. "I also read the blogs, Brenda. I know what's going on."

She made an irritated sound, her brows drawn tight. "Well, regardless. My job is to fix the band and ensure they produce their contractually bound album. Which they can't do if Rhett is locked up in rehab, or worse."

Dead. She meant dead. Was he *that* bad? Fuck me, I felt awful for my part in that.

"Wait, what blogs? You both mentioned blogs. What am I missing here?" I frowned, glancing between them both.

Brenda just arched a brow at Angelo, who sighed. "It's a gossip blog," he told me. "They've been causing a bit of drama for the entertainment industry for the past year or so, but recently the full focus seems to be on Bellerose. And you."

"Me?" I squeaked, panic flooding through me. "Why? Wait, just show me."

I didn't have a phone of my own—prisoner, remember? So I needed Angelo's. He exchanged a long look with Brenda, then reluctantly handed it over.

"It's called *The Dirty Truths*," Brenda helpfully informed me, and I navigated to the blog site in question.

The first article was about Bellerose going into hiding to work on their overdue album and speculation that they were in shit for both canceling the international leg of their tour *and* for excessive partying lately. It hurt to read, seeing these boys I cared for being discussed with such insensitivity, but this was the life they chose. It couldn't be easy to be famous.

I paused on a post that led with a full-page photo of *me*. Me and Angelo. It'd been taken some weeks ago when we were leaving the country club luncheon where that bitch whose name I'd already forgotten dumped wine on me.

I had a coat on when they'd taken the photo, so my bump was hidden entirely, but the blogger was quick to comment that *Billie Bellerose has gained plenty of pounds since leaving the band in disarray, looking festively plump ahead of Thanksgiving.*

"Seriously?" I spluttered. "How do people write this shit?"

At least the author had commented that I looked good with the extra weight.

The next article was much more confrontational, and my palms sweat as I read all about how *I'd* torn the band apart by sleeping around. Fucking hell.

I scrolled down, skim-reading posts about Flo and Tom's breakup and speculations about him taking all her money. Good. Bitch deserved it. I'd have been happier if it was Tom getting his just desserts, but I had faith that karma was coming for him.

Then countless posts about Rhett's drug use and Jace's womanizing. There were even several uncensored photos of him fucking girls publicly, which made me shift uncomfortably in my seat.

After a few more posts, some of which focused on my history with Angelo and Jace—facts totally skewed to favor Jace—I had to stop reading. They'd touched on my parents' deaths, and I just couldn't face that right now.

"Okay, so they're in the media. That's nothing new for Bellerose. What do you need from me?"

Brenda rubbed at the bridge of her nose. "Well, shit. I came here to ask if you'd be open to visiting with them. I thought if you and Rhett could talk, maybe it'd help him heal. But this..." She waved a hand at my belly. "This would be like throwing a can of gasoline on a campfire."

"Maybe that's what they need," Angelo mused.

Brenda's look of shock probably mirrored my own. "I don't think—"

"I do," he countered, smiling an evil smile. "All their best music came from pain and anger, not reconciliations. You want good songs? Let's blow shit up."

My jaw dropped. "What? No. Angelo, I can't meet with them like *this*." I flapped my hands in distress. Had he just had a stroke? In no world was this a good idea.

"Meet them? No, we can't just do that. For one thing, this *Dirty Truths* prick seems to have eyes everywhere, and for another, they're locked away on a writing retreat. We'll have to go and *stay*, of course."

I nearly fainted. "We?"

Angelo's grin spread wide. "I can't let my pregnant

mistress stay with a bunch of rock stars alone. It'd be unseemly. Besides, Brenda, you know all Jace's best shit wasn't *only* about Billie."

I had nothing to say. Speechless. I was fucking *speechless.*

Wait. No, I wasn't. "Why? This makes zero sense, Angelo. I'm sorry but you're fucking up to something and don't for a second try to pretend you want to help Bellerose finish their album because you're a fan of their music. What gives?"

Angelo and Brenda exchanged a glance, then his *don't give a fuck* stare returned to me. He shrugged. "Maybe I do have ulterior motives, but last I checked, I don't have to explain myself. You want to see your boy toy Rhett again, don't you?" I nodded before I could catch myself. "So just go along with it, Bella. My reasons are my own, and Brenda can't afford to question them any more than you can."

Brenda winced, but also nodded slowly and thoughtfully. "You might have a point there, Angelo. Christ, this will either produce some amazing music or end in a bloodbath. Let's do it." They'd both lost their fucking minds.

twelve

GRAYSON

I'd been closely following *The Dirty Truths* as part of my investigation. Their information was only a few steps behind mine, and on the rare times Johnson or I missed something in our surveillance, they tended to find it. I managed to avoid any question from my bandmates about my lack of surprise when Brenda brought it up, and after another couple of days had passed, we were all too focused on the music to worry about the outside world.

Except for my once-a-day updates from the dickhead-of-the-year-investigator, Johnson. In his last update, I'd been surprised to hear that Billie was in Naples, seen exiting the Big Noise head office. Angelo was with her, of course. A captor never allowed his prisoner to roam freely without him.

Speculation of why she was there, and in our label's office, dominated my mind, even as I mindlessly drummed along to the beat Jace was experimenting with for his current song. This house had a basement studio and music room with the most incredible equipment and acoustics. We'd been down here most of the time, only moving to the main level when we needed to eat or sleep.

"It's missing something," Rhett said shortly. "We sound like fucking amateurs." He was more with it on our third day here, but his temper was out of control. If Brenda didn't hook him up with something soon, I was going to be burying a bandmate out in the backyard. Asshole was getting on my last nerve.

He wasn't wrong though. For all of his issues, Rhett had an ear for music that rivaled Jace's. Sometimes it was far greater.

"I think the issue is—" Florence barely got those words out before Rhett growled and stomped off, guitar still over his shoulder. If she added harmony, he didn't flip out, but the moment she offered an opinion, he lost his shit.

Florence sunk into herself, closing her eyes briefly before she took a deep breath. "He's never going to forgive me," she rasped, opening her eyes once more to look between us. "How can we make an album when he can barely be in the same room as me?"

"Rhett's mother went back to her abuser," Jace reminded Florence. "He's been concerned about you for a while. Tom was clearly predatory, but you ignored our advice and asked us to stop interfering, so we left you to it. Now he finds out that you were working with Tom to betray us and get rid of Billie. You've hit on one of the few things he'll struggle to forgive."

"Billie did it too," Florence shot back. "She went to Angelo."

Shaking my head, I stood up from the drums, deciding we were done for today. "She was taken by Angelo. If Billie was running, it was for another reason, probably something altruistic, if I know her at all. Angelo just took advantage of the situation."

I was as sure of this as I was of my own fucked up past.

"No one fucking knows her, bro," Jace shot back. "Billie is an actress who plays her part well, and when she's done with the role, she runs. It happened in the past, and it's still happening now. Stop making excuses for her. Your damage might be different than Rhett's, but it's there and it's clouding your judgment."

Barely resisting the urge to cross the room and

smash his face into a wall, I instead allowed myself two deep breaths before speaking. "If anyone carries damage, *bro,* it's fucking you. I'm not ready to give up on Billie. Not yet. My loyalty runs deeper than that, and until she's standing before me telling me exactly what happened that day, she has my trust."

The. Fucking. End.

Leaving the studio, I took the stairs three at a time, getting to the top as fast as possible. I'd been stuck in this house for too long; I needed some fresh air. Passing Rhett, who was sprawled on the couch, remote in hand, I walked along the entryway until I reached the front door. Hitting the button to release the locks, I stepped out onto the large wraparound porch.

This was a typical ranch house, with two stories and a basement. It was older but well-maintained with quality fittings. At first, we'd thought we were alone out here, but then I'd discovered the barn during one of my nightly walks. Behind it, large, fenced paddocks held quite a few horses. The owners had popped by twice to check on their animals, but only early in the morning, which meant I was free to approach the yards now without pissing someone off over messing with their prized animals.

I'd spent enough time around horses in my youth to know that the multitude of tan, brown, and white quarter horses out there were of the highest quality. They had the strong, muscled hind legs and smooth gait required for competition and breeding. I approached the three-rail fencing, propped one foot up on the bottom post, and stared out across the paddock.

It was beautiful country, and while it didn't remind me of where I'd grown up, there was a similar, relaxed vibe. This was not a land where you rushed. This was a land where you took a moment, smelled the horse shit, and breathed the fresh air. Crusher, the old rock drummer who'd taught me all I knew, had kept horses and often made me help him out as a kid. Payment for free music lessons.

Noticing some partially opened bales of hay just inside the shed door, I moved over to grab up some of the feed, and by the time I turned around, two of the horses were already waiting at the gate.

They were used to being hand fed, and even if they didn't need the supplement feeding in this lush paddock, the owners clearly liked to add a bit of extra to their diet. Or maybe it was part of ensuring they remained calm around people. Animals had a way of going wild when they were left on their own too long, hence why the owners snuck up here every day, despite lending Brenda their house. From what I'd seen, it was an older couple, and I wondered what their relationship was to our band manager.

Fuck, for all I knew, they were Brenda's parents. She never exactly brought us into her personal life, preferring to keep band stuff separate. This house was definitely not on Big Noise's payroll, though, so it had to be known to her from somewhere.

Maybe we'd find out before our time here was done.

The closest horse, a huge bay that was at least sixteen or seventeen hands high–on the larger side for their breed–lifted his head over the railing. He nudged at my hands, seeking the quality alfalfa I held. "You've been feeding in a good pasture," I said with a low laugh, feeling more relaxed than I had in weeks. "Are you sure you need any extra?"

He whinnied quietly, before he all but ate my hand to get to the feed. Opening my palm so it was flat, I managed to save my fingers, meanwhile using my free hand to brush across his soft hair. "Your coat is beautiful," I murmured, pressing my head closer to his, breathing in that earthy scent. There was something calming about horses, and I related in a way I wished I couldn't. Their nature was wild until they were captured and broken in. I'd been tamed early in life, broken in, so to speak, but the true nature inside never changed. I sensed that in other creatures, but especially in horses.

I'd have loved to ride them, but that would be going too far with someone else's prized creatures. Maybe I'd ask Brenda if she did know the owners and if there was any chance of a few riding sessions. The thought of taking off across the open plains was appealing right now.

Footsteps reached me a moment before Rhett slid in beside me, lifting one foot to rest on the lower post. Were you even in the country if you didn't rest your foot on the railing?

Fuck, no, you weren't.

We remained in an amicable silence for at least twenty minutes, giving the horses some love and attention, until eventually they wandered off. In that time, my internal equilibrium returned, and I got the feeling it was the same for Rhett.

"What are we going to do?" he finally said, voice raspy. He'd had a near permanent gravel to his tone since Billie left. "At this rate, this album is never going to get made. Fuck, we'll be lucky if we don't kill each other and burn the house down."

I shook my head and shot him a sideways look. "Speak for yourself. No one is killing me, but I'll happily burn the house down on you fuckers if you try."

Rhett waved me off like I wasn't a complete psychopath when we both knew the truth. "You know what I mean. We've been struggling for a few years anyway, and Billie coming into our lives just exposed our truths. Our *dirty truths,* as that fucking blog likes to point out. We have far deeper troubles than her weakness. It's our voice... We've lost our voice."

Turning back to the view, I leaned forward and rested my chin on my arms, enjoying the brief chirps of birds and whistles of the wind through the grass. "You're right. Our first two albums were hot, filled with passion and a unique beat, but lately it's all on repeat. Change a few chords and words, slap a different bridge in there, but there's no true creative skill in anything we've produced lately."

Our sound had been deteriorating before Billie. We'd fallen into bad habits, resting on our fame and the fact that the fans just wanted whatever we threw out there. "We need a change of pace. New air." I breathed even deeper at the realization. "I think we should move our next session out here. Maybe even tonight. I can start a campfire to encourage our creativity to flow in a new atmosphere."

Rhett didn't argue, choosing to look out across the field with me. "Yeah, I'd like that. I even have an idea for a song. I've been working on it off and on, and I think it can be fixed with your help." He paused. "Yours and Jace's."

"You have to deal with her," I said when Flo's name wasn't mentioned. "Whether you want her to be or not, for the time being, she's part of the band. We'll never find cohesion if you're constantly giving her the cold shoulder."

He dropped his foot and straightened, whatever peace he'd found gone in a flash. "I am dealing with her," he rumbled. "But dealing doesn't mean I have to be fucking polite. All it means is I sit in the same room as her and work on music. As long as she keeps it to music, then I'll keep dealing."

He stalked off, and I decided to follow. It was time to rally the others into our outdoor night session. Maybe none of us had been the "sit around a campfire and sing" kinda kids, but we did gel best when we were taken out of the recording studio. Away from all our fame and glory.

Maybe it was time to get back to our roots.

It really might be the last chance Bellerose had.

thirteen

RHETT

My skin fucking itched. Everywhere. It'd been three full days since Brenda kidnapped us all, and I was one hundred percent feeling the harsh cold of detox. There wasn't even enough booze in the house to get a proper buzz going, just crappy half-strength beer and cider that couldn't get a mouse drunk.

Grayson's idea to take our songwriting session out into nature had seemed like a good one. Until I realized how bitterly cold it was outdoors at night. Thank fuck for the roaring fire, or we'd get hypothermia before ever producing any music.

"The lyrics need more authenticity," Gray

announced after we'd all settled in around the campfire, bundled up in our thick coats. "Right now, this song sounds like it's been pulled straight out of an AI lyric generator."

"Fuck you," Jace spat.

Grayson just arched a brow, then shifted his attention to me. "Rhett, you said you had a song you've been working on. Let's hear it."

"Uh..." I glanced over at Jace, who stared back at me with an intense expression. He'd always written our lyrics. I'd helped tweak a word here and there and contributed on the melody, but writing Bellerose's music was *his thing*. Then again, the shit he'd written these last few days was trash, so surely, I couldn't do worse.

"Fuck it," I muttered, picking up my guitar. "Alright, this is unfinished and shit... Whatever."

Swallowing past my awkwardness, I strummed the opening notes of the song that'd been rattling around in my head lately, then shifted into the intro. I didn't look at my bandmates, but I could tell, I could *feel* that I had them hooked.

"Our hands slipped apart when you betrayed my heart.
Stolen from time, there're no promises to remain.
All the plans we made, lost and destroyed.
Your weakness was mine..." The newfound huskiness

129

in my voice, thanks to how much I'd been smoking lately, added a haunting quality to the lyrics, and I nearly lost my train of thought.

I wavered slightly on the next verse, which was the most personal of all, then all of a sudden, I had backup. But not from Jace, my best friend. Nope, the first one to join my new song was Flo on her bass guitar, picking up the threads of my half-finished melody and weaving them together for a more fleshed-out sound.

Despite how sour I was feeling toward her, my confidence strengthened, and I pushed forward with the song, closing my eyes to block out Jace's scowl and just losing myself in the music.

It wasn't long before Grayson joined in, drumming his sticks on a hollow log, then finally Jace added his rhythm guitar and harmonized the vocals with me. When I ran out of the shit I'd already written, he adlibbed and built on the story I'd started to tell, finishing the remaining verse with enviable ease.

As the last few notes rang out, a weirdly comfortable silence descended over the four of us. For the first time in what seemed like forever, the music felt *good*.

"Rhett, that was amazing," Flo said quietly, her voice as meek as a mouse, like she was expecting me to lash back with cutting words. Again. She was right to feel like that after how I'd treated her lately.

But she was more than just a bandmate. She was part of my Bellerose family. I might shout on about how I didn't do family, but in truth, it wasn't this family I hated. This one was my safe harbor, and that was no doubt why I'd taken her betrayal so hard, so personally. But I needed to get past it if we wanted any hope of finishing this album and buying ourselves out of Big Noise.

So I wet my lips and gave a short nod. "Thanks."

Gray grunted in approval, then pulled a bottle of tequila out of his huge coat. "I reckon we deserve this."

"Oh shit yes, you beautiful, rugged man, you." I eagerly reached for the offered bottle. "If I were gay, I'd probably blow you right now."

Flo snickered, but Grayson shook his head and gave me a look of disgust. "No thanks. You look like you've got an awful gag reflex. I'd hate to choke you with my anaconda."

"Calm down, big man. I've seen what you're packing, and it's nothing to brag about," I teased. Totally untrue, Gray's dick was huge, the lucky bastard.

Jace cleared his throat, drawing our combined attention. His brow was creased in a frown, and I gave a resigned sigh. "What?"

His eyes narrowed at me. "I have some notes."

I scoffed. "Of course you do. Come on then, let's hear it."

For the next several hours, Jace and I did what we'd done a hundred times already. We collaborated and made music. This time, though, he finessed *my* song, not the other way around. It was... nice.

Flo and Gray stayed, adding comments and suggestions every now and then, but the bulk of the creating was on Jace and me. Just like old times.

As the fire started dying down and we all rocked a nice, warm tequila buzz, car headlights started crawling up the long gravel road toward the house. Confused, I checked the time on my watch.

"It's a bit late for Brenda, isn't it?"

"Yeah," Jace agreed, nodding. "It is. Maybe someone from Big Noise came to check on us."

Gray shook his head, rising to his feet. "At this time of night? No way. Besides, Brenda swore they'd leave us alone out here." He reached under his coat and came out with a gun in hand.

"What the fuck?" Flo squeaked, voicing my own thoughts. "Gray, you can't—"

"Quiet," he growled. "Stay here."

He started toward the approaching car, but I rushed forward to grab his arm. "Gray, stop. It's probably someone who got lost and needs directions. Or an Uber delivery with some quality weed for me. Just fucking chill, and put the gun away. Jesus."

"Rhett, don't be an idiot, they're not looking for fucking directions." Grayson shook my hand from his arm, not making any move to put his gun away. "Just stay back here and keep Jace and Flo safe."

"Excuse me?" Jace drawled. "Since when was I so helpless?"

Gray and I exchanged a quick smirk, then Gray was stalking toward the car again. It'd pulled up in front of the house, so we were a fair distance away still. A man climbed out of the driver's side, looking confident and not at all lost.

"Hey!" Gray barked out, drawing the shadowed man's attention away from the house. "Who are you, and what do you want?"

Well... at least he was asking questions first, even if he did plan to shoot second.

I hurried along behind him, eager to know what the hell was going on but not so suicidal that I wanted to catch a stray bullet if shit went sideways.

"Grayson Taylor, I presume," the man called back. His voice wasn't familiar, but it was deep and rich, stained with an edge of an accent.

"Who's asking?" Gray replied, hiding his gun behind his thigh as he strode closer.

The guy didn't answer immediately, then a low chuckle caught my ears as we approached. "Where's Jace?" he asked instead of answering.

Gray paused, glancing back at me. His brow had dipped in a frown, but he didn't seem too trigger-happy. In fact, he tucked his gun back under his coat as he tipped his head toward our campfire. I got the message and backtracked quickly.

"Jace! Some guy here to see you," I called out to my best friend. "Seems super sketchy, though, if you want my opinion. You expecting anyone?"

Jace left his guitar beside mine and jogged across the paddock to reach me. Flo followed slower, like she didn't want to be left behind but also didn't know whether to join us.

"I'm not expecting anyone," Jace muttered, heading for Grayson, who'd just reached the driveway where the man was parked. "We don't even have phones to let people know where we are."

"Well, he asked for you," I replied, hurrying to keep up with his long strides. "And no one knows we're here except Brenda. She must have sent him."

"I guess," Jace agreed, climbing over the paddock fence that separated us from the house area. I paused to help Flo over the wire, so I wasn't close enough to see Jace reach the guy. All I heard was the reaction.

"Get *fucked*," Jace roared, then he must have punched the guy because a second later when Flo and I sprinted over to the car, we found Gray restraining Jace while the stranger sat in the gravel with his hand over his bleeding nose.

"What the shit?" I exclaimed, looking between Jace, thrashing against Grayson's steel grip, and the bleeding dude. He was young, probably the same age as Jace and I, and had tattoos on his hands. The rest of him was covered in winter clothes, but he had a distinctive *danger* look to him.

"Get the fuck out of here; you have *no right*," Jace bellowed at the guy as he struggled against Gray's hold. "No fucking right to be here! I told you if I saw you again, I'd fucking kill you, Angel, I fucking *meant it*. You're a dead man!"

Whoa. *What?*

"Angelo?" I gaped down at the bleeding man. It checked out; he oozed *mafia*. "What are—"

"Where is she?" Grayson rumbled, pushing Jace roughly aside as he hauled Angelo *fucking* Ricci up off the ground by the front of his shirt. "Where's Billie?"

"I'm right here," her achingly familiar voice cut through me like a knife. "Now if you're all done throwing your manly weight around, can we go inside? I'm freezing and tired, and my back hurts."

Her hazel eyes swept over all of us but didn't meet anyone's gaze before she turned away. Her huge, black puffer jacket turned her into a charred marshmallow, all round and squishy. But her hair shone like spun gold and her face held a healthy glow, unlike the hollow, hungry look she'd had when we met. Fuck. Angelo *had* been taking care of her after all.

A small part of me had held a sick fantasy that he'd been holding her captive, but that idea was immediately dashed as I saw how *good* she looked.

"Billie," Flo croaked, her eyes full of tears as she started forward. Billie didn't even *glance* at our bassist, just stomped up the front steps of the house in her fluffy, designer snow boots and let herself inside without waiting on any of us.

I was the first to react, racing after her to find out what the *fuck* was going on. Jace and Gray could kill Angelo Ricci for all I cared. I wanted to know *why* she was here. With *him*.

"I'm wrecked," Billie announced as I entered the house. She was at the base of the main staircase, tugging gloves off her slim, pale fingers. "Can you tell me which bedroom is free?"

I swallowed hard, folding my arms and saying

nothing. If she wanted to talk to me, she could damn well offer the decency of looking at me.

After a moment of my silence, she gave a heavy sigh. "Rhett... please." The pain in her voice gutted me thoroughly. "I don't want to be here any more than you want me here. Just point me to my room, and I'll stay out of everyone's way."

"Why *are* you here, then?" Jace snapped, entering the house behind me. Gray was right on his tail.

Angelo pushed past both of them, blood no longer streaming from his face. "Because my family just acquired Big Noise Records, and now it's my job to make sure you all meet your contractual obligations."

"So you said outside," Grayson rumbled.

"But why is *she* here?" Jace reiterated his point, glancing at Billie like she was a steaming pile of shit on his shoe.

Angelo's smile was pure venom as he smoothed his hands over Billie's shoulders possessively. "Because it wouldn't be appropriate to leave her alone in her condition, would it, Bella?"

He brushed a kiss over her cheek, but her smile was like broken ice. Only then did her gaze lift to mine, only to instantly flit away again, drenched in guilt.

"Here, sweetheart, let me take your coat," Angelo offered.

Billie's jaw clenched like she was grinding her teeth, then she unzipped her puffer coat and let Angelo slide it down her arms. When he shifted out of the way, all I could focus on was her. Her belly. Her *pregnant belly*.

Holy shit.

Darkness swirled in my vision, and my whole body broke out in sweat. My ears rang, my mouth went fuzzy, and then it all stopped.

Crap. I fainted.

fourteen

BILLIE

Raised voices woke me at some point the next morning. After Rhett had fainted on seeing my belly, I'd decided to take the coward's route and scurried away to a bedroom while pleading exhaustion from the trip. No one had argued, so I had to assume they were glad to see me go.

I'd avoided eye contact with fucking everyone and all but sprinted into the spare bedroom to hide. Then I'd fallen asleep—because it was late as hell—and hadn't even woken up when Angelo came to bed. He'd definitely slept in here with me, though, because for one thing, that side of the bed was rumpled. For another, Brenda had warned us that Big Noise had installed several surveillance devices while setting up the recording studio in the basement. No members of Bellerose knew about them, and we weren't to let on. But it was the only way Brenda could convince the band to come here instead of the fishbowl of the content house.

So Angelo and I had to commit to the act. Which meant sharing a bed.

Bleary, I rubbed my eyes and pushed myself to sit up. The shouting was loud enough it could have been right outside the door, but after a moment, I realized it was downstairs. The walls were just that thin. Good to know.

"...seriously want us to believe that's *your* baby?" Rhett was shouting. Ah shit, it was about me.

"...don't really give two shits..." Angelo wasn't yelling back, but his voice was firm. "...nothing to do with..."

I slid out of bed and quickly changed into a warm, oversized knit sweater and leggings. Winter was awesome for covering up. Not so awesome for all the Christmas decorations appearing across the streetlights and in store windows. Nothing like a bit of Christmas cheer to remind you that your life is a bucket full of balls. And not the good kind.

I hurried from the room, needing to get downstairs

and defend myself before shit got worse. If that was possible.

Angelo was insane. So was Brenda. Fucking insane.

Huffing a deep breath, I raked my fingers through my tangled hair and made my way out of the bedroom. Other than the yelling in the living room, the rest of the house seemed empty. Out the window over the stairwell, I could see some blanketed horses in the field nearby, which was nice.

I could see why Brenda had sent them here. It was *soothing* to be in nature. Or I used to think so, anyway. Now I created chaos simply by existing in this space with so many men I'd mistreated. Whether by my own choice or not, the damage was done.

Conversation ground to a halt as I entered the room, and I nervously bit the edge of my lip. Every eye was on me, and I still couldn't meet anyone's gaze. Except Angelo's. He knew what he'd dragged me into, but he also didn't care.

"If you've got something to ask me, Rhett," I said quietly, "then you can ask *me*."

The silence between us was *suffocating*. Then Rhett pushed his chair back with a loud scrape against the hardwood floor.

"Fuck this," he snarled. "And fuck you, Billie Bellerose." He stalked closer, pausing only when he was right beside me, leaning in to make sure there was no mistaking his next words. "Jace was right about you all along. I should have listened to him."

The pure venom in his voice made my knees weak, but he didn't stick around for a response. The house shook as he slammed the front door, and I flinched like he'd physically struck me.

In his absence, Grayson and Jace exchanged a long look. Then Gray sighed heavily and rose to his feet.

"I guess I'll make sure he's safe," he muttered in a resigned voice. "Play nice." That warning was directed at Jace, who ignored him entirely.

Gray shook his head, then crossed over to where I stood frozen near the doorway. I braced myself for more hatred, but instead, he wrapped his arms around me in a gentle hug.

It was unexpected enough that I nearly burst out crying.

"I'm glad you're safe, Prickles," he said quietly, "and well. But you owe me a conversation."

I nodded, not trusting my voice. He was absolutely right; I owed him a whole lot more than just a conversation, but my hands were tied. Especially since Brenda couldn't confirm *where* the Big Noise surveillance was set up. And now that Angelo's father had taken control of the company, Big Noise cameras were actually Ricci cameras.

Gray accepted my silence, kissing my cheek before following Rhett out of the house.

"Billie," Flo said in a weak voice, "could we talk? I need to tell you—"

I shook my head, a flash of ice-cold anger filling me. "No. I have nothing to say to you, Flo."

Crestfallen, she just accepted it, hanging her head and picking at the frayed tear in her jeans. "That's fair," she murmured. Then she got up. "I'll... just go... um... check on Gray and Rhett."

She took off before I could realize that meant being left in a room alone with Jace and Angelo for the first time in almost nine years. Fuck.

Jace narrowed his eyes at me suspiciously. "Why?"

I looked at his collar, not brave enough to meet his accusing glare. "Why what?"

Jace shook his head, then looked from me to Angelo and back again with a suspicious glint in his eyes. "Why don't you have anything to say to Flo?"

I wet my lips. He had me there. If I admitted that she'd set me up... let me get abducted and tortured so badly I thought I would actually die... then I'd also be admitting that I hadn't *willingly* gone back to Angelo because I was pregnant with his baby.

And we were being watched.

I couldn't forget that crucial part. No way in hell were those cameras unattended, no matter what they'd assured Brenda.

"She knows why," I mumbled, keeping it vague, then changing the subject. "Look, before you go ranting about us being here, you should know that it was Brenda's idea." Sort of. "So if you want to yell at anyone, it better not be me."

Jace stared at me for a heavy moment, then flicked his gaze down to my belly. "Is it Rhett's?"

Fuck. I swallowed and just shook my head. What else could I even say?

Jace's lips twisted like he was trying to decide if I was lying. Then he sighed. "He won't believe that without a paternity test."

"We've already done one," Angelo replied, his eyes on me. "My father required one. I can get a copy if Rhett wants confirmation."

Jace's lip curled in a sneer. "Because we trust your family doctors so much."

Angelo rolled his eyes. "Christ, Jace, it's been nearly a decade. Get over yourself; we're all adults now."

Jace bristled with anger and indignation, and I groaned to myself.

"You know what? You two can deal with this

yourselves," I muttered. "I don't have the energy to get between you today."

"Where are you going?" Angelo asked, rising to his feet with a frown.

I sent a brittle smile back. "Figured I'd go wild, hit up some strip clubs, do some drugs. Maybe I'll find another ex-boyfriend from the mafia and get pregnant. Who knows?" Then I snapped my fingers giving a low chuckle. "Oh wait. Bit late for that."

Turning my back on them, I headed back upstairs to the bedroom I shared with Angelo to find my boots. I didn't want to run into Rhett or Gray right now, but I needed fresh air. So I pulled on my warm boots, grabbed a coat, and headed out the back door.

I couldn't see any of the missing Bellerose members, so I zipped up my coat against the cold and set out toward the stables. Brenda had told us before we arrived that this farm belonged to her godparents and that they took care of the animals while Bellerose was using the house. It gave me the confidence to approach the horses and not worry that they belonged to a neighbor.

As I drew close to the stables, though, the low hum of voices made me pause mid-step. Then I did the only mature thing and quickly hid behind a stack of hay so that I could listen.

"...something else going on here," Grayson was saying.

Shit. Of course they were in the stable; where *else* could they have been if I hadn't seen them outside? *Idiot, Billie.*

"Like what?" Flo asked, her voice timid and anxious. "She won't even look at me, let alone speak—"

"She won't look at any of us," Rhett snarled, "because she knows she's got a lot to feel guilty for. Jace warned us, all along he tried to tell us, and *we*—you too, Gray—were too fucking cuntstruck to pay attention to the red flags."

"Bullshit," Grayson growled. "None of this is adding up, and you know it."

"What I *know* is that Billie is fucking pregnant right now. And she's back with Angelo, who she swore— goddamn *fucking swore*—she wasn't with. She lied to me, Gray. To us. She fucking stared me dead in the eyes and said she wasn't with him, and now she turns up carrying *his* baby?"

"Allegedly," Flo commented. "If we're taking their word for it."

Rhett gave a low, humorless laugh. "Great. So that's just fucking great. You think she could be carrying *my* kid and lying about it? I don't know what's fucking worse right now." There was a crash, like he'd just kicked something. Then he swore. "I need to drink something. Or smoke something. Gray, you got any more liquor stashed?"

"Sorry," the big guy rumbled. "Nothing left."

"I have a couple of joints in my bag," Flo offered tentatively. "Brenda didn't even check mine."

"Sold," Rhett grunted.

A scuffle of feet saw me shrink lower in my hiding place, and a moment later both Rhett and Flo exited the stables. Neither one of them looked back to catch me there; they just stalked toward the house with their hands stuffed in pockets and their shoulders hunched.

Grayson didn't leave, though, and after a minute, my curiosity got the better of me. I scrambled awkwardly to my feet, then slipped inside the stables. The lighting was dim in here, and it took a moment for my eyes to adjust enough to see the drummer down at the far end, scratching a chestnut horse's ears.

"How much of that did you hear, Prickles?" he asked without turning to look at me. Of course he knew I was there. Gray was basically superhuman, I was convinced.

I bit my lip nervously, folding my arms under my breasts. "Um, only the tail end. Enough to hear that Rhett hates me, but that's not exactly a shock. He thinks I lied about everything."

Gray gave the horse another pat, then turned around, taking a few steps closer to where I awkwardly shifted my weight from foot to foot. "Didn't you?"

God damn it all to hell. This was harder than I'd ever anticipated. "I hate this," I whispered, dodging the question. "I'm so sorry, Gray."

He closed the gap between us, raising his hand to stroke a finger down the side of my face ever so gently and using his knuckle to tilt my chin up. "You can tell me the truth, Billie. I can help."

Words bubbled up in my chest, desperate to spill out. I wanted to confess the whole messy story to Gray because I believed him when he said he could help. That he *wanted* to help. But just as I parted my lips to tell him all my secrets, my eyes caught on a tiny reflection in the corner of the stables.

A camera?

It could have been my imagination, but I couldn't take that risk. So I pasted on a fake smile and shook my head. "There's nothing to tell, Gray. Angel and I are just here on behalf of Big Noise to ensure the album gets recorded in time for the scheduled release party."

His eyes narrowed, his brow furrowed. "That's it?"

I jerked a nod. "That's it. You should head back in. Rhett will have a window of creativity while he's stoned that you all could utilize in the music."

Gray squinted at me a moment longer, then gave a small nod and walked away.

That was it. Just... took my word and walked away.

I'd thought my heart was done breaking, that there was nothing left to hurt. I was wrong.

fifteen

BILLIE

The urge to get on a horse and just ride off into the sunset was almost overpowering. Freedom was right there, within reach. No more Riccis, no more mafia threats, no more Bellerose... I could just disappear and reinvent myself. I still had a trust account holding a suspiciously large amount of money left by my parents. I'd never touched it before, almost certain that it'd been gained illegally and could be part of the reason someone had tried to burn us alive. But fuck, maybe it was better than getting other people killed as they attempted to help me. Even if it was stolen.

I couldn't make myself leave, though. For one thing, I couldn't leave Angelo to suffer his father's wrath in my absence. No matter how proud Giovanni was of his son, he would still make him hurt. And then there was Bellerose. Rhett, Gray... even Jace. They might hate me now, but a tiny part of me held out hope that we could move past that and get back to how things were.

Also, I had never ridden a horse in my life and wasn't about to learn on the run.

So eventually I had to force myself to go back to the house. I dragged my feet, but my stomach was growling with the need for food, so I had to suck up my courage.

Thankfully, it seemed like all members of Bellerose were in the basement recording studio, so I was free to make myself a sandwich in peace and quiet. The floor creaked as I was cutting my sandwich into triangles, and I gasped when a strong, tattooed hand gripped my hip.

"I was looking for you," Angelo commented, his other hand wrapping around my wrist like he was scared I might try to stab him with the knife I held. "What were you chatting about out there? You didn't go sharing our private business, did you, Bella?"

The dangerous vibe in his voice made me shiver with fear. He was speaking quietly, his lips against my hair as he held me tight. To an observer we might look like a loving couple sharing a moment. That couldn't be further from the truth. I was so focused on the hidden surveillance that I'd forgotten Angelo was not my friend.

"Of course not," I whispered trying to slow my racing pulse. "I'm not stupid."

"No, you're not." His grip on my wrist tightened to the point of painful, and I gasped, dropping the knife. "But you are a hopeless romantic, Bella. We both know this. So sue me for being suspicious."

I whimpered at the pain in my wrist. "Angel, you're hurting me."

He sucked a sharp breath, releasing me instantly. Had he not even realized?

"Just don't forget how much we both have at stake here, Bella," he whispered, taking a step back. "The pain you went through will feel like a tickle fight if my father finds out we fabricated that paternity test."

I swallowed hard, tears pricking at my eyes. "I won't forget." After all, my body bore multiple permanent scars from the torture I'd suffered after being taken from the concert.

Angelo breathed a long sigh. I still had my back to him, so I couldn't see his expression and wasn't sure I would like what I saw there.

"How's Vee?" I asked, for some reason *needing* to get a human reaction out of him. "Does she know where we are?"

He paused only a moment before replying. "Of course she does," he said in a cold tone. "She's my wife, and nothing will change that. You're just my mistress and the mother of my heir. Nothing more."

His voice was hard and clear. I liked to think it was for the benefit of our observers, but... I wasn't sure.

He walked away then, leaving me alone with my sandwich, which I no longer had any appetite for.

Except I wasn't alone. Someone stepped out of the shadows of the door leading to the basement, and I nearly jumped out of my skin with fright.

"Jace," I breathed, pressing a hand to my chest. "Holy shit, you scared me."

"Is that true?" he demanded, moving closer. I spun to face him properly, not wanting him at my back like Angelo had just been. Stupid me, that put us face to face when he braced his hands on the counter to either side of my hips. "I heard what he just said to you, Billie. Is that—"

"Shh," I hushed him, pressing my fingers to his lips to physically stop the question. Angelo had kept his voice low; Jace wasn't even trying. His brow furrowed in confusion, but I locked eyes with him, imploring him to just *trust me* as I gave a tiny headshake. "Please, Jace... you didn't hear what you think you heard."

He squinted hard as I dropped my hand away from his soft mouth. "I see."

Did he, though? Silently, I prayed that he did. That he understood *nothing* was as it seemed and there was so much more going on than just some hurt feelings.

Just as I thought he was going to back down and let sleeping dogs lie, he grabbed my wrist—the same one Angelo had just hurt—and pulled me after him as he stormed out of the kitchen.

"Jace! What are you doing?" I protested, stumbling over my feet to keep up.

He didn't reply, just continued pulling me along until we burst out onto the rear verandah. Then he looped an arm around my waist to lift me effortlessly down the stairs—saving me from tripping and falling —then continued on across the grassy expanse.

"Jace, ow! Let go; you're hurting me!" I tried to pull my wrist free, but it just hurt more, thanks entirely to the bruises Angelo had just left and Jace's unrelenting determination to drag me out into the middle of the field.

"How about now, Billie?" he demanded, whirling around to face me when we were a decent distance away from the house. "*Now* will you be honest with me?

Because you sure as fuck haven't been from the moment you arrived, and I'm getting the distinct impression we're being watched in there. So? What's going on?"

I bit my tongue, torn over what to say. What if...

"Billie," Jace growled, giving me a little shake. "Talk to me. No one can hear us out here. No one is listening. It's just us. You and me. *Talk to me.*"

Panic clawed at my throat, and I swallowed hard to try and catch my racing pulse. Angelo's warning still rang clear in my head and... I was scared.

"I don't know what you want me to say, Jace," I lied. "This whole situation is uncomfortable, I know, but it's not like—"

"Bullshit," he cut me off, shaking his head. "I know you, Rose. I know when you're lying, and right now... all day... you've been *lying,* and I can't work out *why.*" He released me, spinning away to swipe his hands over his face in frustration.

I glanced around. We really were alone. Unless one of us had a microphone physically on our bodies, there was no way we could be heard. Surely, it was safe to let my guard down? But then again, what the fuck had Jace ever done to win my trust? Especially knowing firsthand what might befall me if Giovanni felt duped.

"You don't, though," I said bitterly, unable to keep

the words to myself. "You don't know when I'm lying. You didn't then, and you don't now. So don't go playing the *I know you* card when we both know it's total horse shit. You cut me out of your life when you signed to Big Noise and *never looked back*. Even when Rhett literally saved my life, you didn't stop once to question what I'd been through, so you can take your emotional manipulation and shove it right up your ass, Jace Adams. I know what I'm doing."

He stared at me in surprise and outrage, but I was shaking with emotion and needed to get the fuck away from him before I spilled more secrets than just what Angelo and I were up to here.

I started storming away, but he easily caught up and grabbed my wrist again.

"Rose, *stop*," he ordered, yanking me to a halt. "Just tell me truthfully, is that Angelo's baby?"

I gave a short, cold laugh, then shook my head. "What does it matter, Jace? It's not yours, this time. So what difference does it make? Go back to the basement and record a fucking album so we can all go home. Please."

Panic washed over me in cold waves as I realized what I'd just said. It hadn't clicked with Jace, but I wasn't hanging around to let the pieces connect.

Instead, I jerked my wrist free and *ran* back to the house, not stopping until I was safely back in my bedroom with the door locked.

Holy shit. *Holy shit.* I'd held my secret from Jace for nearly nine years, and just one private conversation almost saw me confess it all?

This time. That's what I'd just said. *It's not yours, this time.*

Because it had been, *last time.* The baby Jace never even knew about. The baby that eighteen-year-old Angelo had promised to raise as his own, lying to his parents that he was the father after I'd already broken Jace's heart.

Angelo and I had both made choices, the only selfless choices we could think to make. Both out of love of Jace. We had wanted him to succeed. We had wanted him to realize his dream of becoming the biggest rock star in the world, and finding out his sixteen-year-old girlfriend was pregnant would have ruined it all.

So we'd lied then, and he'd never seen through the act. He'd never found out what we were hiding back then, just like he'd never find out now.

I collapsed back onto the bed, tears streaming down my face as my chest ached with all the lies I held inside. I hated this. All of it. But given the choice to leave, I wouldn't. There was too much unfinished business with these boys... all four of them.

Somehow, I needed to mend things with Rhett. Gray knew something was up; I could see the questions all over him. But Rhett? He hated me, and that hurt more than it should.

sixteen

RHETT

Flo and I were good again. Maybe I didn't totally forgive her for *trying* to set Billie up, for conspiring to have her kidnapped by the Ricci family mafia, after which fuck knew what might've happened to her. But considering Billie was *clearly* fine, I could relax my grudge against Flo a little bit.

As we'd laid on the carpet floor of the basement, smoking her smuggled joint, she'd explained how Tom had set it all up and used her as a pawn. Tucker had had a hard on for getting rid of Billie by whatever means necessary, and Flo had just been a convenient means to an end in setting her up.

"Tucker is such a fucker," I drawled, feeling my head swim and closing my eyes. Then I giggled. "That rhymes."

"You just worked that out?" Gray asked, finishing Flo's joint, then stubbing it out in the ashtray supplied. It wasn't our first, but sadly it would almost be our last. We needed to take advantage of our newfound chill, which was why we were in the recording room.

We'd taken a break so Jace could go grab his notebook, but it seemed like ages ago that he'd left.

"Where's Jace?" I asked, struggling to sit up. Fuck me, Flo's weed was excellent.

"He went for a drink," Flo said.

At the same time, Gray answered. "Taking a shit."

I squinted at both of them, then looked to the staircase. "Feels like he's been gone a really long time."

Flo snickered, strumming random notes on her bass guitar. "That's the weed talking, bro."

"I have to tell you guys something," Gray said out of fucking nowhere. "I hired a guy to follow Billie. But he never told me she was knocked up. That's bad, right?"

"Uh-huh," Flo agreed. "One star review for sure."

"You need a refund or discount or something," I added, lying back down on the carpet.

Gray hummed a sound of agreement, then yawned and ran a hand through his hair. Fucking diva.

Then I sat back up. "Wait, you had someone following her? All this time? And you didn't tell me?"

"If I did, would you remember?" Gray arched a dark brow at me.

I glared back at him, but he had a valid point. A *lot* of the past few months was blurry and blacked out. So I guess I didn't have any kind of argument for being left out of the loop.

"I guess that explains *The Dirty Truth* post about Billie getting fat, huh?" Flo muttered with a loopy grin.

"What did he find out?" I muttered. It fucked me off that I was curious about her life away from us. "Was she treated okay by *the asshole* and his mafia family?"

Refusing to say *his* name made me feel marginally better—especially if he was the father of her baby when it should be me. Fuck's sake, did I really want to be a dad? I should be celebrating the dodging of a bullet, and instead, I was mourning like a dumb cunt.

"Apparently, I wasn't as informed as I should have been," Grayson bit out, sounding scary even in his buzzed state. "But she seemed to be okay. Happy enough and well taken care of."

The last line sounded rehearsed. Or maybe I was just too stoned to get the subtle hints, but it felt like he was trying to say everything without revealing anything, and I wondered why the fuck that was. Were we not safe to freely talk here?

"So, she left us?" Flo sounded bitter as she strummed the strings harder. "Tom didn't even have to do anything. Billie gave him what he wanted without any fucking help from us."

Grayson grunted before pulling himself up higher. "It's more complicated than that, and it doesn't mean the fucker isn't going to get the beating he deserves, but yeah... it was going to happen with or without him."

Again, there was a tone that indicated he wasn't giving us the entire truth, but who the hell cared about the finer details when the base fact remained: Billie had left us and gotten knocked up by the asshole who broke her heart years ago. Her abuser.

Unless she was lying, and the baby was mine. Why lie, though?

Pushing myself up to sit, I wriggled back to rest against the glass wall of the studio, lifting my guitar as I did. The weed was turning me into a whiny bitch, and I might as well use that to channel some angst into a song. We just needed Jace to get back from his drink and/or shit, whichever one of those was the truth. Or neither.

He was probably hate-fucking Billie against the wall.

Motherfucker.

I'd probably be doing the same. Pregnant with another man's child or not.

It was a new level of screwed up, and I was owning it.

"That's nice," Flo mumbled as I absentmindedly strummed a melody, one with darker, richer undertones than we usually used. Our sound had a hard rock beat, with the occasional ballad for the fans. But this one had a dark, slow, cloying beat that wrapped around you and refused to let go.

"I've slept about three hours sober since Billie left," I admitted hoarsely. "When I find that rest, this is the fucking song that's raging through my head. I feel it in my soul, but I refused to play it out loud because it's damn haunting." And it reminded me of her. Fuck, was I turning into Jace over here?

"It's fitting," Grayson added, already sounding clearer thanks to the rapid processing of drugs in his giant-ass body. "She's been haunting all of us for weeks —Jace for years, and I finally understand why."

I did too. I fucking understood, and I fucking hated it. Jace had tried to warn us, and we wouldn't listen.

Flo picked up on the melody in a few seconds, joining in with me, adding another facet to the story I was telling without uttering a single word. Grayson moved to sit behind his drums, adding a beat to complete the sound. Flo and I got to our feet as well, and the sound grew stronger. This was my haunted melody, but my bandmates were musical geniuses, and by the time Jace walked into the room looking like he'd seen a ghost, we had a new song all but fleshed out.

He caught the tail end, and some of the blank, wide-eyed look faded from his expression, to be replaced by the sort of hunger he used to show every single time we wrote together. Jace lived and breathed music, but somewhere in the last few years, he'd lost some of that drive. Lost the spark. I saw it again today, though, as he stopped in front of us.

"What the fuck was that?" he rumbled, looking between me and Gray. "And can you do it again?"

For the next two hours, we played our "Broken Hearts and Battered Souls" number until we had it perfected. Jace had already thrown a few lyrics in, but we all acknowledged that this was a piece with fewer words. There was just no need. The beat, melody, and guitar riff in the middle that gave me a chance to let fucking loose told the tale of pain without excessive lyrics.

"Fuck me dead," Jace said as he shook his head, all of us gulping water like we'd run a marathon. "Who knew that having Billie back in the house and some quality weed would produce that. Maybe Brenda knew what she was doing."

Grayson lowered the towel he was using to mop up the sweat across his brow, narrowing his eyes on Jace, examining our lead singer for many unnerving minutes. If that look was directed at me, I'd be squirming, but Jace just flipped him off. "Don't analyze me, bro. I can talk about Billie in a somewhat positive light without being struck down by lightning. I don't like or trust her, and that's never going to change, but at some point, I have to move on."

Grayson wasn't the only one eyeballing him now. Flo and I were just as suspicious of this character change. Jace hated Billie with the sort of bitter passion that could only come from loving her with all of his being. One didn't move from love to hate to indifference just because we'd managed to create a truly spectacular song in her presence.

Nope.

What the fuck had Jace been doing during his "drink/shit."

"Come on, once more and we drop it into a track to send to Big Noise," Jace said, shuffling us all back into position as he took his place by the studio mic. "It will get them off our back for a bit since we haven't sent any progress tracks up until now."

He paused, clearly expecting us to burst into fucking song like a cheesy musical movie, but instead, we deadeye stared him down, waiting for him to break and explain *what the fuck was going on*. Something had happened between him and Billie; I knew it like I knew I was going to find her the second we got out of the studio today. An obsessive itch that no scratching was going to help.

"Not now," Jace growled. "Not here."

His expression grew even more serious, and I was struck with the same instinct I'd had with Grayson before. We were not safe to discuss the important shit here, which made me think maybe we were being watched. Or at least listened to. In that case, it was best to act normal until we figured out where we were safe to freely speak.

But also... *what the fuck?*

I strummed the opening chord. Flo joined me two beats later, and then Grayson added his drumbeat. Jace made sure we were recording, and then he jumped in with the chorus, the only lyrics he had so far, but I wasn't worried about that. The rest would come; they were already floating in the air around us, just waiting for a voice. Music was a lot like that; in some ways we created it and in others, it was already in existence, just waiting for someone to give it a voice.

166

When the final note echoed, none of us spoke or moved for a good minute. Music like that lived in your fucking soul, and I'd almost forgotten this feeling. No matter how dark that melody was, it actually filled me with light, and for the first time in weeks, I didn't crave the blissful high of drugs or alcohol. No numbing required for me to exist in my own body.

Music was a high I'd never been able to replicate, not with the best fucking shit in the world.

"Time for lunch," Flo finally announced, removing her guitar and placing it in the case. "I think I might actually be hungry today."

I was in the process of putting my precious guitar away too, but that had me looking up to examine her closer. Since the shit with Billie, I'd been ignoring Florence's existence, and somehow, I'd missed how thin she'd gotten. I'd missed her refusing to eat or function in any productive way.

I mean, fuck, she could have had half her face missing, and I'd have missed it in the drug-induced state I'd been in. I'd been a real piece of shit lately. "Lunch sounds good," I acknowledged. "I'm going to cook, and we should eat together outside. Take a break from this house."

The house we couldn't speak freely in, apparently.

It was time for us to find a place where we could air

whatever bullshit was happening around us and make sure we were all on the same page. We hadn't acted like a cohesive band for a long time, and it was time to get back to that. We might have lost our way—me more than anyone else—but we weren't dead. We could come back from this, and the chart topper we'd just created together was proof of that.

Bellerose would not be broken by outside forces, not while I was still fucking alive. And to stay alive, I needed to sort myself out. Whatever motherfuckers were watching us and controlling our lives had better be careful because Rhett Silver was no longer living in drug land.

Nope, this motherfucker, who spoke about himself in the third person because he could, was done with all that shit.

Except weed of course. Let's not go too crazy.

The rest was done, though. Time to focus on music and Bellerose.

And maybe Billie, until I could cut her from my heart and mind for good.

seventeen

BILLIE

After almost revealing my secret to Jace, I lost my shit for two hours and hid in my room, tears streaming down my cheeks in a relentless emotional release. It was like a dam had been broken, and none of my usual tactics to suppress emotions were working. Was this all just fallout from the years of keeping this secret from Jace and finally, almost anyway, revealing everything to him in one explosive conversation?

Was there even a sliver of relief in my pain, despite my not knowing if he'd even heard that one random line that had slipped out? Maybe, once he knew, we could hash it all out and finally move on with our lives.

I didn't need Jace to love me, but it would be nice if he didn't hate me with the sort of passion that spanned multiple albums and resulted in a ton of Grammies and AMA awards. Fucker.

Thankfully, during my little breakdown, the band was locked in the basement recording, and Angelo was out on the phone, taking care of mafia business. Or whatever the hell he did for hours on the phone. So I got to lose myself in peace, and these days, moments of peace were all I could ask for.

Especially from Angelo. In some ways, we'd never been farther apart than we were right this minute as an alleged couple about to have a baby. I barely recognized the guy I'd once loved. Who I'd once dreamed of spending my life with, along with his best friend.

We were all different people now, shaped through our choices, with many new scars. But that didn't change the fact that our past would always be with us. Haunting our every fucking step, until we finally figured out how to let it go.

If that was even possible.

When my stomach protested loudly, reminding me we had skipped out on the sandwich, I finally pulled myself together and had a quick shower to help calm the puffy, red-eyed look. By the time I emerged, dressed in the same outfit, I felt a little better—definitely calmer, with my game face back on. This was not the time to forget we were in a life-and-death situation, and being surrounded by sexy rock stars who each owned a small piece of me was no excuse to go endangering them all.

That would make my sacrifice, both times, completely worthless.

If that was the case, I wasn't sure I could remain in any sort of mentally stable state.

Entering the kitchen, I tried not to flinch when I came face to face with Rhett. He was the only one there, calmly stirring something on the stove. When he lifted his gaze to meet mine, his eyes were a touch bloodshot, but otherwise, he looked very clear and sober.

My puffy face probably had him thinking I'd been hitting the drugs and alcohol, even with the baby belly sticking out before me.

"Hey," he said calmly.

If he'd have thrown that pan at me, I'd have been a little less shocked.

"Hey?" I replied, a questioning tone slipping out in that one repeated word.

"Are you hungry?" he added conversationally, as if the past almost two months hadn't happened. Along with the angry words he'd thrown at me this morning, which had more than implied he fucking hated my guts.

Unable to help myself, I quickly glanced around, wondering if there was a film crew here or something. Someone had to be supervising to have Rhett's attitude do such a three-sixty from the last time I saw him. I mean, he'd been furious and out of control, and I couldn't blame him for either.

But this... this was calm and domesticated, and it was freaking me the fuck out.

"You look hungry," he continued when I remained in shocked silence. "Take a seat. I'm making a chicken stir-fry, using some of the fresh ingredients from the greenhouse. This place is actually way more self-sufficient than I expected when we were first ferried here. I mean, it was like 2 A.M when we arrived, so we didn't see much, but still... I could get used to this sort of life."

He moved away from the stove for a second and pulled out one of the white leather stools in front of the island bench. "Sit," he insisted, and in my state of shock, I managed to stumble forward and attempt to hoist my bulk into the high-backed chair. After my second attempt, Rhett let out a low chuckle before he wrapped his hands around my waist and lifted me like I weighed nothing.

"Little belly in the way," he said with more humor in his tone. "Bet that takes some getting used to."

No lie. I pinched my arm really hard, wondering if I was dreaming. Or maybe I'd fallen in the shower, hit my head, and now I was drowning while having the most perfect dream.

As Rhett returned to the other side of the bench and stove, his open and friendly expression met mine. "What is happening?" I rasped, desperate for some water. Or vodka.

He lifted the spatula in his left hand and started to stir the very delicious-smelling dish he was working on, before he reached over and stirred the pot of rice with a large spoon in his right. "What do you mean? I'm cooking lunch for everyone." A chuckle escaped him. "Don't look so shocked. Despite the rock star status, I had to learn to cook at a really young age or I'd have starved. This is one of my favorite dishes."

The fact that he could cook only added to the perfection of this guy. The ache in my heart at missing him was like a sharp jab. Just sitting here now, seeing his familiar piercings and blue mohawk, reminded me of how much we'd shared. Hurting Rhett was high on my list of life's regrets, and the fact that I couldn't just spew out all my truths right now was chipping away at the little sanity I still had left.

"It smells delicious." I choked on the pleasant words as I decided to play along with his charade. "It's nice of you to make lunch for everyone."

Speaking of, where the fuck was everyone, and why wasn't Angelo back in the house yet? It was entirely too quiet; this afternoon felt like I'd stumbled into the twilight zone.

"I'm a nice guy," Rhett said simply, focusing on the food as he added a few more spices. "Is there anything I should be aware of in feeding a pregnant person? Are you not allowed specific foods?"

Okay, evidently, we were having *this conversation.* Aware of the cameras, I forced a smile on my face. "Sushi, undercooked meats, some soft cheeses, items that haven't been reheated really well, along with ham and processed meat products. I mean, it's all just a warning, but I've been trying my best to stick with the rules. For once."

It was no huge sacrifice to give up on a few products for nine months of life to ensure a healthy child.

"I'll remember that," he said simply before he leaned down to grab a bowl from beneath the counter. He then dished me up a serving of rice and the garlic-scented chicken and vegetable dish. When he placed it before me, he leaned in closer, his perfect white teeth standing out against his tanned skin as he smiled. "I want you to eat all of this. You need to build up some strength." He played with the ring at the corner of his lips for a few seconds, and I nodded stupidly, still freaking out that this was a trick.

As I scooped up the first forkful, I discreetly sniffed, wondering if maybe he was poisoning me. Or dosing me with some sort of laxative at the minimum.

I thought I was being subtle with my suspicion, until Rhett let out a laugh. "Come on, Billie. I'm not that petty to hurt a pregnant woman. It's safe."

As if to prove his point, he lifted a piece of chicken from my plate, using his fingers, which had to be burning as he held a steaming piece, and popped it into his mouth. "See," he added, smirk still in place. "Perfectly safe. Now eat. I don't like to see you so thin. Makes me think someone hasn't been taking care of you." His voice rose on that last line, and the dig at Angelo wasn't lost on me. I felt no surprise when I looked to the doorway to find the towering mafia man there, a steely glare on his face. Rhett had clearly seen him as well, and that comment had been projected for that reason.

Hoping to lighten the tension before someone got a knife in the chest, I let out a forced laugh. "The media seems to think I look like I was pre-gaming for Thanksgiving , so... I should be okay. But thank you."

Rhett scoffed. "The media create whatever narrative they want to fit the story they want to tell. If it's ten percent true, that would be a stretch. You need more food, not less, trust me."

"She's been well taken care of," Angelo snapped as he pulled out the chair beside me. "You can move on with your life and stop worrying about her."

Rhett met his gaze with a blank one, like he had no idea who Angelo even was. They remained in some sort of odd stare-off, and my stomach roiled. I was not going to be able to eat a bite until one of them left the room.

"I'll see you soon, Thorn," Rhett finally said, without truly acknowledging Angelo. "Need to make sure Flo eats as well. She's had a rough time of it lately."

Anger sliced through my confusion since Florence was on my shit list and probably would be forever. It was hard to forgive a bitch who was so weak that she let her small-dicked boyfriend orchestrate the kidnapping and torture of another woman. And even worse, she'd faked a friendship to help with said kidnapping. Betrayal from girl friends hit differently, and for that, she was permanently dead to me.

And Rhett looking after her... To see his savior complex kicking in for someone like Florence really fucked me off. Not that I could show it.

He gathered up another bowl of the stir-fry, leaving

the room without a glance back, and I silently fumed into my meal, staring at the colorful and healthy-looking food, all the while wishing I was anywhere but here. In a way, it was easier when the band was angry and fighting with me because it meant there was still some sliver of emotion there. They gave a shit, even if it was an angry one.

But Rhett today had been almost pleasant. As if we were strangers, forced to get along for a short period of time until we were free to go on with our lives, never thinking about each other again.

I mean, that was odd, right? Had he really managed to just get over all of it in the few hours I'd spent bawling? Why the hell did that make me feel so terrible, too, when I should be happy that he was at peace with the life I had to live. I hadn't chosen it, but that didn't mean it wasn't my new reality.

"What the fuck was that about?" Angelo asked, lowering his voice as he leaned toward me, so once again it looked like we were having a "couple" conversation.

Pasting a fake smile on, I picked up the bowl, needing to get the fuck out of here so I could eat in peace. Too many meals had been ruined lately by the tension in my life, and I was done with sacrificing food as well. Fuck that. I needed to eat.

"None of your fucking business, love," I snarled under my breath through the fake smile. "Now leave me the hell alone before my pregnancy hormones make me nasty."

Hauling my ass off the chair was a bit of a drop, but I was steadied by Angelo's hold as his hand snaked around the back of my shirt. He leaned in very close, until I could almost taste him on my tongue, and I tried not to let him affect me. Tried and failed.

"Just remember, *love*," he shot back, "that you belong to me now. I own you, since I'm the one person standing between you and the afterlife. I know it's easy to forget, here, surrounded by past lovers, but there's only so many warnings I can give before I need to remind you in another way. Don't make me do that, Billie."

Whatever he was implying here, it was dark, and I wasn't sure if the spike in my pulse was from fear or something else.

This time he let me back away, and I hurried from the room, following the same path Rhett had taken. When I got down the hallway, I happened to glance out the window to see that Rhett had left the house and was striding out toward the barn. Watching him, because I couldn't look away, I finally tasted his delicious dish, and a small groan escaped me as a rich, garlic-and-soy flavor hit my tongue.

He hadn't been kidding about knowing how to cook.

The next bite was just as good, and I was about to take my third when Rhett paused his march toward the barn and, in the next second, hauled his arm back and threw the plate he'd been carrying so it smashed against the wall he was near. From the house, I never heard a sound, but it scared the horses as they took off in the field, galloping away.

It was the first unraveling he'd shown since I walked into the kitchen, and to see that slice of violence made me feel better.

Because I was fucked up like that. But at least his action showed one thing.

He was still bothered by my presence, and that meant I had a chance to fix the canyon sized rift between us.

Before it was too late.

eighteen

BILLIE

After I ate my food, I took another *long* shower. Brenda had been fairly certain that the bathrooms were clear of cameras, so the shower was one of the few places I could relax and *breathe*. Rhett's weird pleasantness in the kitchen had thrown me for a loop. Followed by Angelo's threat...

The hard thing with Angelo was that I couldn't work out if he was full of shit or not. He regularly threatened me but had never followed through. The worst he'd ever hurt me was just how he'd gripped my wrist this morning, leaving slight bruises that Jace had only made worse. Other than that, he was all talk and no action.

Not that I was complaining. I really didn't want to know what he'd do in order to *remind* me that I was little more than a prisoner with invisible bonds. Beat me? Rape me? I shuddered at the idea of either. The Angel I'd known—and loved—as a teenager would never even *speak* that threat, let alone follow through physically. I had to remind myself regularly that this version was *not* the same boy who'd whispered promises in my treehouse hideaway while I sobbed into his shirt.

I was pushing the boundaries, though, and I knew it. With Big Noise—and by extension, Giovanni himself —watching us around the clock, Angelo couldn't be seen to let me off the leash. As far as they were concerned, I was his dutiful mistress. I had no doubt that our lack of sex was already raising flags, but I figured some women hated to be touched sexually while pregnant.

The health of the Ricci heir needed to come first, right?

Eventually, I forced myself to get out of the shower and dress in warm clothes. I'd go utterly insane if I were to just lurk around the house all day, so I decided to go back out and see the horses. Maybe they would want some carrots or apples?

Smiling to myself, I pulled on my boots and coat,

then filled a bag from the fridge to take to my new friends. Maybe Bellerose wanted nothing to do with me, but I could entertain myself. I was resourceful.

I'd overheard some of the new music spilling from the basement earlier, and it'd stuck in my head. I hummed it to myself as I made my way across the grass toward the horses, who grazed in the next paddock over.

For some time, I chatted to the horses and fed them the treats I'd brought along to buy their friendship. They quite liked an ear scratch, so they seemed content to hang around for pats even after all the food was gone.

When the sun began to set, I bid farewell to the horses and started back to the house. Then stopped when I spotted a campfire further in the distance.

Like an idiot, I glanced around. What I expected to find, or see, I had no clue. We were in the wilderness with not even neighboring houses within sight. If someone had set up a campfire, it had to have been one of the band. Maybe Rhett? I needed to talk to him, and what better opportunity than out here away from the watching eyes?

Decided, I changed my path to approach the fire. My fingers were crossed inside my pockets, and my heart raced with nervousness as I approached, but I was soon reassured by the gentle sound of guitar music. That was Rhett, without a doubt.

Choking back my nerves, I approached faster and nearly stumbled when I saw he wasn't alone.

Jace sat across the fire from Rhett, his head resting on a log and his eyes closed as he sang the lyrics of a song I'd never heard before. It was instantly apparent that this was a private moment of creativity between friends that I'd undoubtedly ruin simply by being here.

If I'd been quicker, quieter, I would have just backed away and left them to it. But when Rhett's eyes met mine across the small campfire, it locked my knees and prevented me from leaving.

"*...burn me once and that's your shame. Burn me twice in your fucked up game. The trust is broken, the lies are wishes falling in ashy rain.*" Jace's crooning voice struck me right in the heart, and I gasped at the pain he elicited.

His eyes opened at my small sound, but no surprise crossed his face when he saw me standing there.

"Well, if it isn't everyone's favorite thorny rose," he commented with a yawn. "Come and join us."

I frowned, ready to leave. Then Rhett set his guitar down and held out a hand to me.

I was weak and *so* emotionally drained. Against my better judgment, I took his hand and let him pull me closer. He guided me into the space beside him, tucking me into his warm body as though we were right back where we'd been. Back before Flo set me up, before I suffered indescribable torture, before Angelo offered me a deal to save both our skins.

Back when I'd thought maybe I was falling in love with Rhett and Grayson both.

"Rhett's high," Jace informed me with a pointed glare. "Don't read too much into his behavior. He's an affectionate stoner. Always has been."

I glanced up at Rhett's face, noting the lazy smile touching his lips and the redness of his eyes. Jace was right, but I was okay with playing along. Just for now, where no one else could see us.

"Jace thinks there're cameras or something in the house," he said in a quiet, sleepy voice as his arm draped over my shoulders. "And that you know about it."

I shifted my gaze across the fire to Jace and wet my lips. Sooner or later, I had to trust them. Didn't I? Angelo wasn't the only one I could lean on. Maybe Jace was a bastard who'd happily run me over with his car, but Rhett... he was my knight in shining armor. He'd understand, wouldn't he?

"Jace is right," I whispered after a heavy pause.

Jace sat up, his eyes wide and sharp, but Rhett just

chuckled as his fingers danced a pattern over the sleeve of my sweater.

"Typical," Rhett mumbled. "I don't know why any of us believed the label when they said they'd leave us alone."

Jace shook his head, scowling. Rhett might be high, but Jace was as sober as a judge. And sharp-witted too. "Why would you and Angelo care what Big Noise thinks? I know you two, better than either of you give me credit for. Neither of you are acting like yourselves in that house. Why?"

I frowned. "Angel didn't explain it already?" Jace just lifted his brows, and I shook my head. "Not the surveillance thing, obviously. But, surely, he explained why we're being cautious here?"

"He said that he's here for his father," Rhett drawled.

"Right," Jace agreed. "Then I punched him again."

"You mean he *let* you punch him," I teased, unable to help myself.

A flash of irritation crossed Jace's features, then he smirked. "Right. So... I take it there's more we need to know?"

I nodded. "Yeah, the Ricci corporation—or whatever the fuck they're called—just bought a bunch of businesses from some other dumb-name company, and as Angel said, Big Noise Records was one of them. He got sent to Naples to deal with some guy who was working for some other bad guys or... something." I shuddered, remembering the blood on my skin. "Anyway. It's not *just* Big Noise recording you guys for behind-the-scenes footage. It's Giovanni keeping an eye on his heir."

Jace's eyes flicked down to my belly, and I nodded.

Rhett sighed dramatically. "We need marshmallows. I fucking love toasted marshmallows."

Jace and I exchanged a look of confusion, then I snickered. Rhett really was high.

"I need to take a piss," Jace muttered, pushing to his feet with a groan. "Play Rose that tune we just worked out; see what she thinks."

He was gone before I could recover from the shock of not only hearing my old nickname on his lips, but the fact that he was being even slightly *civil* toward me. Ever since the kitchen incident with Rhett, it had felt like I'd landed in a weird alternate reality.

"Hey Thorn?" Rhett murmured as Jace walked away from the campfire. "You know you broke my heart?"

Fuck. "I'm so sorry," I whispered, shifting my position so I could look up at him. "But Rhett... you didn't love me. You didn't even know me. We'd only been together for a heartbeat, and—"

"And sometimes that's all that you need. When you know... you know." He gave a loose shrug. "Not that it matters now, I guess. You're... living your best life as a mafia mistress. Or whatever the fuck you are to him. He doesn't deserve you, though."

Christ, was he trying to kill me? At a loss for words, and still too scared to admit my truth, I did the only thing I could think of. I cupped the back of his neck with my hand and pulled him down to kiss.

The moment our lips met, I knew I'd fucked up.

Rhett groaned, leaning into me as his hand found the back of my head. His tongue expertly teased my lips apart, and I turned to a puddle of goo. All thoughts of Angelo, the *baby*, all of it just evaporated out of my brain because this was exactly where I was meant to be.

"Fuck, Thorn..." He breathed the words as he hauled me into his lap, his hard length grinding against my crotch, but the swell of my belly between us was like a bucket of ice water over my head.

"Shit." I pulled away, putting my fingers to his lips. "Rhett... we *can't* do this."

His brow dipped in anger. "You—"

"What the *hell* is going on?" Angelo snarled, his hand grabbing me by the back of the neck and all but dragging me out of Rhett's lap.

Then he dropped me when Jace appeared out of

nowhere and punched him right in the face, knocking him off balance and into the campfire.

I screamed, horrific memories of my own burns flashing through my mind, but Angelo was quick to roll to the side, thrashing back and forth in the dirt to put the small flames on his clothes out. Then, instead of striking back at Jace, he rushed to me.

"Hey, hey, Bella. You're okay. It's okay, see? I'm fine. No burns. Just a few holes. See?" he held up his coat to show me, his expression full of concern.

It wasn't until Jace stared at me in bewilderment that I realized I was rocking back and forth, whimpering. Fuck. I'd have to explain this... but not now. Not tonight.

I swallowed back my old trauma and peeled myself out of Angelo's grip.

"I'm fine," I lied. "I just... I need some air." Despite the fact that we were outside. I didn't give them a chance to point that out, taking off into the darkness.

I just needed to be alone.

JACE

Billie took off and Angelo followed her, leaving me wondering what the actual fuck I'd missed in both of their lives. Twice now she'd revealed a piece of her past, a piece of her broken soul, before she'd snatched it back away, and I couldn't stop thinking about the life Billie had lived without me. For years after she dumped my ass, I'd refused to think, discuss, or hear her fucking name. Ironic, considering I'd named the damn band after her, but music was the only avenue of "Billie pain" I'd allowed myself, and it was my nightly torture on stage—hearing *Bellerose* screamed out by tens of thousands of fans.

But the girl who'd inspired it all... I had no idea what she'd been through after her sixteenth birthday.

Dropping down next to Rhett, I looked toward the house, wondering if Billie would reappear, but when two shadows came into sight, it was only Flo and Grayson. They made their way across to us, taking seats on the other side of the fire, which still had random embers scattered around.

"What happened?" Gray asked shortly. I wasn't surprised; that eagle-eyed fucker never missed a thing.

"Rhett kissed Billie, and Angelo lost his shit," I said shortly.

Rhett snorted, rubbing a hand over his face as more laughter echoed from him. "Jace punched him into the fire. It was gold."

Grayson almost looked impressed, and I wondered when I'd become such a pathetic bitch that my bandmates expected me to ignore all the Billie drama rather than fight. It never used to be that way, not when we were growing up. I was the damn hothead, with Angelo the calmer backup. Together, we'd been near unstoppable, which we'd had to be to keep Billie safe.

She was far too fucking desirable for her own good, then and now.

"Why did you kiss her?" Florence asked, arms

wrapped tightly around herself, a position she'd been in a lot lately.

Rhett's laughter died off a touch. "She just... she fucks with my head in ways I never expected. We've all done the rounds with women, right? We've all been *in love* that was only lust, but it was never like this. My soul knows hers. It makes no sense, and yet there's not another fucking explanation I can come up with."

He knew the truth. Billie was a soul destroyer, and the only way that worked was if she owned a part of it in the first place.

Giving Rhett a break from questions, I quickly filled Flo and Gray in on the information Billie had given us about the surveillance and Big Noise buy-out by Giovanni.

"What are we going to do about Angelo?" Grayson turned serious. "How long will we let this shit go on before we say *enough*?"

Angelo, that motherfucker. Part of me wanted to kill him, and another part missed my best friend. We'd grown up together, my family half raising him, since his family was filled with assholes and murderers. I'd never believed Giovanni would get to him, but in the end, Angelo hadn't been able to break free. I mean, it was the fucking mafia, so I shouldn't be surprised, but the idealistic kid in me had expected we'd all make music together forever, with no need for his family.

I'd lost both my best friends that day and, along with it, my moronic naivety.

Probably for the best.

"We can't do anything," I said when no one else answered. "She made her choice, and her choice was him." Again. "So we have to do our best to move on and write more fucking Billie songs to appease our broken souls."

Rhett let out a choked sob but didn't say anything, his stare heavy-lidded as he watched the fire.

Poor bastard, he was too new at this. But it'd get easier.

Yeah, that was a fucking lie.

He'd get better at pretending at least.

"Let's shelve the Billie talk for a beat," Flo changed the subject, "and talk about the surveillance in the house. I vote we leave; I don't want to have to watch everything I say and do so that some perverted cunt can record us. We are too goddamn rich and famous for this shit."

The *rich* was debatable in her case, but for the most part, she was right.

"Let's just stick it out for another week," I said, "so we can get this song down to perfection. I don't want to mess with our vibe, but after that, we're out of here. Besides, it wouldn't be any different in the content house, except we'd have paps camped out on the front lawn."

No one argued, and for the first time in a long time, we felt like the old Bellerose: a cohesive unit that loved to make music together.

"I've got something to tell you all," Grayson said suddenly, and whatever calm had fallen over us vanished in that one ominous statement.

Rhett even pushed himself up, as if the vertical position would help his buzzed brain concentrate better.

"I'm not from a nice family."

One simple statement, and it wasn't that any of us were surprised, considering the scary badass our bandmate was, but he'd never volunteered any personal information about his life before Bellerose.

"Bad in what way?" Rhett asked, sounding clearer.

"Bad in the same way that Angelo's is," Grayson replied. "And when Billie was first taken, I had to tap into some contacts to make sure she was okay."

Part of me loved that asshole for caring so much. The other part hated that he'd even been in this position. Billie fucking Bellerose was a gorgeous pain in our asses. Destructive siren. Minus the singing ability.

"I'm only letting you know on the very small chance that this might drag me back into their world," Grayson continued, staring at his hands. "And if that happens, it could be dangerous. For you all." He let out a deep breath. "I can take care of myself, but it might be a good idea to have extra security until I can ensure that the past remains where it belongs."

"You did what you had to, man," I told him, not remotely upset. Our life was a bag of fuckups this year anyway, so did it really matter if we added one more criminal organization to the mix?

Grayson's gaze met mine, his cool and a little detached. Not quite his scary face, but a close second. "I'll take care of it, don't worry. I just wanted to warn you all so you're cautious moving forward. Don't go out alone. Don't take stupid risks. Don't answer phone numbers you don't know—the usual shit we do anyway because we're Bellerose—but in this case, take extra precaution."

He clearly wasn't asking for input, and when we nodded, it appeared that conversation was done. The night was done, everyone heading back into the dark and quiet house. Billie and Angelo were already in bed, and I tried really fucking hard not to think about them behind that door together. Were they fucking quietly?

His hand over her mouth to muffle her moans as he pounded her tight cunt?

More to the point, why did that mental image still make me sick with jealousy? Once upon a time, I'd been there too, bringing her more pleasure than her small frame could handle.

Fucking fuck.

Probably not a good idea to burst in and beat my former best friend to death in front of Billie. Especially if he was the father of her child. *Child.* She'd said something alarming earlier, and I knew I'd have to ask her about it eventually. I couldn't find the strength to do it now.

I had the sense that the truth would be more than I could handle this week.

In the shower I palmed my dick, wishing that fucker didn't turn into a rock every single time Billie was around, but this was her superpower. Billie Bellerose, the cock whisperer. Closing my eyes and dropping my head against the wall, I pictured her on her knees, perfect fucking lips wrapped around my dick, and it took only a few minutes before the tingles in my balls exploded up the shaft, and I came hard.

Motherfucker. I needed to get laid properly, and soon. This life of limited booze and pussy was killing me, and we weren't even a week in. Too much time to think, too much time to mourn. When I was cleaned up, I pulled on a pair of shorts, since we were in a shared house and my usual naked attire wouldn't work if I stumbled out half-asleep in the morning, and thankfully, fell asleep immediately.

It felt like minutes later that I was roughly shaken awake, heavy hands gripping my shoulders as I jerked up and started to shout. A hand covered my mouth before I made a sound. "There are people outside the house," Grayson whispered near my ear. "They're coming in dark, so I can only assume they're here with bad intentions."

He removed his hold on me, and I shook my head, a new surge of adrenaline helping to clear my sleep-addled state. "What do we do?" I rasped.

"You get Flo and Rhett, and I'll get Billie and Angelo. That fucking gangster should have some weapons stashed in his shit. Then we'll figure out the best route to get everyone to safety."

"Oka—" I couldn't even finish that one word before he was gone, and I was up and moving in the same instant.

Rhett was in the room beside me, Flo beside him, and I managed to wake both of them in a slightly gentler fashion than Grayson had used. We were all confused, pissed off, and more than a little worried by the time Grayson and Angelo strode along the hall, Billie between them.

The guys had guns in their hands, and I could see another weapon or two tucked into their jeans, since they must have slept fully fucking clothed in anticipation of being ambushed.

Thank fuck I'd at least put shorts on.

"Okay, here's the plan," Grayson said shortly in a drill-sergeant manner. "Angelo and I will be the distraction, take out those up front to scare the ones behind into thinking we are more armed and prepared than they expected. That will give all of you time to get out of the house and take off into the paddock with the horses. There's a house three miles south of here, the closest neighbors. From there, you will call the police and Brenda and get a fucking armed guard here if necessary."

"No," Billie said in a croaky voice. "You two don't get to sacrifice yourselves so the rest of us can live. We stick together or—"

"Take her," Angelo interrupted, roughly shoving Billie at me. "Don't let her double back to try and save us. She has a savior complex, and it's going to get her killed."

Billie's fatigue vanished as fury lit up her features. She opened her mouth to shout, so I covered it with my palm, wincing as she sank her teeth into the fleshy part. Little bitch. Fuck, my dick was hard again, and this was not the time.

"Go," Grayson pushed us toward the back door, and we crept along, me half carrying Billie, who, thankfully, wasn't fighting or biting me any longer. Maybe she'd realized that this wasn't a battle she could win.

When we reached the exit out toward the barn, Angelo and Grayson split up, hiding in the shadows either side as they watched silently. "They're out here too," Grayson muttered. "We need to draw them into the house first. You four hide, and when I send out the signal, get the fuck out of here."

"Stay fucking safe," I warned him before nudging Flo and Rhett toward the large closet off the hallway. It'd be a tight fit, but we'd have to manage for a minute.

Damp heat brushed across my hand, and I realized Billie was silently sobbing into my palm. And just like that, it was my heart and not my dick aching. In her state, this was too fucking much, and I had to ensure she survived. Her and the baby.

"I've got you," I crooned softly, using my best weapon to calm her. My voice. "It's going to be okay."

There was no way for me to know that, but I had to reassure her. To be her fucking knight and protector one last time.

When the four of us were squished in tight, Grayson closed the door behind us, and I tried not to react to the feel of all Billie's curves pressed against me. Despite the small belly, the rest of her was thinner than I'd like, as if she'd been starved lately. I couldn't imagine Angelo hurting her like that—we'd both loved her curves in a way that probably should be illegal—so it must be Billie's choice. Maybe grief? Maybe she hadn't wanted to leave as much as I'd initially expected.

The maudlin thoughts vanished when a crash echoed through the house and into our space. Whoever had surrounded the house had finally made it inside, and it appeared Angelo and Grayson, our two criminal masterminds, were making their presence very known. Shots rang out, followed by shouts and cries. I hated hiding in here while my brothers were out there, but I had no weapons or skills to survive in a gunfight, so it was better I spent my time ensuring everyone else survived.

More shots rang out, and I heard Angelo shouting, which faded as he appeared to run from the house. Maybe to clear the outside. A second later there was a knock on the door. Gray's voice floated through. "Backyard is clear. Get outside now."

The door was yanked open, and I exited first, bringing Billie with me. I hadn't been able to see her in the dark, but when her face was visible in the low light filtering through the windows of the house, it was apparent that she'd stopped crying, a newfound determination in her expression.

"Ready to run?" I whispered.

She nodded resolutely, and Rhett and Flo did the same. We were only a few steps from the door, so I picked up the pace, keeping a hand on Billie to make sure she didn't fall behind. She kept pace easily though, and when we got the door open, I breathed deeply as icy air hit us. None of us were dressed to be out in the winter like this, but there was, thankfully, no snow, so my feet wouldn't freeze off. Not immediately anyway.

The light was minimal, but I knew the path to the barn, having taken it twenty times recently. Grayson had said to get out into the field, but there were coats in the barn, and I couldn't let Billie run off into the night without a jacket. She was dressed in pajamas that, while long, were not made of heavy material.

"I'll get the jackets," Rhett said, clearly picking up on my intentions. "You take the girls out into the field and as far from the house as possible."

"Rhett, no," Billie and Florence both said at the same time.

"No point in all of us getting killed for jackets," he continued.

His gaze met mine, and his eyes were imploring me to understand. "Okay," I told him. "Don't fuck around. Get the jackets and get out."

"Understood."

He continued to the barn, and I changed directions, heading for the paddock. More shouts and gunfire rang out behind us, but I didn't look back. With Billie under one arm and Florence at my side, I had responsibilities right here.

Save the girls and then go back for my band.

twenty

JACE

The field was dark enough that I had to slow our pace. There was no way to know what fucking obstacles might be out here, including potholes and some very large horses that were no doubt spooked by the distant gunfire. At this rate, I wouldn't need to find the neighbors. Sound traveled miles in the country, and they'd probably heard the shots already and called someone in. Right? Or was that not something country folk worried about?

"Are they going to be okay?" Florence sobbed when we were a few hundred yards from the shed. "Should we go back for them?"

"We should," Billie bit out.

Flo growled. "Why don't you shut the fuck up. This is all your damn fault. You brought this shit into our lives, you selfish little cun—"

"Florence!" I barked. "Stop lashing out just because you're scared. You and I both know you don't believe that shit, it's just Tom in your head."

She blanched, looking like she'd swallowed her own tongue. Then her gaze dropped guiltily to the ground. "Shit," she whispered. "You're right, Jace. I... fucking hell, I'm sorry Billie. I really didn't mean that, I just got so used to Tom constantly talking shit about you, it's like he brainwashed me. I know this isn't your fault, and honestly I am choking on my own guilt for selling you out."

Tom Tucker was such a fucking snake.

"It's fine," Billie replied quietly, giving a tight smile. "We're both scared. I can forgive some name calling." Why did her forgiveness strike a cord in my heart?

"You're unquestionably a bigger woman than me, Billie Bellerose," Flo muttered, "I'd have probably punched me right in the tw—"

She never got to finish that sentence as a bright light lit up around us and two black-clad men appeared as if by fucking magic. Before I could shout or initiate an attack, one dove forward and wrapped his arms around Florence. My yell echoed into the night as he pulled out a blade, and in the split second it took me to react, he slid it across her throat. Silencing her screams.

Blood cascaded down her front, spilling out of her far faster than anyone could survive.

Our eyes met, hers that had been filled with life now dull, and I shouted her name into the night right as she whispered *"Jace,"* then dropped lifeless to the ground.

Screams rang in my ear along with a clanging sound as I tried to process what the fuck just happened. The shadowy figures lunged for us, and I shoved Billie behind me on instinct, realizing she was screaming so loudly my head rang.

Screaming Florence's name. Sobbing for my fallen friend. My sister.

"No! Florence! *Fuck!*" I raged, losing all conscious thought as I raced toward the closest attacker and slammed my fist into his face so hard that I felt bones crunch. A scrape of his blade crossed my right bicep, but it was a scratch, doing nothing to slow me. I hit him again and again, while red hot rage drove me to murderous new heights.

When the first one was motionless on the ground, I hit the second and knocked him down too, before turning to see where Billie was... just in time to catch sight of a third person approaching right behind her. "Billie," I shouted. "Run toward me, Rose."

She obeyed instantly, sprinting my way when a fist slammed into my side. The second guy from before was back in the game, and he was fighting with his fists this time, having lost or abandoned the blade.

Billie's panicked scream had me losing my fucking mind once more, and by the time the red haze cleared, the second figure was motionless on the ground. But I was too damn late.

Too fucking late again.

I turned to see Billie fighting off the much larger attacker, right before he pulled a blade from his belt and slammed it right into her rounded stomach. Once and then again, and again, over and over in the two seconds it took me to cross the few feet between us and pummel into him, knocking us both to the ground.

Under my bulk, all air expelled from him, the blade flying out of his hand as well. In the dull light of a fallen flashlight, I managed to catch a glimpse of the weapon on the ground and lifted it effortlessly to stab right down into this motherfucker's chest.

I wanted to stab him over and over as he'd done to Billie, but I didn't have the time. I had to settle for slamming it deep and twisting it for extra impact, before climbing off and scrambling my way to where Billie lay motionless.

When I reached her, I brushed her hair off her face, almost losing my shit when she remained motionless, eyes closed. A few seconds of feeling for a pulse, and I found a strong flutter under my fingers. Thank fucking fuck.

Lifting her with as much ease as I'd lifted the blade, I took one extra second to check Flo, my heart shattering at the silence of her pulse. The stillness of her heart.

Florence Foster's light was dimmed this night, and all I could do for her now was ensure that these fuckers paid for their crimes. Every single one of them. But first, I had to save Billie.

If I didn't save Billie, none of us would survive.

Sprinting across the field, I headed in the direction of the neighboring farmhouse before the absolute panic in my mind had me slowing and placing her back down on the field, tearing at the pajama top, trying to determine how much damage had been done. He'd stabbed her so many times that I knew I had to stop the bleeding. If I didn't, she'd die before I got her across this field.

Under the top shirt, there was a second layer, and I tried to be as gentle as possible, all the while cursing myself for not grabbing one of those fallen lights. I couldn't see shit, and it was impossible to tell where the wounds were.

My hands were slick with blood, the rich smell of copper filling my nose and making me gag as I frantically tried to *help her*. When she groaned and opened her eyes, I rasped her name, "Billie, fucking hell."

She groaned and coughed before trying to pull herself up. "No, don't move," I growled. "You were stabbed, Billie. In your stomach. The baby... I need to stop the bleeding."

It was pure blind panic pushing me now; very little could have stopped me in this moment.

She made a gurgling sound, and pure, cold fear chased through me. Was this it? Had he stabbed her lung and now she was drowning in her own blood? I'd never noticed how used to the light pollution of cities I'd become, until now. Out in this cursed paddock with only the light of the half-moon to help us see.

"Billie, Rose, please don't leave me. Please, you can't—"

"Jace," she gasped out, her body shaking under my grip. She wasn't drowning in blood; she was laughing. What the fuck? It had to be shock because it quickly shifted to sobbing, and she threw her arms around my neck, pulling me close as she cried.

I needed to get her medical attention. She could be dying.

"Jace, I'm okay," she said between hiccupping sobs. "I promise I'm okay. My head hurts, but that's all. I'm *okay*."

Confusion wracked through me like physical pain. "What? No, I know what I saw, Billie; you're in shock, but if you don't get to a hospital, you're—"

"Jace!" she shouted, pulling back and clapping her hands against either side of my face. "Listen to me, you arrogant bastard. I'm *okay*."

Nothing made sense. "No, you're not. You got stabbed several times, Billie; your baby is—"

"*Not real*," she hissed, cutting me off. "Look." She sat back on her knees, tearing her pajama shirt over her head and tossing it aside. Underneath, she wore some kind of singlet top that stretched tight over her belly, and then with a tearing of Velcro, she removed that too.

Not just the singlet top. The whole damn belly.

My jaw hit the dirt as I gaped in shock.

"See?" She grabbed my hand, placing it against her smooth, uninjured, *flat* belly. "I'm fine."

"Wh-what?" I croaked. "But... there's blood on my hands and—"

She shook her head. "It's not mine."

My head swirled. I looked from her bare body to the prosthetic belly she'd just taken off. "It was fake?"

Billie nodded, tears coursing down her face again. My heart *hurt* to see her upset, and at the same time, I was so overcome with relief that I could barely formulate words. She wasn't dying, and she wasn't pregnant with Angelo's baby. Holy fuck.

"Rose," I croaked. Then I grabbed her and kissed her. Adrenaline had flooded my entire bloodstream, and now with all the confusion and relief, I was helpless against my baser instincts. And right now, I needed to touch her. Kiss her. Hold her.

And more.

She resisted briefly, squirming in my grip, but I just held her tighter, kissed her harder, and she caved. Just like she always had... back then.

Fuck, we'd just been kids the last time I'd held her in my arms like this, and the memory paled in comparison to the real thing. Holding Billie again was like embracing pure light, like throwing myself into an abyss and not caring if the bottom was full of jagged rocks. The pain of my landing would be worth the thrill of flying, no matter how momentary.

She groaned against my kisses, her lush sounds sparking a fire of fury inside my chest. She'd fucking tricked us all. She'd let us think she was carrying Angelo's baby and *for what?* More fucking games. Always more games with Billie Bellerose.

My teeth nipped her lip, and she inhaled sharply at that pain. Good. I wanted her to hurt, just like she made everyone else hurt around her. Me, Rhett, Gray... I bet she had even done a number on Angelo at some point, too. Now that I thought about it, he was always watching her with that wary caution of a man who'd known pain.

Fueled by my anger, my fingers clutched at her naked waist, my short nails digging into her flesh like I wanted to rip her skin from her body as I bit her lip again.

This time she cried out, and a split second later, her open palm cracked across my face and left my head ringing.

"What the fuck, Jace?" she panted, her face twisted into bewilderment.

Another fucking act. Nothing about Billie Bellerose was real; it was all just *fake*.

Instead of explaining myself, I just grabbed her again, crushing my mouth back to hers and tasting the tang of blood. She fell backwards, and I went with the motion, pinning her to the grass with my body as I circled her wrists with my fingers.

"Jace," she protested, turning her head to the side. "What the fuck is wrong with you?"

I needed to swallow back the urge to scream, I was *so mad.* "You are, Billie Bellerose," I snarled, my lips against her ear. "You're what's wrong with me. With all of us. I thought I hated you before, but that had nothing on what I feel *now.* Right when I started to care about your safety, you reveal that it was all a ruse. You need *help*, Billie."

She swallowed audibly, her head twisting so she could meet my eyes. "You hate me, Jace?"

I studied her cold, closed-off expression for a moment. "With every fiber of my being," I whispered back, my voice like venom.

Her lips curled in a sneer, her eyes flashing. "Oh yeah? Then why is your dick so hard right now? I can *feel* how much you still want to fuck me, Jace. I bet you were watching from the shadows when Rhett kissed me earlier, too."

I had been. I'd been watching, dick hard, waiting for them to take things further.

"Just because my dick is hard now doesn't mean I feel anything but hatred and disgust for you," I growled, forcing myself to sit up and create space between us. She was flat on her back, her blonde hair messy around her head and her perfect tits on full display. *Fuck.* "Believe me, Billie, the moment I tried to fuck you, my dick would go so soft it'd be like trying to shove a noodle into a keyhole."

She scoffed a laugh, making no attempt to get up from where she lay. I still straddled her waist. It'd be so easy...

"You think I'm the liar, Jace? You're so full of shit you're basically choking on it. Go on then, you hate me that much? Prove it."

My brows shot up, and I stilled. "Excuse me?"

"You heard me, rock star. Prove it. Try to fuck me; see what happens."

I swallowed hard. "What? I'm not going to—"

"Because you're scared," she taunted, scoffing up at me. "You're scared that if you fuck me, you'll have to face up to the fact that you don't hate me and probably never did. You'd have to admit that even after all this time, you're still in love with me. Isn't that right?"

My mouth was dry, my palms sweaty, and my pulse racing harder than if I'd been running sprints. "I don't need to fuck you to know that's not true, Billie. You're just easy pussy, nothing more."

"Then what are you scared of, Jace? Put your dick inside me. Prove there's nothing left between us." She locked eyes with me, dead serious and unblinking.

I shook my head, shifting back off her legs to let her

go. "This is stupid. You think you can bait me into doing something stupid? You're even dumber than you look." Christ, I wanted nothing more than to shut her up by making her scream. And yeah, I was fucking aware that made no sense.

She gave a low, mocking chuckle as she wiggled away. "That's what I thought," she sneered, rolling over and pushing up on her hands and knees. "Angelo would have taken that offer without a moment's hesitation."

That was where my control snapped.

twenty-one

BILLIE

It was a low blow and I damn well knew it, but I couldn't seem to stop the words spilling out of my mouth. I wanted nothing more than to see Jace crack, to make him lose control and give in to what we both still wanted so badly. So I played dirty, throwing out that comparison to Angelo as I pushed up off the ground.

No sooner had I reached all fours than Jace's hand snatched up a handful of my hair, pushing my face back into the grass as he ripped my pajama pants down.

I gasped, rocking back as his fingers plunged inside my cunt, filling me up as he held me firm.

"Is that what you fucking wanted, Rose?" he

snarled, pumping those fingers with fury and sending intoxicating waves of pleasure right through my body. "Are you satisfied now?"

My cheek in the grass, I moaned. "No. Not even close."

Jace breathed a curse, his hand leaving my hair for just a moment as he tugged his own shorts down. "Tell me to stop, Billie."

Not a chance in hell.

"Fuck you, Jace," I said instead, clenching my inner walls around his pumping fingers. "You aren't man enough to fuck me properly. You limp-dicked, spineless piece of—*Oh!*"

His thick cock replaced his fingers in the blink of an eye and nearly made me scream at that first thrust. Holy hell, I'd forgotten...

"What was that?" he taunted back, pushing in deeper as I thrashed beneath him. His hands found my hips, holding me tight as he seated his dick entirely. "You were saying something, Billie."

A breathy moan escaped me as he pulled out and thrust back in hard. "Y-yeah," I gasped. "Fuck you, Adams."

He chuckled, and it was one of the single sexiest sounds on this earth. "No, see, that's where you're wrong," he informed me, thrusting hard enough to make my knees scrape in the dirt as I grabbed handfuls of grass. "I'm fucking *you*, and guess what?"

Holy gods of orgasms, had Jace always been like this in bed? Or was this a new skill he'd picked up since becoming a rock star? I was starting to understand the Jace-hype and all the one-night stands. My head was crackling with an overload of endorphins like I'd snorted Pop Rocks, and it was all too hard to maintain our verbal sparring when I was so damn close to coming.

His hand smacked my ass.

"Ow!" I yelped.

"I said, *guess what?*"

Oh, that was right. I swallowed hard, trying to catch my breath—and my wits—while he pounded my cunt doggy style in the grass. "What, dickhead?"

He laughed again, and my pussy clenched up tight around his shaft. "I'm fucking you, Billie Bellerose," he growled, then bent over me as his hips continued to piston, putting his lips right near my ear, "and I still fucking hate you."

An overwhelming rush of emotions clouded my head, but then my orgasm took control. My muscles tensed, and the euphoria unraveled inside my lower belly, making me cry out in undeniable pleasure. Stars lit up in my vision, and my hearing dipped out momentarily as Jace chased his own release, coming inside me with several brutal thrusts as his fingers bit deeply into my slim hips.

"I hate you, too," I croaked as soon as I caught my breath. "Never fucking touch me again, or I'll cut your cock off and make you choke on it."

It took more effort than I liked to admit to move off the dick in question, and I scrambled to pull my pants back up. Instantly the emptiness between my legs made my breath catch, but I steeled my spine and retraced my steps to find my shirt. I left the prosthetic belly where it was, not caring enough to maintain the ruse anymore. At least the sex had warmed me up, since it was blistering cold and I'd been suffering before Jace decided to fuck me.

He said nothing, just knelt there in the grass where we'd just fucked with his head hanging low with defeat.

When he raised his head, the moonlight showed tears streaking his face, but before I could comment— even if I had something to say—a series of gunshots rang out through the night air.

They weren't close, but it was enough to remind us both that we had bigger problems to deal with.

Jace swiped a hand over his face, then pushed to his feet. "Let's go," he said, his voice like a frozen tundra. "I don't want or need your death on my conscience."

He stalked off in the direction we'd originally set out in. I think. I was all turned around after the fight and Flo... *Fuck. Flo is dead.*

Hot tears spilled out of my own eyes, but I said nothing as I followed Jace silently, just wrapped my arms around my rapidly cooling body, trembling and crying as we trekked through the darkness. I lost track of how long we walked, but not a single word passed between us. Jace barely even glanced at me, and several times I vividly pictured what might happen if I just stopped. I was so cold my bones ached, my face hurting from where my tears had chilled on my face, but still I said nothing.

Jace was no better off than me in just a pair of shorts. And I would rather die than seek his pity.

The fact that his cum still dripped out of me was only a harsh reminder of how the two of us were like baking soda and vinegar. Like magnesium set alight. And apparently, I lost *every* shred of common sense around him. So I was better off freezing to death than risking another of those earth-shaking encounters.

Eventually—and I had no idea how—we found the neighboring farmhouse. Whether it was the one Gray had meant for us to go to, I had no clue. It was entirely empty, though. No one home, no cars in the garage... no active phone line either.

"M-m-maybe th-they c-cut the line?" I suggested between chattering teeth. My fingers had bypassed cold and were now numb. That couldn't be a good thing.

Jace didn't even glance my way as he shook his head. "Doubt it. They probably disconnected it because literally everyone has a mobile phone these days, and a landline is redundant. Except now."

"C-c-cool," I muttered, looking around. There was a light switch near where I stood, so I reached out to test it. To my relief, light flooded the kitchen.

"Turn it off!" Jace barked, his voice like a whip, and I automatically did as he said, plunging us back into darkness. "We don't want anyone to know we're here, remember?"

"R-r-right," I chattered, hugging myself harder to try and stop the shivering. It was a pointless effort, though; my arms were just as cold as my body at this point.

Jace turned his head just enough to glance at me. Then he sighed and ran a hand over his face. "Go find a shower, Billie," he said in a weary voice. "You need to warm up. Hot water is the best thing to do that."

Now that I'd tested that the electricity was working, a hot shower was a distinct possibility. Fuck yes.

I couldn't even muster the energy to respond, just stumbled out of the kitchen in search of a bathroom. Thank the stars, the first room I shuffled into was a bedroom with an en suite bathroom.

It just seemed *so* far away, though. And the bed looked so cozy, all made up with a checkered blanket. That would warm me up just as well as a shower, wouldn't it? Surely. Whatever, it'd do.

With a sigh, I collapsed onto the bed and gave a pathetic little roll to wrap myself loosely in the blanket. Then I just... gave up. My eyes closed as my whole body trembled with uncontrollable shivers, and I stopped fighting the allure of sleep. Sleep was safe. Sleep was warm.

"*Shit, Billie!*" I dimly heard Jace's voice, but it seemed like he was at the other end of a tunnel or something. Like he was all echoes. Everything swayed, and dull pressure seemed to imply someone was touching me. Or carrying me? What was going on? "*You stupid, proud bitch. Fucking hell, you're blue.*"

Blue like a Smurf. Or maybe I'd be Smurfette, now that I was the only girl in a band of boys.

That made me want to laugh, but my face didn't work. It was something that should definitely be worrying, but I couldn't muster the energy for all of that.

Hot prickles touched my skin like acid, and I cried out. As dull and useless as my body had grown, I couldn't do anything to get away, but *holy hell,* it hurt. Like being dipped in lava. All I could do was cry and moan as my skin peeled from my bones.

In the background, Jace's voice sang to me. I didn't know the song or the words, but I knew his voice. It gave me something to latch onto, something to ground my mind amidst the pain so I didn't finally lose my last shred of sanity.

Eventually, the pain eased, and my petrified muscles relaxed. Best of all, the trembling subsided, and I could finally breathe again. All the while, Jace continued to sing his song, and like a lullaby, it soothed me gently into sleep.

twenty-two

GRAYSON

The black-clad body rolled over with a heavy thump as I pushed it with the toe of my boot. Yet another anonymous face. No distinctive features or tattoos or gang markings. This one had been stabbed multiple times in the chest, far more than necessary, like someone had totally lost their shit.

"Find anything?" I called out to Angelo, who'd worked shockingly well with me in taking down the attackers who'd swarmed the farmhouse in the middle of the night. We'd handled the worst of them, but when we'd set out to follow the others, we'd come across more bodies two paddocks past the barn.

"Yeah," Angelo replied, sounding grim. "You need to see this one."

Curious, I left the stabbed man and crossed over to where Angelo crouched. He held a lantern, and I had a flashlight. Between us, it was more than enough to see what he thought needed my attention.

"Shit," I breathed, staring down at Florence's vacant eyes. The bloody, gaping wound across her throat revealed the story of how she'd died, and a cold rage built within my chest. Crouching down, I reached out a hand to close her eyes, unable to stomach the nauseating guilt that her death stare elicited. I should have kept her safe.

"Billie?" I asked, nearly choking on her name. Seeing Flo dead was a knife to the gut, but my every instinct was desperate to know if Billie was also lying dead in this field somewhere.

Angelo shook his head, standing up to look around. "No sign, so far. Looks like Jace or Rhett held their own here."

"Jace," I muttered. This had Jace all over it. He spent enough time in the gym and contained enough pent-up rage that he was entirely capable of killing when necessary. Rhett... he was damaged enough already; I sure as shit hoped he hadn't been involved in this.

Casting my flashlight around, I spotted signs of flattened grass leading away from the farm.

"What do you want to do?" Angelo asked, yawning. "Follow them or...?"

I knew what he was asking. Did I want to follow and make sure the remaining members of my band— and Billie—were safe? Or did I want to find out who the hell was responsible for this attack, for killing Flo, and get retribution. What better partner in crime than Angelo Ricci himself? I couldn't think of anyone better suited to vengeance, aside from myself.

Still, it was a bitter pill to swallow that I'd be turning my back on her. On Billie. Did I trust Jace and Rhett to keep her safe now? They'd both be grieving Flo's death; would they blame her?

I shook off my doubts. They were my brothers—by choice, not blood—and I knew their hearts. They were both honorable, even to a fault. They'd keep her safe, even if it meant risking themselves. So I grimaced and ran a hand through my tangled hair.

"Let's explore a little farther into the field to make sure there're no more bodies, and then we find out who ordered this," I reluctantly responded. "They'll try again, no question about it."

Angelo grunted. "Agreed. It's just a shame we have

so very many people who could be responsible. And for a whole host of reasons."

That sounded a whole lot like he knew more about me than I'd even let on to my bandmates. Glancing at him from the corner of my eye as we made our way across the field, I nearly fell over when my toe caught something heavy.

Steadying myself, I sucked in a sharp breath, sure I'd just tripped over another body. But instead...

"What the fuck is this?" I demanded, holding up the... *garment*. Narrowing my eyes at Angelo, I shook my head. "I fucking *knew* it. There was no fucking way she'd let you knock her up so fast. No way in hell. I should have guessed..." It was a prosthetic belly. Billie wasn't pregnant; it was all a sham.

I'd never felt so relieved in my life.

Angelo showed not even a lick of remorse as he shrugged. "It had nothing to do with Bellerose and everything to do with saving Billie's life."

I scoffed. "Bullshit."

Continuing on across the field, he laughed coldly,. "You have no idea, Taylor. No fucking idea. Maybe ask her, one day. Ask her what happened after your backstabbing bitch bass player sold her out to my father's men. *Then* maybe you'll understand the choices she made. That we both made. Until then? Keep your baseless accusations to yourself."

Well. That shut me up.

For about one eighth of a second, before my need to know had me asking, "What happened to Billie when she left our concert that night?"

I'd been able to follow her trail through New York, and then it had gone cold. And stayed cold for days. This was the timeline of events I needed information on. Angelo scoffed as we came across another dead body near the barn, this one with a pitchfork in it.

"My handy work," a low voice said from the shadows as Rhett stepped free with multiple outdoor jackets over his arm. "The others ran, and I went for the coats. But there were a few of these assholes around, so I had to lay low."

He bore deep furrows in his brow as he looked around. "Did you find them? I've been panicked that they're freezing their asses off out there. None of them were well dressed, Flo and Billie especially. I mean, Jace was in shorts, but his stupid muscles should keep him warm. The girls, on the other hand, are both too thin..."

He was rambling, shock over this situation and the dead attacker that lay at my feet clearly kicking in, and it destroyed a part of me to know that I still had to tell him about Flo. Maybe I'd start with some good news first.

"The assholes who broke in are all dead or gone," I said, stepping closer to him. Rhett could be unpredictable in high-intensity and emotional situations. "But they'll be back, so you still need to head for that farmhouse and meet up with Billie and Jace."

I deliberately left Florence off, hoping he'd give me the opening. And he did.

"Flo?" he asked, and I could tell in that one word that he already knew. He fucking knew somehow. That empathetic bastard had probably felt her last moments, even from across the field in a barn.

"Rhett." I breathed through my own pain for a beat. It had been so much easier when I gave zero fucks about anyone. Flo had been a sister to us. "She didn't make it."

He just stared at me, eyes so fucking wide and shiny that I swore the half-moon above was reflected in them. "No," he finally whispered, shaking his head so violently it had to hurt. "No. I refuse to accept that. She's just hurt, badly injured, but we can get her help. There's always help and hope and a fucking chance."

Now he was shouting, the jackets flying off his arms as he raged at the fucked up injustice of the world. I didn't argue with him, but I did do a completely out of character thing when I stepped forward and wrapped my arms around him, holding on tight, letting him rage his pain into the world.

He fought me for a second, and I took a few blows of his fists before he collapsed against me and sobbed. "Fucking hell, man. I can't do this again. I can't."

Rhett's past was almost as mysterious as mine to the rest of the band. He'd let a few things slip over the years when he was drunk or stoned, enough that I'd managed to put together that even his family was a suspect in this current attack. When he was back in his right mind, I'd have to ask if he'd had any contact with them recently. If there was any reason they might be back in his life, trying to take us out.

Tonight had been a coordinated attack, at least twenty attackers, mostly armed with blades for a silent kill. They'd planned on slipping in and out, leaving us all dead in our beds. It was only the few early detection alarms I'd set up around the perimeter, and the fact that I rarely slept heavily, that had saved us all.

It was a hit, plain and simple, and the fuckers here were the hired hands. I just had to figure out who was the money behind it. Then, we would go for them.

Rhett grew silent in my hug, heavy against me as if he could barely hold himself up, but my brother was made of tougher shit than that, and I knew he'd find his strength again. And sure enough, he pulled himself together, and I released him. His face was calmer, the shine of tears the only indication he'd lost it at all. "They need to pay," he said without inflection. "Every single person who had a hand in Flo's death will pay with their lives."

I shook my head, a snort of laughter escaping me despite the seriousness of this situation. "It's fucking done; don't you worry about it. Angelo and I are about to tap into our upbringings and go all gangster on them."

Angelo, who had been silently watching our exchange, remained in the same *arms crossed because I'm a tough guy* pose, revealing nothing of his inner emotions. That was *my* fucking pose.

"You're sure Billie is okay, though?" Rhett asked, stronger emotions bleeding through his tone once more. "You've seen her? And the baby's okay?"

Ah, the fucking baby. Turning to Angelo, I shot him a dark smirk. "Your turn, *bro.*"

"Billie isn't pregnant. The belly was fake."

Angelo didn't even try to lead into it, and there was still no repentance in this piece of shit for the pain he'd caused all of us. And Billie.

I might need his help right now, but sooner or later, I'd have to beat his ass on principle.

Rhett's jaw comically fell open. "It's fake. How in the fucking... Why the fuck? Who and what the actually fucking fuck? You absolute piece of fucking shit. Why didn't you die instead of Flo? I mean, if the universe was fucking fair..."

Rhett's ranting rage this time was different, and Angelo still didn't bat an eye. Not even when Rhett was describing in great detail the many ways he'd off the *Italian motherfucker*. And I actually thought Angelo's lips twitched, and if I didn't already hate him because he'd touched Billie, I might even like him.

"Your time is coming," Rhett spat, pointing a finger right in Angelo's face. "And I'm going to find *my* girl now."

This time the twitch in Angelo's face was of a more serious nature, and recognizing that small loss of control in a very dangerous man, I pulled Rhett back and sent him toward the coats he'd dropped earlier. "Take these to the farmhouse," I said to him. "It's that way across the field." I pointed so he couldn't miss it. "A few miles. Find Billie and Jace, and let them know what we're doing. If they haven't called the cops yet, don't bother. We're going to deal with this our way, and the less law enforcement is involved, the better. You three also need to lay low until I tell you it's safe to show your faces." I hoped they took this part of my warning very seriously. "Don't come back here. I'll work out where you can go, so get in contact with Brenda. She can be our go-between."

I'd normally be suspicious of our manager, since she was the one who'd placed us here, but I'd been over her background multiple times, and she was clean. She had no connection to this darker world of criminal organizations, and with all the surveillance from Big Noise, it could be anyone behind the attack.

Rhett nodded, reaching down to gather up the coats before he shrugged a long parka over his sleep shirt and shorts. "Don't trust him, Gray. Use that asshole to help, but don't trust him. He always has his own agenda, and I wouldn't be surprised if he orchestrated this entire fucking attack."

Angelo lunged forward, the first true break in his steely facade, but I caught hold of him before he could smash into Rhett.

He shook off my hold, leveling me with a *fuck you* glare. "I would never be so fucking sloppy as these assholes were tonight. If I wanted you all dead, you'd be dead."

Somehow, I believed him, and even Rhett looked a touch paler. He leaned in closer to me. "Stay on alert, Gray."

That was his final warning before he turned and

took off into the field, vaulting over the first lot of fences with ease. Rubbing my hands together to get some warmth back in them, I turned to Angelo and crossed my arms into *my* pose. "Alright, we have limited time until this shit gets discovered. I don't have access to a cleanup team."

"I'll deal with it," he said shortly. "Meanwhile, we need to tap into any and all contacts to figure out who set up this hit. Your family, my family, or the—"

"Wilsons," I finished bluntly.

He paused, looking almost surprised I knew that name. "Yes, that's where my money sits right now. They're hungry, ready to take down the old families and criminal organizations. I know who your uncle is, just as you know who my father is. We can easily track through those two groups. Jace is clean, squeaky fucking clean, but what about Florence and Rhett?"

I paused, thinking it over. "Florence is an orphan, and my background checks brought up very little outside of the foster homes she bounced between through the years. Rhett, on the other hand, had a fucked up family life. I don't know the full story, but I suspect his grandfather might be a cult leader and is probably more than capable of taking out the wayward grandson."

Rhett would probably blow his fucking brains out if

he discovered his family was the cause of Flo's death, so I'd do everything in my power to ensure that never happened.

"Then there's Billie," I said, since he hadn't mentioned her before.

Angelo grew even colder, and I wasn't imagining the way he palmed his gun as he faced me. "Billie is mine. We don't delve into her past. It remains where the fuck it is while we figure out which *other* avenue to explore."

His tone brooked no argument, despite her being an obvious target if rival families thought she was carrying the Ricci heir. And I believed he'd walk away right now and take Billie with him if I pushed the agenda.

If only he knew that I would never let it rest, not when it came to Billie.

Because she wasn't Angelo's.

She was mine.

twenty-three

BILLIE

It had been a long time since I'd slept properly. Not since I'd been with Bellerose, before Angelo and the fake pregnancy. Before I'd lost my heart again.

Waking in the cocoon of the bed in the farmhouse to softly whispering voices felt so calming, and I was super rested.

And toasty warm.

Until Rhett's rasp of "...said she's dead" had last night's horror flashing through my mind.

That bubble of peaceful waking I'd found myself in was slashed as I realized multiple things. One: I was naked in bed with Jace. Two: I'd fucked Jace. Or Jace fucked me. There had been fucking, and it was so damn good that my pussy still ached in all the right places. And the wrong ones. Three: I wanted to fuck him again, but I also hated him. Both points were equally disturbing. Four: Rhett was alive, and that made my heart soar. I'd thank God if I didn't believe religion was all horseshit. Five: Florence was dead, and that cracked a little slice through my soaring heart. We'd had our issues, but she didn't deserve to go out like that. It wasn't fair, and I hated to think it had anything to do with me or the Riccis.

My mental list was cut off when Rhett snarled, "But seriously, what the fuck are you doing in bed with her *naked*." He was trying to be quiet, but his anger rang through. "You hate her, remember? Billie will kill you when she wakes up."

"She was freezing," Jace said shortly. "When we got here last night, she was near hypothermic, and I had to get her under hot water to bring her body temperature back up."

"Dangerous to do that so quickly," Rhett still sounded pissed off.

Jace shrugged, moving me with him, since his arm was draped over me in the cocoon. "It was quick or dead. I voted for quick, and thankfully, she feels warm and healthy now, so I think it worked okay." He paused for a beat. "She has a lot of still healing scars."

Fuck. Fucking fuck. Did he see the burn scars too? They were faded, ropey in places but older and not as obvious, especially in the low light. The newer scars from Giovanni's thugs were more obvious at this point, still puckered and red. Still hurting me on occasion. Hopefully, those were the only ones he'd noticed.

"You think the scars are from Angelo?" Rhett continued softly. "Because I will fucking kill him. Or have a very good attempt at it, since that Italian dickhead is almost as scary as Grayson."

Jace didn't answer for a moment, but his fingers were tracing soft patterns across my arm now, and I tried not to squirm, wanting to hear this conversation. "The Angelo I knew would never hurt Billie. He adored her. I always knew his love for her was as strong as mine, but I was a selfish, spoiled bastard, and I kept trying to claim more of her heart." His laugh derisive. "Karma sorted that shit out quick, ripping me to fucking pieces."

"He's not that Angelo any longer," Rhett said. "He's dark now, man. I get that fucking spine tingle, and I don't like the spine tingle."

Rhett might not be a killer like Angelo, but he also hadn't been raised in a white-picket-fence family. I didn't know his history, but it was fairly obvious that he had terrible shit in his past that he was still running from. Only in his dreams did it catch up to him—those moments of broken sleep, which I'd momentarily soothed. Until I'd been the one adding to his darkness.

I must have moved in my distress because Jace's body grew tense, and that touch on my arm faded. "She's awake," he said without inflection.

Weight landed on my free side as Rhett pulled back the blankets that had been surrounding my face. "Thorn, babe, fucking hell. Are you okay?"

I blinked at the sight of his drawn face, surprised when a genuine smile tilted up his lips before he leaned in and kissed me hard. Some of my panicked thoughts faded under his touch, and I found myself relaxing into the kiss, even as I heard Jace curse and untangle himself from me and the blankets, hauling ass out of bed.

"I'll leave you two alone," he bit out, and I managed to catch sight of his perfect, toned, and tanned ass, before he entered the bathroom and slammed the door behind him.

Between that and the taste of Rhett lingering on my tongue, it was no surprise to feel damp heat between my thighs. In other circumstances I'd be squirming and pulling the hot rock star under the sheets with me, but we had a few more pressing items to deal with before any sex could be had. Last night with Jace had been under extenuating circumstances, and it'd probably never happen again...

"Is Gray okay?" I asked him. "Did you see him?"

Rhett kicked off his shoes before he wiggled in under the blankets with me anyway, and I gasped as his colder body came in contact with my very warm one. Another stimulation in my decidedly overstimulated state. "He's fine. They killed everyone, and now they're off to figure out who put out the hit on us."

Angelo and Grayson together. The mental image worked better than I'd have guessed. "Do you think they'll kill each other?"

Rhett didn't answer immediately, his hands tracing across my stomach slowly, and I panicked for a second. He didn't know about the pregnancy. How was he going to react?

"So, yeah, I probably should have mentioned—" I started in a hurry.

"That your pregnancy was a fake," he said conversationally.

In the low light of the early morning filtering through the blinds, I could see his expression, and he didn't appear angry. Well, not as angry as I'd have expected.

"You knew?"

A small smirk appeared. "Gray told me before I hauled ass over to you guys. Why did you lie to us?"

"To protect you," I admitted. "Angelo's family is very dangerous, and there were eyes and ears everywhere in that fucking house. To ensure none of us were murdered in our sleep, we had to play our parts very well."

The irony of almost getting murdered anyway wasn't lost on me. Hence why the belly was gone, never to return again.

"I'd have eventually brought you back into our world, even if the baby was his," Rhett told me seriously, rolling on his side so that we were facing each other, heads cushioned against the pillows. "It fucked with my head that it wasn't mine, but I would have loved that fake little rugrat all the same." My pulse thrummed hard at being back with him like this, and I was desperate to lean forward and kiss him again, play with his lip ring, take all of Rhett. But this was not the time. We had a lot of questions that needed answering first.

"I'm really sorry I lied," I whispered, voice breaking. "Sorry that I did plan on leaving that night in New York, even if it was only to save you all."

Pain crumpled his face briefly, before he swallowed

roughly and got himself together. "Did you plan on going back to Angelo?"

The shake of my head was fierce, disturbing some of the blankets around us. "No. Not a fucking chance. I was taking off to disappear, change my name and hair color, and hope that no one caught up to me. Tom and Flo *did* sell me out to the Riccis. They captured me in the concert, and yeah... let's just say that if Angelo hadn't tracked me down to where his dad's thugs had me chained up, I'd be dead now. I nearly was then, too."

He lifted a hand to cup my face, his touch jagged as if his control was almost shot. "They're the ones who hurt you?"

I nodded into his hold. "Yeah, what's a bit of light torture between friends, right?"

Only they weren't friends, and it hadn't been light.

Rhett didn't smile at my attempt at humor. "And Angelo saved you?"

"He did," I confirmed. "And he killed both of them without asking a single question. I don't know if we can trust him totally, but he's taken a lot of risks to keep me alive. The fake pregnancy thing for one. Mafia mistresses are protected, especially if they're carrying the family heir."

Rhett's eyes narrowed as he did some deep breathing. Probably counting to ten. "I can't say that I will ever like that bastard, but I might worry a little less about Grayson now that I know Angelo has some integrity."

"He'll keep his word as long as they're both working toward the same goals," I assured Rhett. "And figuring out who attacked us is a pretty solid goal."

Rhett nodded. "Yes, and we need to do our part now too."

"Which is what, exactly?"

His thumb brushed over my cheek, sending tingles through my body. "Gray wants us to contact Brenda and then lay low. He said that taking out these guys won't stop the hit. He said he'll get word to Brenda of where we should hide until it's fine to return."

I was nodding, but inside all I could think about was hiding out with Jace and Rhett. What possibly could go wrong?

And should I be angry with fate right now? Or sending her a fucking thank you gift basket?

The door to the bathroom banged open, Jace emerging with a towel around him, steam billowing from the door. "We need to find some clothes," he said shortly. "We can't keep running around in dirty pajamas."

"We can look while Billie showers," Rhett said, rolling out of bed and taking me with him so when he stood, he had my naked ass plastered to his front. Jace's glare dragged across both of us before he let out a huff and exited the bedroom.

"Moody bastard," Rhett said with a laugh, sounding more like his old self. It was only a brief glimpse, but it made me happy. "It's going to be an interesting few days with just the three of us."

We were having the same thoughts on that, clearly.

"Shower, Thorn," he said, then dropped another random kiss on my lips, leaving me a little breathless. "Then we can plan our next steps."

A shower and refresh did sound nice, especially when I had to deal with two rock stars under these circumstances. When he set me down on the tiled floor, his hands lingered on my bare skin longer than was probably necessary, and the look on his face was pained as he finally released me. "I wish I could come in with you," he said softly, "but this is not the time."

It wasn't, but I appreciated the desire all the same. "We'll figure this out," I told him. "We will deal with the assholes trying to destroy us, and then we can finally have some time together."

"The assholes who killed Flo," he rasped. "We can't rest until they're ended."

The heat behind my eyes burned stronger, and I pressed the heels of my palms against them. "I've been trying really hard not to think about it," I confessed. "I know that makes me a shitty human, but... seeing her face when they grabbed her, it's haunting me, and I won't make it through the next days if I keep reliving it."

Rhett nodded. "I understand. There will be time to mourn her soon, but if we fall apart now, we will end up in the same situation. It's survival mode, and once we're safe, then we'll deal with the emotional fallout."

The matter-of-fact way he said that told me this wasn't his first death. Nor the first person he'd mourned. Rhett's scars weren't as visible as mine, but they were as deep.

We all had cuts, bruises, breaks, and losses in our past, and it appeared that the darkness wasn't quite done with us yet. It had already cost us one friend and their band sister.

I just had to hope that there were no more losses. Rhett, Jace, Grayson... and even Angelo, to some degree, were parts of my past, owning sections of my heart and soul, and if I lost one of them... I wouldn't survive it.

twenty-four

BILLIE

There was one small hurdle in our way when we agreed to get in contact with Brenda. None of us had our phones, and the landline for the house was disconnected. The *only* logical ideas we could come up with were that we should either walk out to the main road and hope a passing driver would lend us their phone... or return to Brenda's farmhouse.

I was firmly against going back to the farmhouse, and for once, Jace was in agreement with me. With that decided, the boys outvoted me on who should venture out to seek help. Eventually, Jace left the house just after lunch, and Rhett turned to me with a lopsided smile.

"Just you and me, Thorn. What do you wanna do with our time alone?" His suggestive eyebrow waggle told me he was joking, but *shit*, it was tempting. So freaking tempting. I wanted nothing more than to mend the broken bridges between us and reassure Rhett that I'd *never* stopped caring about him.

Or maybe I wanted him to reassure me.

But the dark cloud of trauma and danger loomed over us, so I just shrugged and headed for the kitchen. Maybe there was a tin of instant coffee stashed somewhere, even if we had to drink it black.

Rhett seemed to follow my train of thought, hunting through the cabinets and coming up with a stove-top kettle and a wide grin.

"Nice," I commented, smiling back weakly. "Rinse it first. Who knows how long the owners have been gone." The fridge was empty and turned off, so it must have been a while.

Now that it was daytime, I felt more confident in flicking on a light to help search the pantry. To my intense relief, I found not only a sealed tin of instant coffee, but also a bag of sugar and some powdered milk packets.

"It's like Christmas," Rhett remarked as I showed him my prizes. He had the kettle already on the stove, heating our water, so he just leaned against the counter and crossed his ankles. "So... *not* pregnant."

Ah, we were back on that subject. I shook my head. "Nope. Not even a little bit."

His lips tugged in a lopsided smile. "That's not a thing, but okay. Good. I mean..."

"I know what you mean." I saved him before he could dig himself a verbal hole. Babies were lovely and all, but being the mother to a Ricci mafia heir, tied to Angelo's family for the rest of my life and forced to live as the "mistress," wasn't in my life plan. Not that I had a plan, but if I did, it wouldn't have anything to do with the Riccis.

I wrapped my arms around myself, thankful for the soft flannel shirt Jace had found for me to wear. It was cozy and warm and covered up all my scars.

"You want to talk about... it?" Rhett asked after several moments of awkward silence.

"It?" I echoed, then shook my head. "No. None of it." Not Angelo or my fake baby or the torture or leaving him or fucking Jace or *fucking* Jace. Or Flo. Shit. Flo was dead. "Do you? Want to talk...?"

He stared at me for a long moment, tugging on his lip ring with his teeth. Then he released it with a sigh. "About some things... no. Other things, yes."

I swallowed my nerves. Why was I so damn

nervous? This was my *Zepp*, bad boy rocker with a heart of pure gold. He'd never hurt me. Even when he'd believed I was carrying Angelo's child, he'd been thinking about winning me back. How could I ever feel anything but totally safe in his presence?

"Okay, sure. That's fair. So, um, what—"

"Did something happen between you and Jace?" he asked, knocking me completely off balance.

My mouth opened and closed like a fish. Then I responded with the full strength of my intellect and wit. "Huh?"

Rhett's eyes narrowed. "You and Jace. This morning it seemed like... I don't even know. Like you both hate each other a hundred times more than before. I'd have thought after everything last night, you guys might have become closer, but it's the opposite. He couldn't have been *more* eager to head out on a solo mission, and it seemed a whole lot like he was trying to put space between you two."

I wet my lips. "Um..."

The whistle of the kettle saved me, announcing that the water was boiling, and I set about finding some mugs for our coffee. Rhett seemed content to let the Jace question drop, and I went back to the pantry to see if there was anything to eat that hadn't expired.

Sadly, my luck had run out with the coffee. The best

I could produce for eating was a couple of tins of tuna in spring water. With a sigh, I showed Rhett, and he screwed up his face in disgust.

"I think I'll wait it out," he muttered, sipping his hot coffee. "Hopefully, Jace can get in touch with Brenda and we won't be here for that long."

I shrugged, grabbing a fork from the drawer. "Suit yourself." It wasn't my favorite food by any means, but it was food. Not that it'd been *that* long since we ate last night, but who knew what the day would bring. What if whoever had attacked the farmhouse—and murdered Flo—was coming after us here? What if they'd already caught Jace and slit his throat too? What if—

"Hey, Thorn baby, are you okay?" Rhett had moved from the other side of the kitchen and put his hands on either side of my face, his eyes locked on mine. "Hey, take a breath. Stick with me, babe. You're having a panic attack, okay? Let's just sit down."

He gently pulled me down to the floor, getting me seated with my back against the cabinets, and guided my head down to my knees.

"Deep breaths, baby, nice and slow, that's it." He rubbed soothing circles on my back as I attempted to get a grip. Eventually that choking panic subsided, and I raised my head back up to give him an apologetic look.

"Sorry," I croaked. "I got caught in my own head."

Rhett's sad smile was full of experience. "Nothing to apologize for, Thorn. It happens to everyone."

I doubted it but also wasn't going to argue the point with him. From where we sat on the kitchen floor, though, I'd just spotted some bottles of whiskey at the bottom of the pantry.

"Look, this is probably a bad idea," I murmured, crawling across to the whiskey to pull it out. "But is it too early to start drinking?"

Rhett barked a laugh, taking the bottle from me. "Tell me something about yourself, Billie Bellerose. Where are your ancestors from?"

Confused, I shrugged. "Uh, my parents are both from Michigan. Mason, Michigan."

Rhett leveled me a dry look, then sighed and pushed up off the floor while unscrewing the bottle cap. "Okay, well you'll probably be shocked to know that Rhett Silver was not my given name."

"What?" I gasped sarcastically. "I don't believe it. You didn't come out of your mother with a mohawk and piercings, rocking a little baby guitar?"

Rhett's smile turned brittle, then he shrugged off the mood shift as fast as it came. "Uh, not even slightly. Anyway, I feel like it's time I told you that *my* ancestors"—he poured a heavy dash of whiskey into each of our coffees—"were Irish." He winked, then handed me my mug. "Cheers."

Chuckling as I understood where he'd been going with that question, I took the mug and held it up to clink his. "Cheers," I replied, then took a sip.

Wow. Strong. Delicious, though.

"Jace is gonna be so mad if he comes back and we're drunk," Rhett warned, leading the way through to the living room with the rest of the bottle in his hand.

I smiled, sitting down on the sofa. "Good. Pissing Jace off is my new favorite pastime, although getting day drunk is not the smartest idea under our current circumstances, I suppose. Working together to stay alive and all that."

"Well, based on how far we drove from the nearest town when Brenda dropped us off, I'd say he won't be back for hours yet. So... we may as well drink now and sober up before he gets back."

I took a mouthful of my Irish coffee. "On a scale of one to ten, how dumb would it be? I mean... after last night, we should stay alert and ready to run and shit. Right?"

Rhett looked me dead in the eye as he answered. "Twenty. But no one other than the people we trust even know we're here. And Angelo. Okay, sure, it wouldn't take a genius to work out we might be in a

nearby house if someone was super motivated but...
live in the moment? Also my nerves could really use
some calming. Yours?"

I grimaced. "Fuck it." The rest of my coffee
disappeared in a matter of mouthfuls and Rhett
followed suit.

"Truth or dare, Thorn," he drawled, taking my
empty mug and putting it on the coffee table alongside
his own.

I chuckled, eyeing him with suspicion. "What are
we, thirteen?"

"Come on, Billie, we've got nowhere to be, nothing
to do"—his gaze turned suggestive—"unless you
wanna just have sex?"

I choked on the mouthful of liquor that I'd just
taken straight from the bottle.

"Too soon?" Rhett mused. "Fair enough. So, truth or
dare?"

My face must have been on *fire,* it was so hot. "Um,
truth I guess." Because I had a feeling he was likely to
dare me to do something like sit on his face. Not that I
was against the idea... but things were still awkward.
We needed to get to know each other all over again, and
maybe a tipsy game of *truth* was perfect for that.

Rhett wasn't easing into anything, though. "How'd
you get the burn scar on your back?"

Shock kicked my pulse into a higher gear, and I bit the inside of my cheek for a moment to try and get a grip. "Just... going for the jugular, huh?"

Fuck. That conjured up vivid pictures of Flo's throat being slit, and *that* was something I'd happily erase from my brain with the help of more booze. I took another gulp, choking and spluttering before handing the bottle to Rhett.

"I was in a fire," I croaked, trying to skate by on minimal information.

Rhett rolled his eyes. "No shit. Give me more than that, Thorn. I saw how you freaked out when Jace punched Angelo into the campfire. I might have been high, but I wasn't *that* messed up."

Fair point. I had to know it was coming.

"When I was sixteen," I said quietly, my eyes on the threadbare couch as though not looking at him meant I wasn't really talking about *my* life, "someone set my parent's house on fire. With us inside. They didn't make it, but Angelo saved me." Tears pricked at the backs of my eyes, but I pushed them away. It was in the past. Ancient history. I was over it... right?

"Someone *set* the fire?" Rhett asked, leaning forward and bracing his elbows on his knees. "It wasn't an accident?"

I scoffed. "Unless it was also an accident that all the

windows were nailed shut and the doors barricaded? Of course, that couldn't be proven when there was nothing left of the house. But I know. I still remember the sheer *terror* of realizing we were trapped in there."

Rhett reached out and took my hand in his, stopping me from picking holes in the seat of the couch with my fingernails. "Angelo saved you?" he asked softly. "Again?" I jerked a nod. I wasn't ready to reveal the rest of that story just yet. "I guess I misjudged him, then. Because it sounds like I owe him a huge debt."

I glanced up at him in confusion. "For what?"

Rhett's stare was dead serious. "If he hadn't saved you then, we never would have met. And that, Thorny Rose, would suck."

I grinned, seeing the attempt to lighten the mood for what it was. "I see why Jace is the lyric writer in your band. You're as poetic as a toad, Zepp."

He grasped his chest in mock pain. "You've wounded me!"

"Whatever. Your turn, wise guy. Ready for a truth?"

"Hit me where it hurts, Bellerose." He said it with confidence, but there was a tremor in his hand as he reached for the liquor bottle.

I wanted to ask a million things but sensed he wasn't even remotely close to tipsy, let alone drunk enough to give truthful answers. So I started easy. "What are you drinking to forget, Rhett?"

His eyes widened, and he gave a visible swallow. "Today? Or any day?"

Fuck. He was holding so much darkness back. "Today," I whispered. "Start with today."

He gave a tight nod, then took another sip. "I killed someone."

I blinked twice, processing. "Last night?" He nodded again, and I exhaled heavily. The way his shoulders bunched with tension as he waited for my reaction told me how much it was weighing on him.

I closed the distance to where he sat, then climbed into his lap, straddling his hips with my knees and cupping his face with my hands. "I'm glad," I said softly. "They deserved to die. Every fucking one of them. But I hate that you have to wear that stain for the rest of your life, Rhett. I hate that any of us were ever in a position that we've needed to make that choice. I'm so sorry."

He gave me a sad smile, lightly holding my waist. "You're right. It was him or me, and *fuck it*, I'm not done with this life just yet."

"Thank fuck for that because I'm definitely not done with you either, Zepp." I emphasized my point by kissing him, but that one taste wasn't nearly enough. I moaned his name as he deepened the kiss, holding me tight as he maneuvered us to the floor.

Screw our bridge rebuilding project. It could wait until after sex. Pillow talk was always the most honest conversation, right? Right.

twenty-five

BILLIE

"Am I interrupting something?" Jace asked in a heavily sarcastic voice, making me jump out of my skin and headbutt Rhett in the process.

"Yes," Rhett snarled. "You are. Fuck off."

He wasn't joking. He'd literally just pushed his fingers inside me, so yeah, the timing couldn't be much worse. Okay, it could be a bit worse.

"Mm, nah, I think I'll stay." Smirking, Jace sat his ass down on the floral armchair and snatched up our forgotten bottle of whiskey. We hadn't had a lot... just a little.

Face flaming with embarrassment, I wiggled out

from under Rhett and tugged my pants into place. "We didn't expect you back so soon," I commented, smoothing my hair. Fucking hell, Jace.

Jace's gaze was dark as he stared at me, then gave a slight shrug. "There was a little gas station not too far away; I managed to plead a free phone call from the cashier. Luckily, I had Brenda's number memorized."

That hadn't even occurred to me. Good to know one of us was thinking, though.

"So? What did she say?" Rhett adjusted his pants, not appearing to give any shits that Jace could see his hard outline. "She coming to get us?"

Jace shook his head. "Not yet. She knows the owner of this house, though. They're on an extended vacation in Spain right now, so we're safe to stay here a little longer while she sorts out what we do next." He paused, his expression saddening. "She's pretty upset about Flo."

Rhett cleared his throat, his eyes downcast. "Yeah."

He didn't need to say it. *Everyone* was upset about Flo, and we were all largely trying not to think about it. We could process and grieve when our lives were no longer at risk. Or maybe that was just easy for me to say when I hadn't been close to her like they all had. She was family to them...

"So, chill here?" I asked, giving a weak attempt at shifting the subject.

Jace nodded. "For today at least. She's been in touch with Gray already, and he asked for us to stay in hiding. Buy him a little more time before letting anyone take another shot at us."

"Which is all well and good if it's one of us three that was the target. What if Gray is the target? Or Angelo..." Rhett tugged his lip ring thoughtfully. "Angelo seems like the most obvious choice."

Jace shook his head. "No way. He's the *least* likely. Anyone trying to kill him is sparking a mafia war with the Riccis, and no one is that stupid. If they wanted to take him out, they'd be damn sure to succeed. No, my guess is that someone wanted Billie—and the fake baby—dead."

"What about Gray's family?" Rhett asked, threading his fingers through mine and giving a small squeeze of reassurance. "He said he'd been in touch..."

Jace shook his head. "We're famous. If they wanted to hurt him, they didn't need *him* making contact. Same goes for any of us, you included. Changing our names means nothing when our faces are all over billboards and magazines."

"What about Flo?" I suggested, my voice quiet and cautious. I didn't want to speak ill of the dead and all, but... "She and Tom seemed like they were into bad shit. Could it have been about her?"

To my surprise, they didn't immediately shut down my idea, just exchanged a long look, then Jace sighed and took a gulp of whiskey.

"So, our instructions are just to lay low here. Any ideas on how to pass the time?" He arched a brow at Rhett.

"Well... Thorn and I were playing truth or dare, until we got a little, uh, distracted." Rhett gave me a heated smirk, and I squirmed in my seat. "You game, Jace?"

Jace's lip curled in a sneer. "No thanks. I'll find something else to do." He started up out of his seat, and my mouth moved faster than my brain.

"Chickenshit."

Jace froze halfway to his feet. "Excuse me?"

I shrugged, backing myself. "You heard me. You're *scared*. Again." Whoops, there I went making a reference to our little argument in the field last night. I was wholeheartedly blaming adrenaline and shock for *that* tryst. So what was my excuse now?

"That's how you wanna play this?" he challenged, eyes narrowed as he glared across the coffee table. I made a casual *if the shoe fits* kind of shrug, and Jace sank back into his seat with a cold laugh. "Fine. You asked for it. Truth or dare, Billie?"

Shit. Um... "Truth," I croaked, instantly regretting my big mouth.

"Why did you break up with me? The *real* reason."

Nope. No way. Not for all the whiskey in Scotland. "*Dare*," I conceded, making it clear that I wouldn't answer that truthfully.

Jace rolled his eyes, leaning back in his chair. "I'm shocked. Billie Bellerose can't even be honest in a game of truth. Some things never change."

"Don't be an asshole," Rhett growled. "She's allowed to switch to dare. Just pick something and move on."

Jace scoffed. "Sure, so she can flake out of that, too. Alright then, Billie. I *dare you*..." He paused then, like he was having an internal debate over how far he wanted to push me. The darkness in his gaze told me he was ready to blow shit up, though, and that terrified me.

"Sometime this year," Rhett drawled, yawning dramatically, then reaching for the booze.

I arched a brow at Jace, challenging him right back. "Go on, Adams. Dare me to *what*?"

His eyes locked on mine, his lips curled in a cruel smirk. "Suck my dick, Bellerose."

For a second, I thought he was telling me to go to

hell. Then Rhett choked on his mouthful of whiskey and spluttered dramatically.

"Look, before anyone says anything," Rhett croaked out between coughs, "I'm okay with this. I'm into the threesome thing. But Billie is not gonna suck your dick on a *dare*, Jace."

Jace shrugged, looking smug and superior. "Told you. Can't answer a truth, won't do a dare. The Billie I knew used to have at least a little bit of spine. What happened to that girl?"

She died in a fire, then again lying in a hospital room for a month without even a get-well card from the boy she loved.

Furious, I glanced at Rhett. He was no help, just shrugged and shook his head. "Jace is an asshole. We can play without him."

I looked back to Jace, and the desire to wipe that smug-fuck smile off his face was so potent I could taste it. "Screw it," I muttered, getting up from my seat and crossing to where Jace sat. "Go on then, get it out. Show us what you've got, tough guy."

I dropped to my knees in front of him, planting my hands on his thighs to spread his legs apart.

"Whoa, um..." Rhett's protest made me look over my shoulder at him. If he wasn't *actually* cool with it, then I'd let Jace take the win. But otherwise...

"Chill, bro. Billie's just trying to call my bluff. She doesn't have the backbone to follow through." Jace was pure arrogance as he met my gaze. "All talk, no action."

"Okay, sure bro." Rhett chuckled. "I think you're way out of your depth here, but I'm totally turned on already, so just ignore me."

I arched a brow at Jace. "Your move, Adams. Whip it out."

He stared back at me a moment, then seemed to decide I was still bluffing. He shifted in his seat, stuffing his hand into his borrowed sweatpants, and tugged out his already hardening cock. His fist pumped a couple of times, getting it fully up as I watched with wide eyes. I couldn't tear my gaze away, and goddamn it, my pussy was wet.

"Go on then, Bellerose," he taunted, "suck it."

Sexual chicken, such a dumb game. But I sure as fuck wasn't backing down, so I batted his hand out of the way, replacing it with my own smaller one. Then before Jace could even draw a gasp, I leaned down and closed my lips around his tip.

"Sh-shit," he stammered, his fingers threading into my hair like on reflex.

Rhett laughed. "Told you she wasn't bluffing. Fuck, I'm hard."

I had plenty of gloating in mind, but Jace's hips

rocked up, and I took him deeper into my mouth, my tongue exploring the silken planes of his cock. He gave a helpless little moan as I sucked, and smug satisfaction warmed my belly. Meanwhile, I tried really fucking hard to ignore how my cunt throbbed in response, blaming it on how Rhett had gotten me worked up earlier.

"Jesus, Rhett are you—" Jace's question cut off as I pumped with my hand and with my mouth, making him gasp.

Rhett laughed again, "Fuck yeah, I am. As if I'm just gonna sit here and watch without jerking it."

With that visual, my stomach flipped and twisted, like my body was planning on getting off without even being touched. Was I into this? Yes. Yes, I was.

Jace's grip on my hair tightened, his hand pushing my head down and forcing me to take more of him. I'd rather cut my own foot off than admit I liked it when he was rough. It did unspeakable things to my dirty mind, and my nipples were hard enough to cut glass. His thick tip pushed against the back of my throat, and I gagged a bit before relaxing into it.

Saliva was drenching his cock and my hand, but it only added to the sensations. He was losing it, I could tell by the way his hips bucked against my face and the desperate way he tried to increase my pace.

"You gonna come like that?" Rhett asked, sounding devious and horny as hell.

Jace's breath was coming in harsh gasps, but he gave a grunt of denial. "Doubt it," he lied. "I've gotten better head from a blow-up doll."

I laughed and nearly choked, then released him from my mouth. "You ever get tired of being such a fucking liar, Adams?"

His gaze as he looked down at me was pure fire. "Prove me wrong, then."

I smirked. "Nice try. The dare was to suck it, not make you come." Licking my lips, I extended my middle finger as I shuffled over to where Rhett sat with his pierced cock in hand. "Zepp, baby, mind if I help out?"

His answer was a wolfish grin as he gathered my messy hair into a one-handed ponytail and pushed my mouth onto his dick. Fuck, I missed him. My tongue played with his piercing bar, tugging it gently before taking him deeper. My fingers wrapped around his base, squeezing a little as I worked my mouth up and down his length.

"God, yes," he groaned, keeping his grip on my hair to hold it out of the way while I sucked him hard and fast. "Okay, this is the kind of *laying low* I can get on board with. Holy shit, Billie... that mouth..."

Jace muttered something, but I was too engrossed

in blowing Rhett to hear what he'd said. It wasn't until his hands rested on my hips that I suddenly paid attention.

"You're asking to get stabbed, bro," Rhett chuckled, groaning as I slowed and teased his tip with my tongue again. "She'll turn violent if you push her too far..."

He wasn't wrong, but I was curious and aroused.

"Nah," Jace murmured, his lips right by my ear as his hands worked my pants down. "She won't bite until after she comes. Isn't that right, Rose?"

Excitement made my pussy clench. "One way to find out," I taunted, barely removing Rhett's dick from my mouth long enough to get those words out.

Rhett met my gaze as I closed my lips around him once more. The question in his eyes was crystal clear. Was I okay with this?

Yes. Holy shit, yes.

twenty-six

RHETT

Not even the slightest hesitation crossed Billie's steady gaze as she teased my dick piercing with her teeth and smiled when I groaned. She was on board, but at what cost? Even an idiot could see how much bad blood lay between Jace and her. The romantic in me, the silly optimist who couldn't be silenced, hoped this might be a step forward for them, though. Like maybe if they could admit how much they still craved each other—even just in a physical sense—then they could mend the emotional hurt.

I'd already made my peace with sharing Billie's heart—and cunt—when she and Gray grew close. I barely even had to adjust to allow for Jace in that equation. Hell, he'd always been there, even before Billie and I got together. This was inevitable.

She gasped a breathy sound and my balls tightened. Jace was toying with her, if the expression on her face was any indication. He'd tugged her pants down to her knees and had his hand buried between her legs. I bet she was soaked right now; she already had been when he'd interrupted us.

"If you're joining in, bro," I panted, wetting my lips as Billie took me deep again. Holy fuck, she did that well. "Then you better play nice."

Jace smirked, doing something that made Billie tighten her grip on the base of my dick as she shuddered. "Nice is overrated, right Bellerose?" He kissed the bend of her neck, but then she flinched and made an angry sound with her mouth full of my dick. Fucking asshole had bitten her.

Laughing to himself, he shot me a pointed look, then grabbed Billie's thighs to pull her pants off entirely and spread those legs wide. With my grip on her hair, I pulled her up off my cock while Jace got situated in his new position.

"Wh-what?" she stuttered, looking between us in bewilderment.

I smiled, flicking my lip ring with my tongue. "Sit."

Her puffy lips parted in shock, but Jace grabbed her hips and pulled her down onto his face. The strangled moan that escaped her lips as his mouth met her cunt was pure heaven, and I needed to bite down on the inside of my cheek to keep from blowing my load. I wasn't anywhere even close to done with her yet. The fun had just started.

"You good?" I asked as her eyelids fluttered closed and her breathing sharpened.

She nodded, licking her lips. "Uh-huh."

"Good," I purred, smacking my dick against her mouth to remind her what she was in the middle of sucking. She grinned, then took me so far into her throat I worried my piercing might get stuck on her tonsils. Not that it was actually possible, but that one movie made out like it was and the image had been stuck in my brain ever since.

I lost myself in the euphoria for a minute, until the sound of a hand slapping flesh brought me back to earth.

"Sit, don't fucking hover," Jace growled, pulling Billie down firmly.

I chuckled, stroking her face. "If he can breathe, you're not sitting hard enough." Her eyes widened, then her long lashes fluttered shut once more as Jace got back to work. "That's better. Come on his face, Thorn.

Fucking drown him; he deserves it for being such an asshole."

A visible shiver ran through her, and I smirked. Violence and hate was their love language right now, and I'd just given her the visual she needed to get off. Barely a moment later, her spine stiffened and her mouth released my dick with a wet pop. Good thing, too, I didn't want to risk her biting me as she came.

"Fuck," she gasped, her fingernails biting into my thighs as her body quaked with her climax. "Oh my god, *shit*. Jace!" I cupped her face, smoothing her sweaty hair back and reveling in the pure bliss radiating from her features. Then she trembled and moaned, her orgasm ebbing and her pretty hazel eyes opening to lock with mine once more.

"Holy shit, you're perfect," I muttered, swiping my thumb over her lower lip. She flashed a grin, then caught my thumb between her teeth and bit me teasingly. Yep, I was about to lose it.

Shifting my grip to her ribs, I lifted her straight up off Jace's very wet face and repositioned her across my lap. If I didn't get my dick inside her *right fucking now,* I was likely to come all over the old floral couch. And that'd just be a waste.

Her pussy was slick with her own release but clenched up tight from her climax, making my first thrust in something straight out of a dirty dream. By the time I got her seated on me entirely, I needed to pause a beat to get a grip. I wanted to make her come again... if I could hold out that long. Holy hell, it wasn't easy, though. She was so fucking sexy.

In an attempt to distract myself, I focused on unbuttoning her flannel shirt. That only made the situation worse, though, when I pushed it off her shoulders and revealed her perfect, naked breasts right there in my face.

"Rhett," she gasped, bracing her hands on my shoulders and rising to start riding my cock. "Rhett, oh my god, *fuck,* I missed you." She picked up the pace, and I grasped her mouth with my own, kissing her like I could swallow a piece of her soul. I wanted to carry it with me always, never to let her go again.

Fragments of lyrics crowded my brain as she fucked me faster, rising and falling as she chased another orgasm and dragged me along with her. I was fucking lost to her, my whole body pulsing with the need to come. But *dammit,* I wanted to feel her sweet release, that glorious way her inner walls gripped onto my dick like her body didn't want to let me go. I needed it.

"Come for me, Thorn," I ordered. Begged. "Let me feel you coming on my dick."

She whimpered, her pussy throbbing as she rode

me hard and fast. Then we had an extra hand. Jace's long fingers slipped between us, and she slowed right down to let him find her clit. It took no time at all, then she sucked in a harsh breath as he found that delicious spot to drive her over the edge.

Her nails bit into the back of my neck, her entire body tensing up and her cunt damn near choking my dick out as she cried out. Wave after wave, pulse after pulse, she came *hard*. Longer than her first one and more intense, I liked to think. I held out as long as I could, my balls drawn up so fucking tight it hurt, but then I exploded. My release poured into her with such force my own vision blacked around the edges and my breathing stuttered with harsh gasps.

She kissed me as I jerked and pulsed, our tongues dancing together in unity as my soul recognized her as *mine*. No matter who I shared her with, she was still *mine*.

Billie gave a small gasp as Jace grasped her hips in his hands. He lifted her only just enough that my cum-soaked cock slid free of her pussy, then he thrust his own thick cock into her, and she cried out in ecstasy.

"Fucking hell," she moaned, wrapping her arms around my neck to hold on as Jace pounded her cunt from behind. Her tits bounced in my face, and my dick twitched, even as it was still softening from my climax.

"*Jaaace...*" It was a plea and a protest, soaked in desire and damage.

"Shut *up*," he growled, fucking her harder. "This changes nothing. I still *hate* you."

Her moan was long and low, sweat running down her throat. "Noted. Ditto. *Fuck!*"

He slammed into her with enough force that her pussy ground against my dick, and I grinned at Jace over her shoulder. He shot me a smirk right back, knowing exactly what he was doing. Then he smacked her ass hard and made her scream. Damn, I bet that felt amazing. She would have clenched up tight at the shock of pain.

"You gonna make me come this time?" Jace taunted her. His balls slapped against mine, he was that close now, and I wrinkled my nose. It was a small price to pay to have her sandwiched between us, and all I could think about was whether she'd be game to let us fuck her at the same time.

Did Billie Bellerose take it in the ass? I couldn't wait to find out.

"Jace, quit being a cum-tease, and finish already!" She was frustrated, wrung out, ready to come again. My girl was a fucking goddess. Eager to get back in on the action, I cupped her bouncing breasts in my hands, bringing one of those hard nipples to my mouth.

She cried out as I sucked it, and I got the feeling she was ready to blow. So was Jace, based on the horrified look on his face.

A few short moments later, Billie exploded, and Jace followed a split second later. Like they were still in sync, even after all these years, their bodies remembered.

There was a brief moment of utter peace as everyone's breathing gradually slowed. Then Jace lurched to his feet and snatched up his pants from where he'd discarded them.

"I'd have had a better time with my hand in the shower," he lied, casting a disgusted look Billie's way.

My anger sparked, and I drew a breath to tell him to *fuck himself,* but Billie started laughing where she'd collapsed boneless in my arms.

"Good, do that next time, and leave me and Rhett to it. Oh, and by the way, Adams? I've gagged harder on a throat swab than your micro-dick. Surely, with all your money you could get that thing enlarged?"

Jace's expression was pure thunder as he flipped his middle finger up at Billie, but she wasn't even looking at him, snuggling her face into my neck with a blissful, exhausted sigh.

"You're an idiot," I told my friend.

He just shrugged, his jaw set in a stubborn tilt. "I'm going for a walk. Don't go anywhere."

Like there was anywhere *to* go. After all, orders were to lay low, so that's what we would do. All the more enjoyable now that Billie was back in my arms. Jace was a goddamn fool. A potted plant would have been more in touch with its emotions than he was at this stage.

So much for sex mending their broken bridge. If anything, that might have just tossed a grenade at it. Whoops. My bad.

twenty-seven

BILLIE

I expected to be in shock. I'd just fucked Rhett *and*
Jace all but at the same time. After jumping from
one of their cocks to the next, and three orgasms
later, Jace was out of here like the huffy bastard he was.
Huge shocker there.

"You okay, Thorn?" Rhett was watching me, gaze
gentle, as he gave me a moment to sort out my messy
thoughts.

"Surprisingly... yes. I'm actually more than okay."
Probably couldn't walk, and I'd be leaking cum for a
week, but other than that, I'd had way worse
afternoons with the Bellerose boys. "I expected to feel

more freaked out by what just happened, but maybe I'm as rock star as you guys now."

I shot him a flirty smirk, and he returned it in full. "You think I'd slap balls with Jace for just any chick? Fuck no, I wouldn't. You're special Thorny Rose, and I will pitchfork the next fucker who disagrees with me." His smile fell rapidly as he grimaced.

"Too soon," I said softly, reaching out to hug him tightly. We needed to clean up, but comfort was first.

"I joke through my pain," Rhett admitted. "But yeah, some shit is too soon."

My reply was to hug him harder. "It's going to be okay. We just have to stick together."

It was a cliche, but in this situation, I strongly believed that if we were to survive the next few days, we had to start working as a team. Jace continually heading off without us wasn't safe, and this had to be the last time he did so.

"You're never getting rid of me now," Rhett said, and when I pulled back to see his expression, it was serious. That part hadn't been a joke. "And we should get cleaned up."

It took more effort than it should have to pull myself away from him and stand on somewhat shaky legs, the aftereffects of that sex session—*along with the booze*—enough for my limbs to feel tingly, almost as if they were a little outside my control. We headed for the same bathroom we'd already used, determined not to mess up these poor people's house any more than we had.

Rhett followed me straight in, and no lie, the cleaning up process took a whole lot longer than I'd anticipated, as he stroked calloused fingers across my skin. Sending spikes of pleasure through me.

"Fuck me," I groaned, and his answering smile was so goddamn smug.

"Baby, I will fuck you here, there, and everywhere."

A snort escaped me, before I groaned when his fingers reached the junction of my thighs. "What, are we in a Dr. Seuss novel now..." I trailed off as he slipped one and then another finger inside me, pumping slowly, before he ramped up the movement.

"Jace cut us off before," he murmured, pressing his lips to my shoulder before sliding his tongue across my wet skin, tasting as much of me as he could reach. It was a tiny shower stall, and we were crammed in. Not that either of us was complaining.

"I— I think we managed to— fuck."

His laughter was low against my throat as he scraped teeth across my jugular. "We certainly managed to fuck, but I need to one up that bastard. You'll come on my hand, and then we'll call it even."

It really shouldn't have been possible after the multiple orgasms in the living area before, but already I was clenching around his fingers, riding his hand harder and harder as I chased the fucking pleasure thrumming through me.

"Rhett... Zep!"

He groaned, his cock growing harder between us as I jerked against him. "This is how you tame a rock star," he groaned again.

Breathy laughs and moans escaped me. "By fucking them?"

Rhett shook his head. "By owning them, Thorn. By owning every single fucking part of them."

The tingles in my center expanded through the rest of my body until I could feel it in my limbs, and as my clit throbbed, I exploded, jerking violently into Rhett. He held me up with the hand not thrusting deep in my pussy, and I had my fourth and equally as impressive orgasm in thirty minutes.

A girl could get used to this sort of pleasure. Might even grow a little addicted to it.

When I finally stopped clenching and shuddering all over him, he slowly eased his fingers from me, and when I reached for him, he stopped me with a forceful kiss. "There's no time for me," he said. "They're probably on tank water here. I'm more than fucking satisfied watching you come apart on my hand."

Despite his logic, I was disappointed to have this moment cut short. There'd be others though, and with that in mind, we hurried to finish *actually cleaning ourselves* this time, then jumped out and dried off quickly.

We dressed in the same clothes, since there weren't a ton of options, and headed downstairs just in time to hear a shout from outside. Rhett stepped in front of me, blocking me from whoever was hollering as they pounded up the front porch and through the door.

I managed to peer around him in time to see familiar broad shoulders appear. Jace had returned, in usual dramatic fashion. "We've gotta get out of here," he said, his hollers from before clear now. "The farmhouse has a couple of cop cars parked out front, and I saw one searching the barn. It's only a matter of time before they find *everything* and then expand their search to this place."

Shit. Fuck. There were so many dead bodies, and Bellerose was too goddamn famous to be associated with that scene. Not to mention that I knew enough about the police and their position in the world of crime to know that if we got taken into custody, our ability to protect ourselves from attack would lessen.

Ironically. Naples's police were as dirty as Siena's these days.

Until Brenda contacted us with a story, we had to lay low. "What do we do, then?" I asked, stepping fully out from behind Rhett. I appreciated his protectiveness, even if it destroyed me to think of him getting hurt trying to save me. "Where can we go?"

"I managed to sneak in and grab some tack so we can ride the horses," Jace said coolly, refusing to look at Rhett or me. He was staring at a spot between us, and it'd be amusing if we weren't *once again* in another sticky situation. This one far less pleasurable. "I let a couple of them into this paddock, so if you two clean up the evidence that we were here, I can entice them over with some hay. We can use them to get out of here."

"I can't ride," I reminded him, wondering if he'd thought this through. Jace had taken lessons when we were growing up, but my mother had been terrified of horses. So it'd always been a very firm no when I'd asked.

"You can ride with me," he said, still focused on that spot. "We'll go straight to the gas station again to contact Brenda. She can direct us to where we go next."

Ride with me. Hadn't I done enough riding with Jace already? Okay, I could probably fit some more in.

"You plan on throwing me off at some point and trampling me to death?" I asked, only half joking.

Jace's gaze jerked to find mine. When our eyes met, a thousand memories exploded up between us. Or at least in my head they did, and I swore I saw the same happening to him. Our fucking might have been hate-fucking, but it had broken the seal we'd had on our feelings for each other. Hate was still an emotion, and a strong one at that. Would we actually survive being in close proximity for the next few days?

Jace's gaze told me that we'd either kill each other, or fuck again. Maybe both.

"Meet you outside in five minutes," Rhett said, breaking up the awkward tension. Part of me wished that I was going to ride with him instead, but Jace was clearly in a mood, and it was easier to just go along with his wishes.

As I turned to leave, I thought I heard Jace say something, but by the time I turned back, he had already gone to get the horses.

Rhett and I didn't talk as we made the bed, gathered up the towels to hang on the bars, and tidied the kitchen where we'd fucked each other near into a coma. By the time we were done, wearing the coats that Rhett had brought from the other barn, Jace was standing out the front with a brown and a gray horse, both harnessed. But there were no saddles.

"The gear I grabbed doesn't fit these two," he said shortly. "They're for smaller horses, so we'll just have to improvise."

Improvise meant riding fucking bareback? My vagina was already reminding me that we'd been fucked within an inch of our lives and that some close contact with a horse's back wasn't really the best idea. *Harden up,* I mentally warned her. It was this or jail.

Jace got on first, using an old stump that was about the right height so he could swing his long legs over the brown horse. Rhett mounted the gray next, and he did it so smoothly that I knew he was a competent rider too. It made me wonder about his past.

It appeared I was the one in need of some lessons and was about to get schooled today.

Jace used the bridle rope thing he had in his hands to direct the horse over to the stump once more, indicating I needed to get up. When they were close, I gulped at how huge the animal was. "Uh, maybe I should just run along behind."

His gaze trailed down my body to my bare feet. The guys had found shoes in the house, but nothing had fit me. "Get the fuck on, Rose."

He held a hand out, and there he went looking

like a fucking god sitting on top his noble steed. My breaths grew rapid, and I was going to pretend it was from fear. I placed my palm into his, stepped up onto the stump, and then choked on a gasp as he hauled me across his hard thighs, settling me in front of him.

My body slid in against his like I'd been made to ride with Jace just like this. The horse shifted only a touch beneath us, and its back was as firm as the man behind me.

Talk about a rock and a hard place. It really should have been uncomfortable, but instead, I was wondering how it'd feel if Jace slipped his hands down from where they were wrapped around my waist to palm my cunt as we rode this hors—

"Everything okay, Billie?" Rhett sounded amused. "Your cheeks are a little flushed."

Every fucking part of me was flushed. "Yeah, fine," I managed to say. "Just freaking out at being up this high. I've never ridden a horse before."

Rhett's smile was knowing as he expertly led his horse closer. "Right. Well, it feels a little odd to let your legs hang without stirrups, but you'll get used to it soon enough. You already have the necessary skills for"—he cleared his throat—"horse riding."

Jace let out a snort behind me. "Enough, Rhett. I

need her focused. We have to get the hell out of here before the police search reaches us."

That sobered all of us up, and when our horses started to move, the gait was more uneven than I was expecting—yeah, the ground was uneven, but shouldn't they adjust for that or something? If Jace's arms hadn't been around me as he gripped the rope, I'd probably have fallen off, but I figured it out eventually, and soon we were moving a little faster than a walk.

The gas station was fairly close, just down a few winding dirt roads, and when we paused in the shade of a few trees on the perimeter, it was decided that Rhett would be the one to head in. "It's just easier for me to get on and off," he said, already dismounting his horse and handing the lead to Jace.

"Yep, okay. Memorize Brenda's number," Jace said quickly, reciting the digits and repeating it a few times.

Rhett nodded once. "I'll see if the clerk will take her payment over the phone so I can get us some food as well."

My stomach grumbled at the mention of food, and I really hoped that Brenda came through once more. We wouldn't last long on the run if we didn't have a few provisions. At least I had Jace and Rhett, though. Having been through a lot of terrible shit in my life, I knew that *not* being out here alone made a huge difference.

Jace's hands tightened around me as he held us steady, and I couldn't help but wonder if maybe during this time we might repair some of the broken strands in our relationship.

Before the hate was too strong to ever reverse.

Unless it already was.

twenty-eight

BILLIE

Rhett returned in about twenty minutes, and if I'd been able to get off this horse, I'd have kissed the hell out of him. Not only was it a very awkward silence out here with Jace refusing to speak, but my ass was growing steadily numb as we remained on horseback.

"We're set," Rhett said shortly, and I could have cried at the sight of the two plastic bags he carried. "Brenda apparently knew that we'd have to bail soon and is already on her way to get us."

"So we wait for her?" Jace asked.

Rhett shook his head before leading his horse over to a built-up dirt pile that was his only option for mounting it. "No, since we called, she decided to keep to the original plan and instead directed me to a new safe house. There's an Airstream trailer stashed about two miles from here. It's on the edge of the neighbor's property, and she said it's usually used by their kids when they visit but is a great place to hide out because it's off the beaten track."

I felt Jace nod from behind me. "Makes sense; I doubt the police will investigate much farther than the original farmhouse and the neighboring ones."

"How do we find this trailer?" I asked, my butt almost completely numb now.

"I've got vague directions and some provisions," Rhett said, managing to pull himself halfway up on the horse, who was starting to shift on the spot. It was clearly much harder to mount a horse while trying to hold two bags, but eventually he seated himself correctly again and shifted the reins into his hands.

He took off in front this time, leading the way, and I tried really hard not to focus on the numbing pain in my ass. Among other places. The feel of Jace against me was almost too much, especially when the horse started to move rhythmically, picking up the pace. At first I was moving against Jace, and it was awkward and dangerous as I almost fell twice.

"Rose," he breathed, free hand pressing to my

JAYMIN EVE & TATE JAMES

stomach to slow me. "Move with me. Feel the stride of the horse, and stop fighting the rhythm."

My initial instinct was to say *fuck you, asshole.* I didn't ask to ride on the horse with him, and he knew I had no experience with them. But arguing was not going to help the situation, so I decided to just pause a moment and listen.

Jace picked up the pace again by gently kicking his heels into the horse's side, and we moved together, slower at first, until eventually I was sliding with him and not against. Sliding and grinding, and biting my tongue, because there was a sensuality to horse riding that I really hadn't expected.

Especially not with Jace, but as the weak sun beat down on us, the cool wind whipping over our faces, a peace settled between us. It lasted until we entered a thicker patch of forest, following a small river that must have been part of Rhett's directions. Once the canopy covered us, the light faded a touch, and I caught sight of a glint of silver on the horizon. That shiny exterior of the RV returned Jace and me to reality. Reality and our near decade-long feud.

"Why won't you tell me why you really left?" he asked as we slowed once more, the brush around us too dense for a faster gait. "I mean, we can't go back in time to change anything, so what does it hurt?"

It hurt me. That's what it hurt.

"I don't talk about that year," I said, clenching my teeth so hard that I almost bit my tongue off. "I can't relive it. I won't."

I waited for him to curse and demand the information from me, but he didn't. He dropped his head against my shoulder, and my heart lurched in my chest. "Whatever it was, Rose," he rasped, "it broke us. I don't know how I'm supposed to get past that."

Whatever pain I'd been experiencing in my lower half was forgotten as my throat tightened to the point I couldn't breathe. His words, indicating that at some point we'd permanently part ways, never to be Jace and Billie again, broke me. Fuck, I hadn't even realized there was still enough of us left to break, but apparently, I'd been holding on in ways I'd refused to acknowledge.

Jace's raw honesty today forced me to.

"I don't know either," I managed to choke out, the burn of tears clouding my vision, even as the silver Airstream grew closer. Rhett was already there, so we had these few seconds of privacy, and it appeared I was going to use them to bawl my eyes out.

Jace lifted his head, cleared his throat behind me, and the angst that had been holding us vanished. He pulled himself together so quickly that it was as if a magic wand had been waved over the top of him, bringing forth the rock star bad boy once more. When we came to a halt, he slid off, and I wondered if he was just going to stride away and leave me stranded on the big beast, but thankfully, enough of his decency remained that he reached up and slowly dragged me off and down his body.

When I landed on the ground, my legs were weak, and he held me steady. "Take a second," he said flatly before he released his hold. "You need to get the blood pumping through your legs again."

I nodded, my eyes burning so badly from holding back tears that it was growing quite painful. Jace didn't bother to hang around to see my breakdown though, as he turned to help Rhett, who was attempting to find the key to the trailer. When I was alone, just the untethered horse behind me, I gulped in some air, but it didn't help.

The tears were too hot, too painful, too explosive to stop. I had to let them free, or I'd choke on the sorrow. I'd learned that the hard way when I'd tried not to fall apart eight years ago.

Losing a baby was an agony like nothing I'd ever experienced, but losing Jace and Angelo had been a close second. Losing all three... it was half a miracle I was still even in this world, walking around and breathing. I'd had to be hospitalized back then, and if I didn't deal with my sorrow today, I'd likely find myself right back in that bed. Sedated. A shadow of myself.

The first tear felt like acid against my skin, hot and painful, burning a path until it hit my lip and rested there. I could taste the saltiness, and I closed my eyes against the memories. The next tear fell faster, and the rest followed in a relentless assault that would be stemmed by nothing but time.

Time to release the pain, time to breathe deeply, time to mourn another loss.

When gentle hands wrapped around my shoulders and pulled me against a hard chest, I expected that it would be Rhett.

"Rose," Jace rumbled, and I choked on a sob as he pulled me tight against him. "Fuck. Don't cry."

I'd cried fucking oceans over this guy, and here he was, all *don't cry.*

The intensity and sound of my sobs increased, partly to spite this asshole and partly because the pain in my chest kept growing stronger. Had I let this go on too long?

His hands tangled roughly in my hair as he closed his fist and jerked my head back. Firm lips crashed against mine, and the salt of my tears mixing with that familiar taste of Jace jolted me from my state of painful brokenness.

A moaning sob escaped, and I opened my lips further, needing more. "It's going to be okay," he murmured in that sexy-as-sin voice. "I promise. Just... don't leave again. Give this time to heal."

Jace's continued anger toward me made a lot of sense when I looked at it through his eyes. I was the chick who kept leaving, and in doing so, I'd damaged his ability to trust or believe in us.

His damage was on me, and it was up to me to fix it. Only there was no way I could when he clearly thought we were past the point of repair. That's what he'd said on the horse, and yet here he was, asking me not to leave again so we had time to heal. Dude was giving me whiplash.

When he pulled away, that coldly blank expression was back on his face, but he did stroke a thumb across my cheek to remove the last of my tears. "We're in survival mode," he reminded me, straightening. "There's nothing else to deal with until that passes. No more truth and dare. No more revisiting the past."

Two statements I could agree with, since I wasn't sure I could handle more dredged up feelings. Not after the emotional turmoil of the last few days. Fuck, who was I kidding. The last few months and years.

He left me again, but this time it was to deal with the horses, as he found a small dry trough that he filled from a tap. I guessed they had a tank somewhere or maybe a well had been dug, but thankfully, there was enough water for the horses to drink and enough grass for them to graze on the spot. As I moved closer to Jace, Rhett returned from the RV, having figured out how to open the door. "Will you tie the horses up?" I asked when Rhett stopped by my side.

"I can't really keep them tied up for days," Jace answered, patting one on the side of the neck. "I think I'll just leave them to graze and hope they come back for water. Chances are that we won't need them again, since Brenda should be here in a few days as planned."

That made sense, and I was sort of glad to know the horses would be close by. Maybe they'd give us an early warning if any police or assassins came sniffing around. Like guard-horses. That'd be cool, as long as they didn't get hurt. No more innocents could die around me, or I'd lose my shit.

"We should get inside," Rhett said quickly, glancing around. "I checked, and outside of being a little stale, everything in there is clean and secure. This is not a cheap structure, but one designed to withstand all the elements."

As if he'd called the storm with those words, there

was a rumble above us, and the previous blue sky was now a distinct gray color. Winds picked up as we stood there, disturbing the leafy undergrowth, and I shivered in the thick coat.

Rhett wrapped an arm around me, directing me toward the steps of the RV. They were situated halfway along the smooth, silver body, and when I entered, I was surprised by how nice and modern it was inside. The right end of the trailer had a small bench with a table. Rhett had set the bags there, and my stomach growled once more as if to remind me that we were very hungry. Next to the table was a small kitchenette with enough appliances to get by.

When I turned to see the other end, I almost ground to a halt in surprise. Rhett paused behind me, and I heard his low chuckled. "Ah, yes. Our one small issue, but we've all shared a bed before. We can make do for a couple of nights."

One. Bed.

Ah, come the fuck on. This beaten and broken chick only had so much willpower, and being sandwiched between Rhett and Jace for hours every night was going to lead to one thing. There was no use lying to myself about it. I had no strength to resist these two, and if they wanted to use my body to pass the time, who the fuck was I to say no.

Jace thought he hated me now... just wait until we'd hate-fucked our way through the next few days.

All of a sudden, this little escape from reality had gotten very interesting.

Very interesting indeed.

twenty-nine

GRAYSON

S ounds of pathetic screaming bounced off the walls of the soundproof room, hurting my head and making me wince slightly. Any more of this and I was likely to lose my ear for music; then I'd really be pissed off.

A gunshot rang out, and the man I'd been chatting with fell backward, his blood and brains leaking out all over the floor. With a frustrated sigh, I turned to glare at Angelo.

"Do you fucking mind?"

The mafia prince just shrugged, tucking his gun away once more. "He wasn't talking; we're wasting our time here."

296

I pushed to my feet, feeling my spine click as I stretched. "Not *yet*, but he would have eventually."

Angelo shook his head. "Disagree. That guy didn't *know* what we want to know. He'd have just made something up that sounded plausible and set us on a wild goose chase. No thanks. Come on, we need to get to that meeting with Brenda before she strings us both up for keeping her waiting."

Giving the dead man another annoyed glance, I followed Angelo out of the room and closed the door firmly after us before pulling off my gloves. "Your cleaners are on the job here?"

He jerked a nod, his eyes on his phone screen. "Should be here any minute."

We both got into Angelo's Porsche, then waited silently for another minute until a white panel van pulled up outside the warehouse. The logo on the side of the truck read *Rat-Zap, rodent and pest removal.*

I snorted a short laugh. "Cleaners with a sense of humor, huh?"

Angelo just arched a brow. "What? It's what they do. Remove *rats.*"

Satisfied that his cleaners were taking care of our mess, he started up the powerful car and drove us out of the industrial area where we'd been torturing that whiny dick from the dark-web muscle-for-hire site.

That was where we'd traced the attackers at the farmhouse back to. All of them were anonymous grunts, not even particularly well paid, which explained why we were all able to escape.

Well, most of us.

Poor Flo.

"Brenda said to meet her in the park near the fountain," I told Angelo, tucking my bloody gloves into his center console and pulling out some wet wipes.

"Got it," he replied, driving us toward that area of town. We were back in Naples—home of Big Noise Records—and following up on any lead we could find. So far, all we'd managed to do was rule out a couple of options.

Maybe it was too soon to *really* rule anything out, but we'd tentatively crossed off the Riccis. They would never put their heir at risk. Not Angelo *or* Billie's fake baby.

We'd also cautiously crossed out my family. Were they capable? Hell yes. Would they give any shits about killing a Ricci and starting a war? Not a chance. But they'd had *plenty* of opportunity to get at me without resorting to such extreme measures. It just didn't add up.

Because of those two points, Angelo and I had reached a temporary truce, an unspoken agreement to work *together* for the safety of those we loved. It helped that we were both particularly trigger happy, him even more so than me since I was eight years out of practice.

"What's the deal with you and Brenda?" The question that had been bouncing around in my brain all day. "You seem close."

Angelo just shot me a sideways look. "And?"

"Closer than I'd expect. You met her when she first negotiated the Big Noise contract, yes?" I was well aware that Angelo had been part of the original Bellerose before things fell apart with Jace and Billie.

Angelo nodded. "She picked us up at an open mic night in Siena. Jace thought she was totally full of shit, so he wouldn't hire her as a manager until she could get us a meeting with some labels. Stubborn prick."

"Uh-huh," I agreed. "But you seem more familiar than that."

He arched a brow. "How would you know? You haven't seen us interact in person."

I grunted. "Call it intuition."

He was silent a long time. Long enough that I thought he wasn't going to answer my question. Then as we turned into the parking lot beside the park, he sighed.

"We stayed in touch," he admitted grudgingly. "Jace would fire her if he knew, so I trust you won't tell him."

Dammit. I should have known what I was getting into there, and now I had a secret to keep from my brother.

"You stayed in touch *because*...?" I prompted, wanting to know the whole story if I was already neck deep in secrets.

Angelo chuckled, turning off the car and getting out. "None of your fucking business, Taylor. Hurry up."

He set a brisk pace across the snow-dusted park, pulling his coat closed, and I followed a little slower, taking my time to assess all our surroundings. I'd gotten so used to keeping an eye out for paparazzi since Bellerose hit the big time, but now I wasn't totally sure what I was looking for. Paps? Shooters? Cops? All of the above.

"You're late," Brenda announced when we reached her beside the frozen duck pond. She was bundled up warm, and her baby was sleeping soundly in a winter warm buggy. Cutie.

"Lovely to see you too," Angelo replied sarcastically, dipping to kiss her cheek.

Brenda blushed slightly and shot him a smile. Were they sleeping together? I kind of hoped they were... it'd mean he wasn't such a threat against Billie's heart.

"I had a call from Rhett this morning," she told us without any other small talk. "For some fucking reason,

Jace ventured back to the farmhouse and found cops all over the place. They panicked and left the house they were at."

My brow dipped with irritation. "Dumb fuck. What part of 'lay low' was hard to understand?"

Angelo sighed. "Probably not the dumbest decision. Cops would likely visit neighbors to ask if they heard or saw anything suspicious. They might have been found there, and that'd seem even shadier."

Okay, good point. "Where are they now?"

"I gave them directions to an Airstream parked in the forest behind that property. They took some horses and should already be there by now. Rhett grabbed food on my credit card, too, so they're fine for now." Brenda sniffed, her nose red from the cold. She paused, her lips tight, then looked up at me. "What did you do with Flo?"

Christ.

"Dealt with," Angelo answered for me. "She'll be found soon, if she hasn't already."

We'd made the joint decision to move Flo's body from the farm to her apartment where Angelo's people had staged it to look like a home invasion. It sucked, I hated it, but we also couldn't go implicating ourselves, Jace, and Rhett for all the various hitman deaths at the farm. So we'd cleaned things up to a degree and changed the narrative of Flo's death.

As easy as it would've been to make her disappear —like all the other bodies—she deserved better. She deserved a funeral and to be mourned by those who loved her. She deserved her death to be recognized.

Brenda gave a long exhale, looking for a moment like she was about to start crying. But she pulled herself back together with a tight nod and professional smile. "Good. You two are the best people for the job here." Little James stirred in his sleep, whimpering, and Brenda rocked the buggy back and forth to send him back to sleep. "Okay. Good. It seems that the cops went to check out the farmhouse, thanks to that fucking gossip blog. They posted a story about a *crime* occurring that involved Bellerose, and enough people blew it up that the cops had to do due diligence."

"*The Dirty Truths* again?" Angelo scowled. "They seem to have a lot of inside access for Bellerose in particular. Any ideas who's behind it?"

Brenda shook her head. "None."

I couldn't say the same. Ever since reading all the blog posts about us, and Billie, and comparing them to older posts about other celebrities, I was pretty confident the blog had changed hands some time in the past months. Or maybe there were several contributors.

Either way, Tom Tucker was my number one suspect for those leaks.

"Well, whoever it is, they're really starting to piss me off," Brenda muttered. "Anyway, here's the coordinates and directions for where I sent Rhett, Jace, and Billie. Also, Rhett told me the belly was a fake, so thank you a whole lot for that one, Ricci."

Angelo just smirked. "It was a need-to-know subject. You didn't need to know. Also, tell Rhett to keep his dumb mouth shut. The last thing I need is my father catching wind of that little lie."

Brenda flapped a hand. "Please. I'm a vault. You know that. In this situation, I won't even let my husband know. Okay, I'll let you two get back to whatever you were doing." She gave the visible gun at Angelo's waist a pointed look. "And I'll be in touch if I hear anything more. Try not to leave the other three in the forest too long, or we might have more bodies to clean up."

Angelo shook his head. "Jace is all talk; he still loves Bella. He just can't swallow his own pride long enough to admit it."

Brenda winced. "He's not the one I'm worried about."

James started stirring again, so she quickly bid us both farewell and pushed her buggy away at a brisk pace, leaving Angelo and I standing there in silence.

"Now what?" I asked him after a beat.

He glanced over at me. "You mentioned that Flo was broke, didn't you?" I nodded. "How is that possible? I know what you all get paid."

"How you know that is an issue for another day," I muttered, peering out over the empty park. "But we think her boyfriend—ex-boyfriend rather—somehow drained her account when they broke up. She wouldn't give us the details, but he seemed like the type."

Angelo nodded thoughtfully. "Let's shake that tree. See what falls out."

I smiled. "I knew I liked you, Ricci. Come on, I know where he's been staying since Flo kicked him out and the band strong armed the label into firing him."

We'd barely made it five minutes into our drive, though, when Brenda called my phone.

"They found Flo," she told us in a curt voice as I put her on speakerphone. "Big Noise execs want to see the whole band. They're talking about a press conference already."

Angelo and I exchanged a hard look, and I shook my head. "Not a chance. That could be a ruse to pull the others out of hiding. I don't trust it."

"Me neither," Brenda agreed. "Gray, will you do it

alone? You can just say Jace and Rhett are overwhelmed with grief and..." She trailed off with a sigh. "Jesus. I dunno. You two chat about it, but meet me at the Big Noise office tomorrow morning at nine, alright? I'll stall until then."

She ended the call without saying goodbye, and I looked to Angelo for his opinion. When I'd started caring what he thought, I had no clue. But the arrogant dick knew his shit.

"Big Noise had at least one Wilson employee on the books," he told me in a carefully calm voice. "I killed him before Billie and I came out to the farmhouse. It stands to reason there might be more."

That was news to me. "Why?"

Angelo laughed. "Why does anyone do anything? Money. Money and power and influence, but always money. The root of all evil."

Fuck. How right he was about that.

thirty

BILLIE

Noone of us addressed the single bed situation again as we went about opening windows, airing out the Airstream, and making it as habitable as we could. Rhett had grabbed a decent array of food from the gas station, including some bread and fruit, but obviously nothing that would require a fridge. There was one in the vehicle, but like the other house, it was off.

"Canned beans or canned spam for dinner?" Rhett said, upending his bags on the table so we could see the full range of potato chips, crackers, cheese, fruit, and canned goods. Along with as many bottles of water as he could fit in the second bag.

"Also got some dessert," he said with a smirk, pulling a third smaller bag from under his shirt. A dozen or so candy bars spilled out of it. "We can live on the chocolate if all else fails."

It said a lot about our current situation, but the sight of my favorite candy bar lying there had real happiness filling me. Sad as it was, there hadn't been much to celebrate in my life lately.

This almost felt like being handed an all-expenses paid vacation.

"I'm used to living on very little food," I reminded them. "My ration can be pretty small."

Jace, who had been sitting on the bed away from us, grumpy as per usual, let out a growly, pissed-off sound. "You will get the largest portion because you have no weight to spare."

When our gazes met, I couldn't quite figure out what I'd said that was pissing him off. Probably all of it, knowing Jace. "I'm also the smallest, so it stands to reason I *need* the least amount of food," I pushed back, and he got to his feet and stalked forward, the magnetic presence he was born with suffocating in this close proximity.

Rhett continued to sort the food and water into piles, while Jace leaned over the top of me, bracing a hand on either side of the chair so that he was caging me in completely. Signature fucking move of his, apparently. When his face was mere inches from mine, he said, "What happened to you, Rose? Why are you used to living without food? Your family was not poor, and they'd never let you starve, even after their deaths."

My breath stuttered in my lungs, the air constricting until I felt faint. This conversation was skating way too close to the edge of topics I could never discuss with Jace. With anyone. "Thought you said no more past," I managed to gasp, and his lips flattened into a line of annoyance.

"Maybe you shouldn't mention things like *starving when you weren't fucking with me,* then."

Another rumble rocked his chest, and I was close enough to see flecks of darkness in his blue eyes. "Didn't think you'd care," I told him, and it wasn't a dig. It was the truth. "It's been a long time, Jace. You never checked in before; why are you giving a shit now?"

He stared into my soul, and it was painful sitting there being dissected by a man who used to be a boy I loved. He never said another word, and I was about to shove against him, when he let loose a string of curses, pushed off from the chair, and stalked from the trailer.

The storm had passed by quickly before, so he'd be safe out there. But would *out there* be safe from him?

Rhett chuckled lightly, and for the love of rock stars

everywhere, I'd actually forgotten he was in the room. And considering how much of my attention Rhett often had, that said everything about how fucking all-encompassing Jace could be at times. "Poor little guy," Rhett said with another laugh when we heard a crash. "His big-boy emotions are too much for him."

Swallowing hard against my dry throat, I shook my head, confusion pulsing within me. "I don't really understand what his issue is... It's been a long time since we were in each other's lives, and he's never once sought me out. Never once checked to see if I was even alive."

Rhett's amusement dried up then. "Don't kid yourself, Billie. Jace might not have been in your day-to-day, but I know for fucking sure that you were on his mind more than he'd ever admit. I'm pretty sure he always intended to track you down one day and likely would have bulldozed through whatever life you'd built when that happened."

Toxic motherfucker that Jace was, that didn't surprise me in the least.

"I've been near homeless and starving many times in my life. Are you saying that Jace was aware of that and never tried to help me?" I mean, if that was the truth, then he was the worst kind of human. I'd never have done that to him if I'd been in the same position.

"No, god no," Rhett assured me. "He's not *that* much of an asshole. He just never truly got over you. I think a part of him was waiting for you to run back to him for help. His ego couldn't handle you dumping him and then him chasing you. It's all fucked up, but the truth of it is, you are his muse and destruction, and that will never change. Jace couldn't truly let you go, even if it cost him his life."

Being someone's destruction sounded terrible, and yet I couldn't argue. "I don't want his life," I whispered, my pain too great to put into words. "It would just be nice not to have his hate. Fighting with Jace is exhausting."

Rhett leaned forward and wrapped his arms around me. "Peace might not be in the cards for us, but you can be assured, Billie Bellerose, you'll never face your trauma alone. Not while I'm here."

And that made all the fucking difference. Some people weren't built for a life of peace, and clearly, both me and the boys of Bellerose were in that category, but as long as we were together, we would be okay.

"Let's go find Jace before he punches holes through multiple trees," Rhett said against my neck, placing a gentle kiss there. I sighed at the sweet touch.

Rhett got to his feet first, pulling me up with him,

and together we left the trailer. Outside there was no sign of the horses—huge shocker with the raging fit being thrown by Jace. Speaking of, Bellerose's lead singer was also nowhere to be seen, but I could still hear him crashing around in the underbrush. If the police were anywhere close by, we'd just blown our hideout for sure.

"I'll get him and be right back," Rhett told me. "You return to the RV and keep the door closed."

I wanted to protest, but I was just too damn tired. "Come right back," I ordered.

Rhett grinned, the silver of his piercing twinkling in a ray of sun that managed to make it through the afternoon clouds. "There's no getting rid of me now. I'm not Jace, and I don't give a fuck if you dump me. I'm just going to follow your ass until you realize that you can't live without me."

I already realized it. Just like with Jace and Angelo, there was a part of me that belonged to Rhett now, and that would never change. Grayson too, if I was being completely honest, even if that big, scary bastard was a complete unknown.

"I'll be waiting inside," I told him before hurrying back into the Airstream and closing the door behind me. I hated to shut myself off from Rhett, but I also needed Jace back here before he brought the fucking police, army, and navy down on us with his impressive vocals.

No wonder he was a damn rock star; his lungs worked far beyond what was natural. Especially when he was pissed.

Part of me struggled to believe that this reaction was all thanks to him not knowing about my past and the years we were apart. Did it really bother him so much that I'd had a tough time of it while he was living it up as a famous millionaire? When, clearly, he'd been such a prideful prick that he was prepared to leave me in any variety of shitty situations until I was desperate enough to reach out to him. Until I crawled back on my knees.

I wasn't sure what part bothered me the most... All of it, really. Typical when it came to dealing with Jace Adams.

There wasn't much to do in the trailer outside of moving bags of chips and food around and opening a few random cabinets in the hope of finding something cool. I was surprised when I explored a tall, thin cabinet tucked in beside the bed and found a guitar. It was an old acoustic with steel strings, and when I pulled it free, a large cloud of dust followed. I'd guess that someone had shoved it in there long ago and forgotten all about it.

I sat on the bed and rested it on my lap, memories filling me of sitting with a guitar just like this when I was ten, Jace beside me, holding my fingers in place as he taught me basic chords. He'd continued to give me lessons for years, and I'd forever associate the weight and sound of music with him.

I hadn't touched a single instrument since the day he walked out of my life.

Knowing this was a bad idea, I still strummed a few chords, my fingers falling back into position like I'd never stopped. I mean, sure, I was super rusty and slow in transitions, but it didn't take me long to get the feel for it.

This particular acoustic was older and probably needed a decent setup, but it still made beautiful music, especially when I adjusted it slightly. Jace always did say my superpower was in my ear, as I'd fine-tuned his instruments growing up. It was just a running joke that I couldn't sing for shit. Angry cats sounded better than me.

Letting myself lose my love for music had been almost as heartbreaking as allowing myself to disappear into a shitty existence without ever attempting to change my own fate. While Jace might have been waiting for me to run back to him, I'd had enough of my own pride that I'd never do that, but in the end I hadn't really fared any better on my own.

I'd failed. In all fucking ways I'd failed.

Dropping the instrument on the bed, I had to breathe through tears because there was no way I was going to fall apart again. Nope. Not a chance. It might be volatile up in here with this forced proximity, but I had to keep it together. Just for a few more days.

Rhett and Jace weren't back yet, so leaving the guitar on the bed, I continued my search through the cabinets. In a small set on the floor, I hit the jackpot, finding three heavy, cast iron cooking pots, along with some matches and fire starters. Amazing. We weren't having cold beans from the can tonight.

We were having hot beans from a pot, and we'd think it was a fucking five-star meal.

Wanting to head outside and check on the boys anyway, I lifted one of the heavy pots and ferried it out to the cooking area set up a few meters from the trailer. The previous occupants had built a small circle of stones, leaving some cut-up firewood beside it. The timber was old and brittle now, and a little damp from the storm earlier, but I thought with the fire starters I could get it to burn, helped along with some dried leaves and grass and protected as it was from the elements by scrub and trees.

The boys weren't in the clearing, but Rhett's voice drifted to me every now and then, followed by the rumbles of Jace, so I knew they were okay, just talking it out. So I might as well make myself useful by preparing dinner.

A few more trips in and out of the trailer, while tending to the small fire, and soon I was ready to cook. The pot had a stand and hook to hang over the top, and I made sure nothing green was added to the fire to limit smoke, which could reveal our location. Unless someone was close by, they wouldn't really see anything.

When I had the beans on and bubbling away, I grabbed the guitar and brought it out to the cooking area. The few chords I'd strummed before were still in my head, and I needed to keep bringing the music to life. It demanded to be released, and despite the emotional pain in making music once more, I felt like it was time.

The first steps to healing weren't just letting go of the past, but in embracing the parts of it I'd already let go. The parts I loved more than life. The parts that made me Billie Bellerose.

thirty-one

JACE

Blind rage drove me from the Airstream. From the clearing. From her.

Fucking fuck. There was a reason I'd cut her toxicity from my life long ago: She was the one person in this goddamn world who was capable of destroying me. The one who could render me a broken, pitiful mess on the floor, while she stomped her shit-covered shoes all over me.

I was Billie's doormat. And the moment she'd thrown us away so easily all those years ago, I'd known that I had to do the same. No matter what happened, what I heard about her, I had to close my fucking ears and eyes and pretend I didn't give a fuck.

Her parents had died, that much I'd heard, but only years after the fact. Before that, any time my mom had tried to tell me about Billie, I'd cut her off. *Not my fucking business,* I'd snarl.

I knew Billie was alive, and that was all that mattered. I'd made sure to know she was alive and her rough geographic location—mainly to avoid her—but her day-to-day...

Yeah, if I'd known that too, I'd have gone after her.

Rhett might think he couldn't make music without weed and booze, but his minor addictions had nothing... fucking nothing on Billie Bellerose. A fact he'd discovered himself not that damn long ago. The only way to be without her was to shut her from your mind and never think about her again, but it fucking killed me to know she'd suffered without me. The physical scars she bore spoke of a life I couldn't understand, and when I thought about the scars I couldn't see... I wanted to burn this fucking forest down.

Fuck.

Slamming my fist against a tree, the bark crumbled under my hit, and I relished the bite of pain in my knuckles. It helped me deal with the raging emotions inside. A large part of me hated her so much, while another part that was growing in strength wanted to storm back to the RV and bury my dick inside her. Twice in the past two days I'd felt her cunt pulse around my cock, and it was messing with my head. I'd thought our sex was intense back in the day, but we'd been kids compared to what had happened between us in the field.

Jesus. I was so fucked up.

"Bro."

Rhett's amused tone distracted me from trying to level a few more trees, and when I spun on him, he held both hands up, huge fucking smirk on his face. "Don't kill the messenger. I'm just here to make sure you're okay and let you know Billie is fine. No need to go all Chuck Norris on the forest."

Screw this asshole for being funny and likable. I didn't have to wonder what Billie saw in him—he was my best friend for a reason. Today, though, I'd have preferred Grayson. Someone to smash trees with.

"I can't fucking do it," I snarled, rubbing a hand across my face as I desperately sucked in air, needing to calm down. *Right.*

"Do what?"

Rhett didn't step closer, instead he leaned back against the nearest tree like we were just two friends having a casual conversation. Not one friend trying to talk the other friend off a metaphorical cliff. "Stay in that RV with her. Be forced to fucking see her day in and out. Feel her damn presence."

Touch her. Smell her. Bury my face in her puss—

Rhett laughed, and I wondered if I'd manage to get a hit in before he moved. Maybe if I really ran at him.

"Just give in to the thrall that's Billie," he said. "Admit that you were kids in the past and that both of you fucked up—Billie in not trusting you with whatever truth she's hiding, and you in letting her just walk away without so much as questioning her actions for even a second. You were—*still are, actually*—a prideful bastard, and holding onto your hurt has impacted the best part of you for nearly a decade. It's time to let it go."

It sounded so fucking easy when he said it like that. "I can't," I told him truthfully. "It's burned into my being, into my blood, into my music. I don't exist without this pain, and I've grown with it, so there's no cutting it from my soul."

Rhett was still smiling, but his eyes were flat. "Then you'll lose her again. And having experienced it once myself—admittedly nowhere near as intense as you have—I'd say that for you, there'd be no surviving a second time."

As desperate as I was to argue with him, I couldn't. He spoke the truth.

"She was hurt," I whispered in a rage. "She starved. I let that fucking happen, and there's no taking it back."

The fact that Billie didn't appear to hate me as much as I hated her astonished me when I took into account the life she must have lived. "What the fuck are all her scars from?"

Rhett's humor was completely dried up now. "I think that's her story to tell, don't you? She gave me some of the pieces, more than you've got for sure, but it feels wrong to go sharing her secrets behind her back. Ask her again, maybe when your tempers have cooled down. I know right now you're thinking the worst and probably want to raze this forest to the ground."

"And kill every motherfucker who ever laid a hand on her," I agreed, grimacing. I couldn't push him to tell me; he was right to respect her like that.

He nodded, darkness casting shadows across his face until he was near unrecognizable.

"If I find out Angelo is responsible for even one of the marks on Billie, I'll destroy him," I said. The Riccis' wrath would be a small price to pay if it came to that.

"I'll help you bury the body," Rhett said, voice dropping lower. "But... as much as I want to see that handsome bastard removed from her life, I don't think he'd ever hurt her."

I fucking hated that he was right. Or I thought he

was. The Angelo I knew, my best friend for the first eighteen years of our lives, would rather kill himself than harm Billie. I just had to hope some things hadn't changed.

We remained in a testosterone cloud for a few seconds before managing to calm down. There was no one to kill at the moment, so we'd have to save our rage for another day.

Maybe the day Billie finally revealed all her secrets.

"How do I get through the next few days?" I asked, my thoughts tumultuous. A dozen or more song lyrics raced through my mind, and I hoped there was some paper in that RV, because I needed to write this music down. Release it from my mind before it drove me insane.

"With earplugs because I'm going to be fucking our girl every chance I get, making her scream my name," Rhett said, his smirk back in place. Then he gave a joking imitation of a girl's voice as he moaned, "Oh Rhett, yes, harder, Jace never fucks me this good. His dick is so tiny compared to your weapon, Rhett!"

Laughing at his antics, I punched him in the arm. "Shut up, asshole. You know that's not true."

He snickered. "Come on, we should get back. I don't like leaving her alone for long. Not since she disappeared on me the last time I did."

If I was being honest with myself, and I fucking hated doing that, it also bothered me to be so far away from her when there were killers out there hunting for us.

We both started back together, and when the silver trailer came into sight, guitar music drifted toward us. Along with the scent of cooking.

"Who started a fire?" I said, panic hitting me that maybe someone had found us. Found Billie.

But why the fuck would they start a fire? Was Grayson back, maybe?

A second later a pitchy voice drifted along with the chords.

Rhett paused, tilting his head to the side. "Is Billie... singing?"

Despite my complete lack of humor at the moment, a short chuckle escaped me. "Billie is a lot of things, but a singer is not one of them. Girl can't do much more than hum along in time, but she has an ear for music writing that makes the rest of us look like amateurs."

Rhett joined me in laughing. "Look, she sounds adorable. Off tune as fuck, but adorable nonetheless. And that melody is fucking catchy. No wonder you managed to write some of our greatest hits with her help."

I had. And I'd never captured that same magic

again, not even with my band. Billie and I made perfect music together, and when we were done for the day, I'd strip her bare and fuck her to the sound of our tracks. Often right there on the floor of our makeshift recording studio. Sometimes with Angelo watching, sometimes with him joining in. It was a part of my life I never wanted to revisit, and yet here the hell I was, making music again and fucking Billie. I'd just swapped out one guitarist best friend for another. Some asshole was having a great laugh at my expense.

Rhett picked up the pace, clearly wanting to catch Billie in the middle of her song. I kept pace because it made sense, not because I was in a rush to do the same. Fuck no. Billie and I were toxic, and I just had to make it through the next few days without losing my shit at her again.

Surely, I could manage that. We were adults. It was time we started acting like it.

When we rounded out the front of the RV, we saw the small fire she had going with a pot hanging over the top. Billie had an old acoustic on her lap, eyes closed as she hummed along and strummed a few more chords, before she found the sound and rhythm she was looking for.

There were no lyrics now, and in my head the words were already forming to match her song. It was just how my brain worked, a gift that I'd had long before I ever received any formal training in music. My half-sister was the same, and despite us only knowing each other for the past five years, it turned out that we had more than music in common.

It was odd to me that Billie and Michelle had never met, considering how close I was to my sister now. I wasn't sure they even knew about each other since I never spoke of Billie if I could help it.

"Billie," Rhett called as he dropped down on the log beside her. "You compose like a fucking wet dream. Why didn't you tell me you were a musical genius?"

Her eyes flew open, and she looked relieved to see him beside her. Her face softened, the pink tinting her cheeks when she was happy. Billie was beautiful, but more than just her heart-shaped face, full pink lips, and large hazel eyes. It was the warmth she exuded when she gave you all her focus. Billie had this way of drawing people in, wrapping herself around them, and making them feel like the sun rose and set in her expressions.

She snared you like a black widow, and then just as you were getting cozy in her embrace, she struck and killed you.

It would be foolish in the extreme to fall into her trap once more, and yet I found myself crossing around the fire to drop down right across from her. Right where I would be forced to stare at her all evening. "Sorry, I wanted to have some dinner going by the time you got back," she said softly, letting the guitar fall against her legs. "I don't think the fire is large enough to call attention to us."

It wasn't, but we probably shouldn't let it burn too long.

Rhett must have agreed. "Let's just finish heating the beans, and then we can use some of that bread I got to mop it up."

Here we were, the picture of domestication, and I knew for a fact that if we weren't out of here in the next few days, I was in real fucking trouble.

Not of falling in love with Billie.

But in falling out of hate with her.

An emotion I couldn't afford to lose, not if I wanted to make it through the rest of this week... and the rest of my life.

thirty-two

BILLIE

Domestic bliss was a crock of shit. It actually required all parties to act like sane, mature adults, and that was something severely lacking in our little campout threesome. Shit, not *threesome*. Threeway. Nope, not that either. *Throuple?* Fucking hell. My brain needed some bleach so I could stop thinking about fucking Jace and Rhett together at the same time.

Trouble was, it was far from the first threesome Jace and I had been participants in. So my mind had plenty of reference points to weave into my vivid daydreams.

The guys had returned from their little bro-bonding moment in the forest seeming determined to play nice.

Which was great and lasted all of an hour while we ate the beans and bread for dinner, then Rhett insisted on cleaning the dishes in the little stream we'd passed on our horses this morning.

Which, again, was great. Except that left Jace and I alone in uncomfortable silence.

"So... I guess you kept up playing the guitar, huh?" he asked, nodding to the old instrument now propped against the side of the trailer.

I frowned, confused. "No, I didn't. Not since..." Not since I broke up with Angelo, who'd been the original Bellerose lead guitarist. My heart couldn't take the memories of Jace teaching me and Angelo finessing my style. "Just... no."

He narrowed his eyes. "Uh... it didn't sound rusty. You were pretty good." The suspicion was so clear in his voice it snapped my temper.

"Oh, so now I'm lying about playing guitar? What the shit, Jace, why would I even do that?"

He shrugged. "Beats me, you're the one claiming you haven't kept up on lessons, but you obviously have. That sure as shit didn't sound like you hadn't played in nearly nine years, Billie."

Outraged at the stupidity of the argument, I pushed to my feet. "Ever heard of riding a bike, Jace? It's called muscle memory. Jesus *Christ*, do you have to start a fight about literally everything? I was going to give you that song for this album you're all woefully behind schedule on, but now I think, hmm, maybe... *get fucked.*"

His jaw dropped, but he made a quick recovery as his expression shifted into irritation. "I wouldn't have wanted it anyway. It sucked, and I never could have made lyrics that fit with Bellerose's aesthetic."

"Bullshit," I snapped back. "Do I need to remind you that I *am* Bellerose? Why the fuck did you feel the need to steal my damn name in the first place, Jace? You signed to Big Noise under *Snake Soup.*"

He scowled back at me. "I think we both know *Bellerose* sounds a hell of a lot sexier than *Snake Soup.*"

I couldn't deny that; his original band name was one they'd come up with as twelve-year-olds. It was awful. But that didn't mean he'd had to steal *my damn name.* "You did it to piss me off, and you know it. You wanted to send a giant *fuck you* every time you appeared on a billboard or poster or side of a fucking bus. It's pathetic and childish and you need to stop thinking so fucking highly of yourself. You barely even crossed my mind over the years."

With that, I stormed inside the trailer and slammed the little door before he could see the lies all over my face. How I even had the audacity to spew such rubbish was beyond me, but... fuck it. Jace's ego needed a pin stabbed through it.

Shoving my hands into my hair, I let out a silent scream. He made me want to break something, but I wasn't a fucking cavewoman. I could control my violent impulses a touch better than that.

I'd left the guitar outside, and my pride wouldn't let me go back out there, so I just gave up and got ready for bed. And by that, I meant I just took off my borrowed sweatpants and crawled under the covers in my panties and flannel shirt. It wasn't like I could brush my teeth or change into clean clothes. Maybe in the morning I'd wash some of our clothes in the river before we really started to stink .

Silence weighed down heavily as I lay there, and it wasn't long before exhaustion set in and my lids drooped.

"Where's Billie?" Rhett's question woke me up from my half-asleep doze, and it took me a moment to realize he was talking to Jace outside. The trailer might as well be made of cardboard for how much sound insulation it offered.

"Inside," Jace replied, his voice low and quiet.

There was a pause before Rhett spoke again, and I tried to convince myself not to listen. But it was hard *not* to, so...

"Did something happen?"

Jace grunted. That was it. Just a grunt. What was he, a pig? *Use your fucking words, Adams.*

Rhett sighed, sounding frustrated. "I love you, Jace; you're my best friend and brother. But fuck *me,* you're an asshole."

"No disagreement here," Jace muttered back. "She brings out the worst in me."

Rhett scoffed. "Don't blame her. You're a man. Man up and take responsibility for your own choices."

Oh snap. I braced, waiting with bated breath to hear Jace start a fight that I'd be forced to break up. But to my shock, he didn't. He just grunted again.

They fell silent, and I nearly drifted back to sleep before the sound of guitar music reached my ears. It was my song, the one I'd just been making up while they were off in the woods. But I'd bet my shorts it was Rhett playing, not Jace.

"I wouldn't," Jace said, confirming my guess. "She said we can't have that song for Bellerose."

Rhett scoffed, still playing my tune on the guitar. I could so vividly picture his long fingers plucking at the strings just like he played with my body... "Why'd she say that, hmm? You must have pissed her off. Besides, I like it."

"Doesn't matter," Jace muttered.

"Do you remember any of the lyrics she'd already put to it?" Rhett asked, continuing to play and adding his own creative spin on my original tune. "I couldn't hear what they were."

Jace groaned. "No. But..."

Rhett chuckled, pausing his playing. "Oh, here we go. You've already written lyrics in your head, huh? Well then, spit it out. I'll start over." He didn't wait for Jace to argue, just started playing again.

There was a moment's hesitation, within which I didn't even breathe, then Jace started singing.

"Pain written in my soul, the blade too blunt to cut you free,

Even as I crave the agony. It feeds my being. My being.

This is the end of something real, of the moment we're desperate to save.

Desperate to save."

Fuck. Now I was crying. Unable to face hearing anything more, I pulled the blankets up and dragged a pillow over my head. I could still hear them, but now it was muffled and incomprehensible. Thank fuck for that.

I must have fallen asleep, because I woke again to Rhett climbing in beside me, his cold hands finding my waist and pulling me into his embrace. Then the

331

mattress dipped on the other side, and I stiffened up like a board.

"I'm not sleeping on the couch," Jace muttered quietly. "It's too short, and this bed is more than big enough if you're not a bitch about it."

"Jesus, bro, can you not?" Rhett groaned, holding me tighter like he could somehow physically fend off the insult.

I was sleepy enough not to give a fuck about petty insults, though. "Just don't fucking touch me," I mumbled, snuggling into Rhett's chest. "Or I'll kill you."

"Likewise," he replied, getting comfortable.

Rhett sighed, then kissed my hair. "You two are insufferable. Sweet dreams, beautiful."

"Sweet dreams, handsome," Jace replied, sounding smug, like he was *so funny*. Dick.

I was already drifting back to sleep, though, so I just intertwined my legs with Rhett's and let myself relax. Really relax. Fuck, I had a lot to be thankful for, and his forgiveness for the fake baby ruse was high on that list.

My dreams when I fell back to sleep were fucked up to say the least, full of masked men armed with knives that turned into bananas before they stabbed me, which then resulted in me all covered in mashed banana while the masked men skipped through a field singing songs from *The Sound Of Music*.

It was a stressful, confusing, and ridiculous dream that then morphed into a seriously X-rated sex dream involving all three members of Bellerose... all three of them inside me at the same time... with no one in my mouth. Was that physically possible? My dream said yes, and I was pretty game to find out for myself.

I groaned as my dream shifted gears again, my imaginary partners all moving to different positions, and I reached down to stroke the hard length rubbing between my legs against my soaking panties.

"Fuck," Jace whispered, his breath warm against the back of my neck. "Billie, we can't—"

Then my panties were pushed aside and he was sliding into me. Only *then* did I fully realize I wasn't dreaming anymore. I gasped, arching my spine to push back on him, and my lids fluttered open a millimeter. Just enough to see Rhett had gotten up already and sunlight was streaming through the half-open door of the Airstream.

"Jace," I breathed, my pussy throbbing hard as he fucked me slow and steady from behind.

"Shut up," he muttered back, his arm banding around my body to pull us closer together. "Just... shut up. I need to get you out of my head, Rose, and how do I do that while you're flicking your clit in your sleep right beside me? Huh?"

Oh shit. Was I?

"What were you dreaming about, Billie?" Jace pumped harder, our skin slapping together. "You came in your sleep, did you know? Fuck, it was hot."

Ah, that explained how achy and wet I already was. Oops, my bad.

"Sorry," I panted, already feeling another orgasm curling through my belly.

"I said, shut up," he whispered back. This time, his hand covered my mouth to physically keep me quiet while we fucked. Or while he fucked me and I just went along for the ride. And holy shit, what a ride it was.

I bit down on his fingers when I came, my toes curling into the sheets and my stomach muscles tensing up as I swallowed back the need to scream.

"Quiet," he growled in my ear as I gasped and writhed, his hand still clamped across my mouth. "Rhett's making us coffee, and he doesn't need to know."

Guilt and shame washed through me, but it was quickly smothered by arousal as Jace's other hand found my clit. Rhett wouldn't actually mind... I didn't think. Or was he only okay with it when he was joining in? Shit, that probably needed to be discussed for clarity, but right now—

"Come for me again, Rose," Jace ordered in a low, quiet voice, his fingers pinching my clit harder than strictly necessary. "The way your tight cunt milks my dick while you come is beyond addictive."

I was tempted to tell him to go to hell, that I wasn't his puppet or sex slave. But it felt *so good* I was helpless to deny that request. Hell, I'd have come again whether he wanted it or not.

He fucked me harder, his shaft probably getting fabric burn from my panties, and then my climax locked my muscles up once more, my inner walls gripping him like a vice and dragging him into his own release. Hot cum filled my cunt as his abs flexed against my back, whispered curses falling from his lips in lieu of a louder reaction.

Then the second he was done, he released me, pulling out and climbing out of the bed in one smooth motion. I'd barely pulled my panties back into place, and he was already gone, storming out of the trailer before even bothering to pull his shirt on.

What the fuck?

My breathing was still jagged and quick, my cheeks undoubtedly flushed, and I sat up in confusion. Swallowing and trying to get control of my racing heartbeat, I raked my fingers through tangled hair. Ouch.

"Good morning, beautiful Thorn," Rhett called out, poking his head back through the door. "I just grabbed fresh water from that stream I found yesterday. Coffee will be ready in no time!"

My responding smile was wobbly. "You're the best."

He really was. And he had no idea that Jace and I had just hate fucked while he was doing something sweet. Damn Jace Adams right to hell for making this *my* responsibility. I had to talk to Rhett.

After coffee, though.

thirty-three

BILLIE

The rich smell of coffee reached my nose before I stepped outside. I'd cleaned up as best I could in the tiny bathroom, beyond grateful to the owner for leaving it stocked with toilet paper. Even so, I could *feel* Jace all over my skin as I joined Rhett beside the tiny campfire he'd lit to heat the water for coffee.

"Figured this was a necessity," Rhett said with a smile, handing me a tin mug of steaming coffee. "You know how Jace is in the morning, I'm sure. Coffee makes him a fraction more tolerable."

I couldn't even muster up a weak smile in response

to that, so I covered my guilt by taking a sip. Then I winced.

"Ah yeah, sorry, no cream or sugar." Rhett grimaced. "But... caffeine is still a bonus."

"It's great," I croaked, taking another sip. This one went down easier, now that I was prepared for the bitterness. "Um, so, I wanted to ask you something..."

Better now than never, right? Rip that Band-Aid off. He *had* said he was "okay with it," so... maybe I was panicking for no reason?

"If it's about you and Jace fucking through your problems, I'm going to politely request no details," he told me with a crooked grin. "Unless it's an invitation to join in, in which case consider me there with bells on. But what you two do in private? It's private. Just as I'd like to think our private moments are."

My mouth flapped like a fish out of water for a moment as I tried to switch gears. Then I quickly nodded in response to his statement. "Absolutely. And for what it's worth, Jace and I... we're just..." I trailed off, having no fucking clue how I explained that mess. So I shrugged and wrinkled my nose. "We're just seeking closure."

Rhett looked unconvinced, sipping his coffee. "Uh-huh. Well, we're cool. He's my best friend, and you're the girl who stole his heart long before we ever met.

Whatever you need to do to stop bickering constantly, do it."

I swallowed hard, my cheeks heating with embarrassment. "So, I guess you know we just—"

"The walls are *really* thin, Thorny Rose. Paper thin." He held my gaze, his expression amused and warm.

Taking a gulp of coffee to cover my awkwardness, I tucked my knees up to my chest. The seats we'd found in the trailer weren't amazingly comfy, but they were better than sitting on the ground.

"Cool," I murmured, at a loss for what else to say. This was all new territory for me... kind of. Jace and I had already been dating when Angelo became involved in our relationship. Angelo and I were never together one-on-one, not until after I'd destroyed things with Jace. Even then, it hadn't been the same. We tried, but we both missed *him* too much—regardless of what Jace *thought* had happened.

"So, speaking of the paper-thin walls, I heard you playing my song last night." I raised my brows at him as he grinned.

"I like it," he said by way of explanation.

I shrugged. "Tough, I told Jace he can't have it."

Rhett laughed, shaking his head. "You don't mean that. If he apologizes for being a turd, can we have it? You must have heard the lyrics Jace put to the tune last night. It's a fucking number one hit just begging to happen, and you know it."

He wasn't wrong. But I couldn't make things *that* easy. "He has to apologize, admit that he's a stubborn, prideful fuck, and kiss my ass. But we both know that's not happening."

"You'd be right about that," the sour-faced dick himself agreed, striding back into our little camp looking fresh with damp hair all sticking up in spikes. He'd opted for the freezing river bath. "The song isn't *that* good. Rhett and I can write better shit while he's tripping on acid."

Rhett just shook his head and held out the spare mug of prepared coffee. "Sit down, shut up, and drink this."

For several minutes—painfully awkward ones—no one spoke. I buried my face in my mug and tried to take small sips to make it last. Then my stomach rumbled louder than a stomach had any right to rumble, and both guys stared at me.

"What?" I murmured. "I got used to the Ricci staff making breakfast, I guess."

Jace rolled his eyes—of course he did—but Rhett just smiled and pushed up from his seat. "I'll grab you something. I would have cooked but didn't want to interrupt anything."

I cringed at the reminder that Rhett had known we were fucking, but Jace choked on his sip of coffee, which entertained me to no end.

"So, what do we do today?" I called out to Rhett as he ducked into the trailer to fetch food. "Just sit around and pick fights with Jace over his crappy tattoos or...?"

"Hey!" the abrasive wanker protested. "These were done by—"

"No one cares, Adams," I drawled. "Literally no one. I was talking to Rhett."

His glare was hot enough to power up the sun a few notches, and I found myself smiling in joy over *the little things in life.* Like ensuring that Jace Adams never got to exist in a pool of admiration, as per the last ten-ish years of his life.

"I don't remember you being such a snarky bitch, Billie," Jace snapped, leaning back in his chair.

"Your memory isn't as great as you think it is," I replied flatly. "Neither is your reasoning ability. Let's take our breakup for example. I mean, fuck, a comatose person would have been able to read through the lines of my pathetic excuses that day, and yet you just flipped me off and walked away."

I shrugged like it didn't bother me any longer. More lies he wouldn't see through, no doubt.

A cold gaze was leveled on me, and swear to the

rock gods, he was trying to laser fucking fry my brain. "You could have reached into my chest and ripped out my heart, and I would have been in less pain than I was that day. Sorry I didn't fucking stop to analyze every word while you were stabbing me over and over."

There he was, my dramatic guy. Well, not mine any longer, which was kind of our point of argument here. "You've had eight—nearly nine—goddamn years to analyze the conversation. More than enough time to pull your head from your ass."

I jumped to my feet, wincing a little at some aches and pains in my body. It had been banged up a little lately, from the attack at the farmhouse to the intense sex to the sharing of a bed not quite big enough for three. Not to mention the bareback horse ride.

My body was finally saying enough was enough and I needed to chill on the abuse.

Ignoring this warning, I glared down at Jace, which apparently didn't bother him at all. He remained sprawled back in his chair, face now blank, as if he was waiting to see what I'd do or say next. The door to the Airstream banged open, and out Rhett strolled, carrying more bread and some cans that probably held spam. We weren't big on options here, and my stomach growled once more to let me know it didn't really care.

"Sit down, Rose," Jace drawled. "We can continue our pointless fight once you've eaten."

Wrinkling my nose at him, I took a few seconds to sit, just so he wouldn't think I was obeying a command. "Don't act like you give a shit if I starve. We've alread—"

Rhett cleared his throat, cutting me off, and I, for once, actually shut the hell up. Because the look on Jace's face now told me he clearly wasn't in the mental space to hear about me starving once more. I'd forgotten about him losing his shit yesterday, and with that, my anger dried up.

"Let's eat," Rhett said cheerfully. "I found this nifty wire rack that you can toast bread over the fire in. This camping shit is fun."

Jace grunted, and I crossed my arms. Cheerful Rhett was my favorite, but I also hated knowing he was working so hard to compensate for the tension between Jace and me. Vowing to do better, I pasted a smile on my face and leaned out of my chair, closer to the fire. "Show me this toaster," I said, and his return smile was warm and genuine.

For a beat, he just held me captive in his fucking presence. Somehow.

We hadn't brushed our teeth, there was no real way to shower, and Rhett hadn't had any hair products for days to spike up his blue hawk. Still, he'd never looked hotter than he did smiling at me in the early winter sun.

"If you keep looking at me like that, beautiful," Rhett drawled when my gawking went on too long to be ignored, "you're going to receive your meal in bed."

"She's already had breakfast in bed," Jace cut in, but for once he sounded amused, rather than perpetually pissed off.

Rhett didn't remove his gaze from me as his lips twitched. "That was such a small snack," he replied. "She needs a proper meal."

Well, fuck me twice in the morning. Like, literally. Because the tension up in here was starting to throb in my lower half. Fuck, even the fighting with Jace was stimulating, and I wasn't sure how I'd survived so many years without this spark in my life.

"Just focus on the food, asshole," Jace shot back.

Rhett winked at me and then went back to what he was doing, placing the bread between this wire contraption that closed in on either side of a piece, and then he held it over the top of the coals until it was lightly toasted. The spam went into the pot, still strung over the small flames, and in no time we had some hot food.

While we were eating, the campsite was peaceful, but as always, it didn't last long.

"You sounded like you were having a nightmare last night, Billie," Rhett said, the green in his eyes very clear as he stared into his toast, before he lifted his head to meet my gaze. "Anything you want to talk about."

No, not really. But I was still going to reply, when Jace jumped in with his usual fucked up attitude. "Bro, you know Billie is the queen of secrets. As if she'd reveal her dream. What if we possibly inferred a truth from it? Something to explain her cagey actions in the past. Shit, I doubt Angelo even knows the reasons she fucked me over. Poor schmuck probably just fell for some bullshit sob story about me beating her or some other fabric—"

The scream ripped from me before I could stop it, and I actually scared myself with the intensity of that noise. It had been drawn up deep, from a place I'd locked away for years. A place where the pain was so intense that on the rare occasions I released my hold on it, I would end up hysterically crying and screaming for hours.

Looked like it was time for one of those events.

Jace fell silent at my outburst, and I found myself back on my feet without consciously knowing I'd jumped up. Rhett was at my side too, trying to hold me, but I brushed him off, unable to be touched at this moment.

"You are the *worst fucking human*, Jace," I sobbed, my chest heaving. Weirdly, no tears were leaking yet; I was almost too worked up for them. "After everything I did. Every fucking sacrifice I made. Gods, I wished that day I'd just told you the truth. I wish I'd told you I was *pregnant with your child*, and it was time for you to accept that responsibility and not be a rock star. Nope, you've got to be a teen father, stuck in a dead-end job, watching your dreams slowly die."

Neither of them said a damn word, both boys frozen on the spot. Rhett was at my side, and I couldn't see his expression because all I saw was Jace. This moment had been a long time coming, and I, honestly, couldn't take the secrets for one more second.

"I was pregnant that day," I continued, each word shaky. "With your child. Not Angelo's, yours. When we met out the front, you were so excited... you'd just had your big break. I'd never seen that level of pure joy in you before, and I knew if I told you, you'd stay with me. And we might have built a great life, but fuck, it was more likely you'd eventually resent and then hate me and our child. I couldn't do that. I couldn't take your big break away from you."

Jace's face was so pale he looked like he was about

to faint. He just stared at me, unblinkingly, as if he couldn't quite comprehend what I was saying. Of all the scenarios that must have run through his head the day I'd left him, clearly me being pregnant was not one of them.

When he finally reacted, it was to whisper, "What happened? Where's my child now, Billie?"

The next words filled my throat, and I really wanted to scream again.

This was the moment I said it out loud. "She died."

She'd died, and so had a part of me.

thirty-four

BILLIE

Jace was on his feet in the next heartbeat, and as he all but jumped the fire to reach me. Rhett stepped in between us, and while the expression on Jace's face gave me no indication what his intentions were, I had no fear that he would hurt me.

"Move. The fuck. Aside," he snarled at Rhett. "I would never hurt Billie. You fucking know that."

Rhett hesitated a second. "You're not thinking clearly, Jace. Take a second. There are more ways to hurt someone than just physically."

At this point I'd caved in on myself, arms wrapped so tightly around my center to try and prevent my body from crumpling to the ground. Sobs continued to choke me, and my eyes burned like someone had a blowtorch on them, but the tears remained at bay.

When Rhett finally stepped aside, Jace got very close to me. I could feel his energy. When I was near Jace, my body reacted like I'd stepped a little too close to electricity, sending sparks across my skin. "Rose," he breathed, and I couldn't keep looking at my feet. I had to look at him. "How did she die?"

Die. Dead. Dead dead dead. Our daughter died.

"There was a fire," I choked out, the words barely understandable. "At my old house on the hill."

Jace made a sound of disbelief. "The house is still there. I've seen it."

Moron. Just... fuck. "They rebuilt it. I guess you didn't bother to visit for a few years after making it big, and by the time you could fuck with coming home, it was like nothing had happened." Except everything had happened, and I'd been broken beyond repair. "I can't believe your parents never told you."

He ran a hand over his face, none of the lines smoothing, as his pain visibly showed. "No one was allowed to mention your name. Not for fucking years. It was the only way for me to keep moving forward."

That explained his absence in my life. Explained

why I'd been alone, going through the worst event that ever happened to me. Jace screwed up his face tightly, as if fighting off tears of his own, and that was when the floodgates released for me as audible sobs shook me so hard that I could barely breathe through them.

"My parents died in the fire," I choked out. "And I fell trying to escape and almost died too. When I woke up in a hospital, I had burns, some lung damage, and our—" I couldn't get more words out. I tried to say it over and over, and in the end, I mouthed it at him. *Our girl didn't make it.*

Rhett, who had been giving us space, must have had enough, as he stepped in behind me and wrapped his arms around my body, holding me through the shaking sobs that were rattling my body. "Your parents died in that fire?" Jace rasped. "When I allowed Mom to speak about you, she just said your parents passed years ago. Way too late to offer condolences."

This dumb fucking fuck had wiped me from existence to the point that he'd never even listened when his parents had tried to tell him. "Yes. They died, and I was alone. I was in and out of the hospital for months, getting multiple skin grafts on the burns, and I fucking waited for you to find me. I waited for you. But you never showed your face."

"What about Angelo?" he shot back, ignoring the rest. "Why wasn't he there for you? Did he know about the baby?"

Were we still doing the Angelo thing? After everything I'd just revealed?

I sagged against Rhett, who was so quiet as he held me together. "Angelo knew everything," I rasped. "And he was there for me. Or at least he tried to be, but I was so fucked up, Jace. I can't explain what it's like to go to sleep pregnant, feeling your baby kick, and then have to deliver her tiny, lifeless body. She was gone, just like that. Ripped from my life like everything else I loved. Angelo tried, but I was too broken, and I pushed him away. By the time I had myself together, he'd moved on with his life. He was a mafia prince, married to Valentina, with no room for me in his life."

That was the point I'd truly been alone.

Jace's chest heaved as he sucked in breaths, and if I had to guess, there was a war inside his huge body. I recognized the rage... and the pain. I was waiting for his next line to cut me deep, and he didn't disappoint. "If you'd have told me about the baby, you wouldn't have lost her," he snarled, before he clenched his fists tightly, arms visibly shaking. "I would have been there to protect you both. This is all your fucking fault."

Right. I pressed a hand against my chest, expecting to feel a gush of blood from that slice. Jace had delivered his usual deep cut, touching on the very accusation I'd butchered myself with over the years. The blame game was a fun one because there was literally no way to know what might have happened if I'd made different decisions.

"Jace, you're way the fuck out of line," Rhett snapped, his calm gone as he held me tighter. "It was a tragic accident, and you should just be damn grateful that Billie is still here." Jace's shaking got worse, and the look on his face... I'd never seen him wear that expression, not even the day I ended our relationship. This was the pain of death, and I recognized it intimately.

If I'd thought Jace Adams hated me before, it was nothing on the white, hot, raging inferno of hate he was directing my way now.

"I'm sorry," I whispered, just too broken to fight any longer. "I was sixteen. A fucking child myself. I thought I was doing the right thing, trying to save your future, and I promise you, my punishment has been to live in the worst torture of a hellscape for the following eight years."

He wasn't hearing me, his eyes stormy but glazed, like he'd disappeared into his own head.

As angry as I also felt, I wanted to go to him. To offer the comfort that no one had offered me when I'd dealt with her death. *Penelope.* I'd given her a name; it had been mandatory to get her paperwork. Didn't feel like the right time to tell Jace though, especially since it was his grandmother's name, one of my favorite people in the world, who had passed away when we were twelve.

"Jace," I said softly. "I know how you feel—"

"Shut the fuck up, Billie," he snarled. "You don't have a clue."

This knocked me out of my own empathetic state. "Oh, right. Of course. I forgot that everything is worse for you than everyone else in the world. I forgot that poor little Jace Adams is the most important fucking being to exist, so of course his pain is above all others. Hey, it's almost as if you were growing the child in your stomach, feeling her kicks. It's almost like you had to push her out of *your* vagina while feeling your heart tear into pieces, knowing you'd never hear her cry or laugh or *anything*. Sorry, my bad." Hot, bitter tears rolled down my face in twin streams of pain.

Yeah, my pain and anger might turn me into a sarcastic bitch, but at least I wasn't a narcissistic cunt.

We were definitely a match made in hell these days.

"Wow. Okay, I think we all need a breather," Rhett,

the peacemaker, tried to interject. "Why don't we take a minute and..." He trailed off at the sound of crunching steps, and a second later both boys were in front of me as a huge, black-clad dude burst into the clearing.

Despite Jace's absolute fury with me, he'd still stepped between me and whatever was heading for us, and I clung onto that fact through the intense pain assaulting my chest.

It had hurt as much as I'd expected to reveal the truth, and he'd taken it about as well as I'd expected. As an adult, I understood that taking Jace's choices away by lying to him was probably not my finest hour. But I'd had good intentions. For what that was worth.

No time to worry about the past, though, when the present continued to try and kill us.

It took a second for the guys to relax their pose, and when they moved aside, a familiar figure came into view. Before I could stop myself, my legs were moving as I pushed through Jace and Rhett and all but threw myself at Grayson. He caught me easily, hauling me up, and my legs wrapped around his waist as I sobbed into his chest.

He grew tense under me, and I was about to release my hold, thinking I'd made him uncomfortable, when he snapped, "What did you two do to her? I swear to fuck, I will beat the shit out of you both if you hurt her."

Jace snarled. "Billie is a big girl. She doesn't need you to defend her lying, deceitful ass."

I couldn't see any of them; my head remained buried against Grayson, and I just breathed in his cool, clean scent. Unlike the rest of us, he'd had a chance to shower and change his clothing, and it was comforting to be held against him. To know he was safe.

"You better cut that shit out," Grayson told Jace. "Your issues with Billie happened eight years ago. We are in a new crisis, and it's going to take all of our time and focus to get through it."

"He knows," I whispered against his shirt. There was no way Grayson should have been able to hear me, and yet he did.

"Knows what?" he asked.

I couldn't say the words out loud again. The last thing I needed was to trigger myself back into the need for hardcore pharmaceuticals to get through the day.

"Billie was pregnant with my baby when she left me," Jace said, trying and failing to sound casual. "She lied so I'd have *a better life without them,* and then she managed to almost die in a fire."

He didn't mention Penelope dying in the fire, as if he was more upset that I'd almost died. But shit, that couldn't be the case, because he hated my guts and made no secret of it.

Grayson's hand came up and threaded in my hair, holding my head as I continued to cling to him like a weird monkey. "Oh, Prickles, baby. I'm so fucking sorry to hear that."

Crap on a cracker. This was too much to handle.

Squeezing my eyes closed as hard as I could, I forced the tears to disappear. I forced them back down inside, where they could stay for another near-decade.

Jace must have made a move to say something else because Grayson took a step forward, and I swore I could feel Jace at my back. So close that I was almost sandwiched between them. "Don't make this about you, Adams," Grayson ordered him. "For once in your damn life, don't make it about you. I'm not saying you don't have a right to mourn and feel the pain you clearly are in, but in that same vein, you don't have a right to take that pain out on Billie. She hasn't taken hers out on you. Repay that fucking favor."

A deep exhalation of air washed over my back, and I was desperate to know what expression Jace wore, but at the same time I wasn't quite ready to stop hiding. "I'm taking Billie to the car," Grayson said abruptly. Rhett gave an *okay*, but there was nothing from Jace. "You two assholes clean up here and grab your shit. Meet us through the trees over there in a few minutes."

He started to walk, and two minutes later, the light

grew brighter around us. I lifted my head to find we were in an open part of the forest, Grayson striding along like he wasn't carrying me in his arms. His vehicle came into sight soon after that, a large army-style jeep, and after he opened the front door, he deposited me easily into the seat.

"Buckle up, Bellerose," he told me. "We're getting the hell out of here."

Swallowing roughly, I lifted my face, wishing it wasn't all blotchy and tear-stained. I didn't need a mirror to know how rough I looked, but it didn't appear to bother Grayson as he reached out and brushed a thumb across my cheek, chasing the moisture there. "It's going to be okay," he murmured. "Secrets are the death of love, but once they're out in the open, you can start to heal. Jace is a stubborn bastard, but when his shock wears off, he'll realize that you've both been hurt and suffered over the years—you much more so than he ever did. It might not feel like it now, but this was an important step forward for you both."

He was right—it didn't feel like a step forward. It felt like I'd been run over by a damn truck, which then proceeded to back up over me to ensure the job was done right.

"What's happening with the hit out on us?" I asked,

my voice rough as shit, but I desperately needed a subject change.

Grayson nodded, accepting that I wasn't ready right now to dig deeper into my soul. He allowed my subject change, and I was grateful for it. "I'll fill you all in when the guys get here," he said quickly. "Suffice it to say, we're not out of danger yet, but the time for laying low has passed. We can't keep hiding you guys indefinitely, so we're going to try and turn the tables."

He paused, and I raised an eyebrow, encouraging him to continue. I didn't have his background to figure this shit out on my own.

"Flo's funeral." He grimaced, and guilt flooded through me all over again about her death. What was being said about how she'd died? "It'll be the first time we're all together again in the public eye and the perfect opportunity for someone to take another shot at us. Only this time, Angelo is going to have his people surrounding the area."

Angelo. It wasn't that I'd forgotten about my fake baby daddy, it was just that there were other pressing things on my mind. But with Grayson's reminder, I was also reminded of one additional thing...

I was no longer fake pregnant. Shit, did the Ricci family know?

And if so, what was the fallout?

Whoever set up the hit at the farmhouse, if I'd been one of their intended targets, might have some competition soon. Giovanni would not take kindly to the subterfuge, and the moment he found out, my life would be forfeit.

Fucking great. Just what I needed.

thirty-five

GRAYSON

Flo's body had been discovered at her apartment, just as Angelo had arranged. He'd greased the right hands to ensure it wasn't investigated *too* thoroughly, because it was impossible to stage a scene without any flaws on such short notice. For now, she was in the city morgue, but we had assurances that the case would be closed within the week.

Our task, assigned by Brenda and the Big Noise legal team, was to stay out of the public eye and write our speeches for her funeral. The actual ceremony planning was being handled by Brenda, for which we were all thankful.

Technically, yes, it would have been fine for Billie, Jace, and Rhett to stay in hiding up in the forest for a few more days. But a gut feeling had told me I needed to rescue them from each other, and it seemed like I'd arrived right in the nick of time.

"Big Noise called a press conference last night," I informed my bandmates as we drove away from their hiding spot. "Big Dick ran most of it, telling the press that Flo was the victim of a home invasion. Did you guys know she had a mountain of debt?"

Big Dick was the label CEO—who was now so far under Giovanni Ricci's thumb he'd never escape—and a real arrogant bastard. He'd been beyond pissed when I was the only member of Bellerose to show up for the press conference but couldn't say anything about it publicly.

"No, what from?" Rhett asked, his worried gaze meeting my eyes in the mirror. Jace was sulking, his jaw set as he stared out the window and seemed to pretend he was anywhere but here.

I shrugged. "No clue. But according to Big Dick, she'd taken out some loans from the Vegas crew, and they'd come to collect." That wasn't the truth... loan sharks didn't expend that many men just to claim a bad debt. But maybe there was something else there that needed investigating.

"Bullshit," Rhett grunted. "Flo didn't have a drug problem like me or a pussy problem like Jace. Her only lapse of judgment was Tom, and he..." He trailed off with a groan. "He must have made her borrow on his behalf. She said he'd taken everything; I assumed he'd just drained her bank account before she cut him off."

Billie had been silent the whole time, but now she turned to look at me with a worried frown. "Has anyone spoken to Tom?"

I shook my head. "Much to my frustration, we haven't been able to find him. Slippery shit is in the wind, which is suspicious all on its own."

Rhett snorted a short laugh. "Slippery shit. Apt. He doesn't have the balls to plan an attack like that."

"Agreed," I muttered, my hands tightening on the steering wheel like I'd like to tighten them around Tom Tucker's throat. "Angelo thinks this was an attack on Billie and... the baby."

"You don't sound convinced," she said softly, her face still blotchy from the tears I'd found her crying. My little hedgehog was fragile right now; I needed to tone down the discussion about hit men and mafia wars.

I just opted for a shrug. "We'll see. For now, I'm taking you back to my place. I have security."

"Drop me home," Jace snapped, his voice cold.

I wanted to argue that we shouldn't separate, but of

all of us at the farmhouse that night, Jace was the *least* likely target. If he wanted to be a little bitch, then it was better he stay at his own apartment and give Billie some breathing room.

"Fine," I agreed. "But don't leave. Brenda gave us *strict* instructions not to be snapped by press before the funeral. Lay *low*. Got it?"

He met my eyes in the mirror, his lip curled in a sneer. "I'm not an idiot, Gray; I can handle myself."

Well... that was debatable. But I kept my mouth shut and jerked a nod.

Everyone lapsed back into silence, and Billie tucked her knees up to her chest a few minutes later. Her arms wrapped around them, and her head rested against the window as her eyes fluttered closed. Poor thing. Strong emotions like she must have just gone through with Jace were exhausting.

She fell asleep quickly as the car rocked her gently, and a glance in the mirror told me Jace was also asleep with his arms folded defensively over his chest.

"Anything I need to know?" I asked Rhett quietly when I was confident they were both deep enough asleep not to be woken easily.

He gave me a long look, then glanced at Jace and back to Billie. "Yep."

I waited for him to elaborate on that, and when he

didn't, it was easy enough to guess. Rhett wasn't the kind of guy who kissed and told, and this seemed to fall under that category. Somehow, more must have happened between Billie and Jace.

I didn't like that development, but it wasn't exactly unexpected. Their roots ran too deep for them to ever move on entirely.

"What about Angelo?" Rhett asked after a minute of silence. "Should we be concerned?"

I didn't have an answer for that, despite how hard I'd tried to work it out. "I don't know. I do wonder if something is going on between him and Brenda. Maybe his feelings for Billie are purely platonic or, at worst, self-serving." Or maybe they weren't. Maybe he, like Jace, was still head over heels in love with her, but he was better at hiding it. Fuck, I had no clue. Spending the last few days torturing bastards with him hadn't given me even a scrap of understanding about what went on in his head.

"The sooner we get her away from him and his fucking family, the better," Rhett muttered, running a hand over his floppy, turquoise mohawk.

I just grunted a response because I had a feeling it wouldn't be so easy. Not while she was tangled up in his marriage politics or while his family owned our band's contract.

"What's the story about her fake baby?" Rhett asked after another long silence. "I assume one of you has come up with a coverup on that."

I sighed, exhaustion from days of stress weighing me down. "Yeah. The story is that she lost it and has been in the hospital these past few days. The Riccis know about the farmhouse attack—their resources were needed to clean it up—so it was easy enough to make out like Billie got hurt and miscarried. Angelo has a paid doctor who fabricated a medical certificate verifying the baby's delivery and death, and Giovanni is mourning his heir's loss. No one knows it was faked."

Rhett winced like that information was painful. "I wonder if he forged the paperwork or just edited the dates on her legit medical records."

Shit. What a clusterfuck. Billie was carrying so much on her fragile shoulders; I desperately needed her to let me ease the load. For her sanity and mine.

For a girl I barely knew—prior to her disappearance in New York—she'd well and truly hooked me. Billie Bellerose was a special breed. Our muse, for far longer than Rhett or I had ever known her. Maybe that had contributed to how quickly she felt familiar.

"Will you stay with Jace?" I asked sometime later, as we drove back into Naples. It was a bigger city than Siena, but close enough that the Riccis rule had extended over here. Which, admittedly, had helped a lot in recent days.

Rhett made a frustrated sound, looking over at our sleeping friend. "I guess I have to. He'll spiral without someone there to smack some sense into him when he's wallowing."

"True," I agreed, recognizing how tortured his eyes had been while spitting those hate-filled words at Billie.

"Maybe Angelo wants to take one for the team and play best friend again while I snuggle Billie in your bed," Rhett mused aloud, and I gave a quiet chuckle. "Yeah, I didn't think so, either. Damn it."

I smirked, glancing at him in the mirror. "Don't worry, Silver. I'll snuggle her twice as hard to make up for your absence."

Rhett's eyes narrowed, and his middle finger extended. Cute.

We remained quiet for the rest of the drive, then, when I pulled up outside Rhett and Jace's condo, Rhett poked Jace awake.

He jerked in shock as his eyes snapped open, but he quickly registered where we were and relaxed slightly. He cast one long, pained look in Billie's direction, then got out of my jeep without even a single word.

"You're welcome, dickhead," I growled out the

window as he headed for the lobby with his head down. Probably wise so no one recognized him.

"Thanks Gray," Rhett said quietly, clapping me on the shoulder. "Call me when you get her home to your place. She's had a rough few days."

That was for sure. "Will do," I murmured. "Don't let him hit the bottom too hard. We need to stay alert in case Angelo is wrong about Billie being the target."

"Understood," he replied with a nod. "Take care of our girl."

Our girl.

"I will."

I waited until Rhett was safely inside the building and out of sight before pulling back out into the street. My home was about a fifteen-minute drive away, and I took it slow, not risking a crash with the precious cargo sleeping in my passenger seat.

I drove straight into my secure garage when we got there, then drew my gun to sweep the house for intruders before returning to Billie. She sighed softly in her sleep as I unbuckled her seat belt and lifted her into my arms. She was so small I could hardly believe I'd been fooled by the fake belly.

Fucking Angelo. What a dick plan.

With long strides, I carried Billie up the stairs to my bedroom and laid her down on the bed.

She stirred as I released her, her fingers clutching at my shirt like she didn't want me to let go.

"Shh, little Prickles," I breathed, peeling her fingers off. "I'm still here, baby; I'm not going anywhere." I kicked off my shoes, then quickly stripped down to my boxers before placing my loaded gun on the bedside table.

Tugging the blankets down, I climbed in and pulled her into my arms. Right where she belonged.

"Gray," she mumbled, her sleepy eyes blinking up at me. "I'm so sorry. I lied... and I left..."

Anger burned through me, but I bit back the need to release it. "No, you survived," I corrected her. "Only an idiot can't differentiate."

Sadness swamped her expression. "But—"

"Shh," I shushed her, placing a finger over her lips. "Sleep now. You're safe here."

I flicked the lights off, but it was only midafternoon, so the room was far from dark. As a musician, I was used to sleeping in daytime, and Billie was tired enough for it not to matter.

She was here. With me. Safe. That was all that mattered today; everything else could wait.

Like what'd gone down with Jace and whether she still had feelings for any of us. For me. If she still wanted to explore things between us... or if that paled in comparison to her first loves dominating her heart once more.

Fuck, I was turning into such a sap. Good thing I'd done enough work on my maturity that I didn't view tender emotions as such a threat anymore. My uncle would have killed her already, just for being a distraction.

There was a reason I'd left my family. He was a huge part of that.

thirty-six

BILLIE

It wasn't like two days in the wilderness was long enough that I'd forgotten what the more comfortable side of life felt like, but when I woke in Grayson's bed, it was as if I woke on a bed of clouds. Very expensive clouds. I was so damn comfortable that I wanted to cry at the sheer joy of being here.

Maybe it was that Grayson was the only one in here with me or maybe it was that he was in here and wrapped around me so tightly that I'd never felt quite so snug and protected in my life.

Not wanting to wake him yet, I didn't move a muscle, content to just lay in his arms. Even if they did feel a touch like steel bands enclosing me. Luckily, my many issues didn't include claustrophobia. If anything, I enjoyed this sensation more than sleeping on my own.

"Prickles," he rumbled. "It's the middle of the night. Go back to sleep."

Middle of the night... I would not have guessed that. Somehow, this clever bastard knew I was awake and what the time was without even opening his eyes.

"Can I shower?" I asked him, feeling super awake now and hating how gross my body was. My skin had that layer of ick on it that only came from infrequent washing. "I'll be back to sleep soon."

His response was to pull me closer, and if he didn't stop pressing his hard cock against me, I was going to moan and wiggle against him. It was the rule. The shower was a good escape from the needy-pussy situation I had going on. Apparently two rock stars wasn't enough for her.

She needed a third. One that was six-foot-five and built like a fucking linebacker.

"Wait for morning," he rumbled, and there was no way I could escape unless he released me.

"Please," I pleaded. "I honestly can't stand how dirty I feel."

He buried his face harder in my neck, breathing me in, his lips caressing my skin. "You smell delicious," he said, "but if you insist, then let's get you clean."

He rolled over, taking me with him, and when he reached the edge of the bed, he stood and kept me tightly bound in his arms.

"I can walk, you know," I said with a laugh.

His reply was a grunt, and I was starting to think that all of Bellerose had a small grunting problem. "I spent months stalking the Ricci family to ensure you were safe," he told me. "Then days killing motherfuckers to ensure you were safe, and now that I have you safe in my arms, I'm disinclined to release you out into the world again. Maybe if no one tries to kidnap or kill you in the next week or so, I'll reconsider my stance."

Was it possible to fall in love with someone over a matter of weeks? Because it had happened so fast with Rhett, and now Grayson, that I was starting to wonder about my sanity.

Or maybe this was just more of the *soul, fate, and music brought us all together* thing.

"I do feel safe with you," I admitted as he crossed the large, dark room, heading for a doorway that I couldn't make out until we were almost at it. "A concept I haven't felt since I was... shit, probably a teenager." Asleep between Jace and Angelo. Not that I was going to mention that to Grayson. We were going to ignore the past few days with Rhett and Jace. Fucking Jace.

Then I sighed. "That's not completely true. Rhett..." Rhett made me feel safe. It was just a different sort of safe.

"I get it," Gray rumbled, leaving it at that.

When he got us through the bathroom, he hit a light that just turned on two small sconces on the wall on either side of the mirror. It was a soft light that didn't hurt my eyes, even after near darkness, and I could have cried at how perfect his bathroom was. Huge bath, even bigger shower stall, with at least four glorious showerheads.

These were the parts of being rich that I would enjoy. The luxury bathrooms and state-of-the-art kitchens. Maybe the nice cars too.

Who the hell was I kidding, all the parts of being rich looked nice. Except the fame part. I never wanted to be someone who walked down the street and got mobbed like Bellerose did. It honestly appeared so invasive and scary. Anonymously rich was the way to go.

"You still with me, Billie?" Grayson asked as he reached in and turned the shower on, sending water out of all four—yep, I'd been right—showerheads, along with steam that shot up from some metal joins on the side. He stepped right in, even though I was fully dressed and he was in boxer briefs.

"I'm burning these clothes anyway," he said when I laughed about being clothed. "We'll get you all new stuff, and it'll be like the attack at the farmhouse never happened."

"Except Flo died," I said softly. None of them had dealt with it; that much was obvious. I had the sense that unless forced to, Grayson would never deal with it. He was a compartmentalizer. I recognized the trait since it was a strong one I possessed as well.

"She did." He breathed deeply for a moment before he continued. "And whoever is responsible will pay with their life. No matter how long it takes to track them down."

He would do that for her. And me. I knew that without even having to ask him.

We were fully under the water now, and I tipped my head back, letting the warm stream cover me from head to toe. Grayson stepped back and gave me space for the first time, and I kind of wished he wouldn't. But I'd demanded my independence, and I wasn't about to whine now. I'd just wash off the last few days of grime, and then hopefully, we'd get back to snuggling.

First, though, I needed out of these clothes. "I'm going to strip," I warned him, and he just leaned back against the white-tiled wall, watching me with a half smile.

"You won't get an argument from me," he drawled. The water poured down his head, and he'd pushed back his hair, so I could see the masculine planes of his face without any interruption. His body was ripped; all those long-muscled limbs containing lethal strength was definitely my aphrodisiac. And I was about to strip for him.

I grabbed the hem of my shirt, and his dark eyes remained on my face as I lifted it, and my bra, free from my body, my tits jiggling as I dropped the shirt on the floor. His gaze darkened when I reached for the band on my shorts, and he got there first, moving so quickly that I hadn't even noticed the transition from wall to me. "Let me help you out," he said softly, tilting his head down so our faces weren't too far apart. Poor guy had to nearly bend himself in half to achieve such a feat.

My breathing got a little faster when his thumbs replaced mine in the band of my pants, sparks lighting up my skin where he touched me. Slowly, oh so torturously slowly, he started to work the shorts down my body. The need to pant was strong, but I forced myself to remain calm and keep all the horniness on the inside. Well, most of it. If he'd slipped his fingers in my needy cunt right now, he'd know for sure that I was far from feeling the calm facade I presented.

"I was worried about you, Prickles," he murmured, still working that band down. "When you were with Angelo, when you were taken from me, no matter how much you fake-smiled, your eyes were screaming in pain, and I couldn't fucking get to you."

The bite of his hands against my skin grew a little stronger as he tightened his hold, and I couldn't help the moan that escaped. "Leaving you all was the hardest decision of my life," I choked out. "And in the end, they took me before I even got a chance to play hero."

My pants finally hit the stall with a soft splat, and then I was completely naked before him.

"Heroes work together," he told me, staring down into my eyes, his gaze darker than ever. "Don't do it alone, little one. That's not how this works."

I was about to promise him anything if he'd just kiss me, when his chest rumbled, and he leaned down into me, lips crashing against mine. I was instantly reminded of how dominating he was in a kiss, and how much I liked it. He took control of my mouth, his tongue tasting mine as my knees went a little weak. He backed me against the shower wall, and I used it to keep me standing as I pushed up on my toes to try and bring our heads closer together.

There was just too much height difference to comfortably do that, and I was more than thankful when he looped an arm around my back and used it to slowly drag me up so that I could wrap my legs around his waist. From here I could explore his mouth thoroughly, tasting him, our tongues crashing together in a dance that wasn't gentle and had me rocking against him.

"Gray, please," I gasped as we pulled apart. I was begging for relief, and I didn't care how that arrived.

"Little hedgehog," he rumbled back. "I'm keeping you locked in my bedroom and bathroom for a year, no exceptions. And the next time a fucker puts his hands on you, I'm going to kill them where they stand."

When he went caveman on me, arousal dripped down my thigh to join the water streaming to the floor.

"What about Rhett and..." *Jace*. Shit.

His reply was a slow laugh. "The only exceptions. That warning is for everyone else. Anyone you *don't* want touching you."

That was good to know. Very fucking good to know.

Grayson kissed me again, and then when I was gasping for breath, he palmed my ass with both hands, lifting me higher as he dropped to his knees. "Legs over my shoulders," he ordered.

That had me pausing as I tried to figure out the logistics of what he was doing here. "Shoulders?" I squeaked.

He lifted a hand and palmed my ass hard, the sound loud in this tiled room. "Shoulders, Prickles."

I thought for sure I was going to slip and fall, but he was so strong that I hardly had to do anything to get my legs over his shoulders, my back braced against the tiled wall. Still worried about falling, I grabbed onto the shower faucet above my head and prayed it was strong enough to hold.

It was a position I'd never been in, with my entire weight resting on his shoulders, but Grayson acted like it wasn't even straining him at all. "Fuck," he breathed, when my pussy was in his face. He leaned back to catch my eye. "Been daydreaming about this for weeks."

Me and him both.

His tongue tasted me in a slow sweep, starting from the bottom of my slit and sliding all the way to the top. This time his groan was louder, and from this angle, the size of his cock tenting his wet boxers had me feeling all kinds of things. Like, would I survive this, and would I care if I didn't?

"Gray," I moaned, rocking my cunt against his face,

one of my hands threading into the wet, silky strands of his hair. "I'm going to need you to use that talented tongue with a little more force."

As I said that, the sound of a phone ringing cut through the haze of arousal in my head. He let out a curse, fingers biting into my ass as he pushed me a little higher. "You're going to have to be quick, baby," he warned me. "If someone is calling at this time, it's an emergency, and I need to get it."

His tongue plunged into me before he'd even finished that sentence, and I was crying out and rocking the best I could while sandwiched between him and the wall. "Quick won't be a problem," I cried out.

Not a problem at all.

thirty-seven

BILLIE

Grayson left me in the shower with strict instructions to take my time. I got the impression he was only partially concerned about my hygiene and relaxation, and partly worried about what crisis needed his attention in the middle of the fucking night.

Admittedly, I was curious. But not curious enough to rush my shower. I did exactly as I was told, cleaning every inch of my body, shaving my legs, shampooing and conditioning my hair... Thank fuck Gray understood the necessity for quality hair products and didn't have some of that horrific 2-in-1 shit that some boys used.

The best part, though, was when I got out of the shower and hunted unashamedly through Grayson's vanity. Somehow, he just struck me as the kind of guy who always had spares of everything, and to my utter delight, I quickly located a toothbrush still in its packet.

Clean teeth. Pure bliss.

My clothes were sopping wet and left in a pile at the base of the shower, so I just wrapped the towel around my body to leave the bathroom. Grayson had taken the time to leave some clothes neatly folded on the end of the bed, which I had to assume were there for me.

It was one of his Bellerose tour t-shirts and a pair of boxers—way too big for me but better than being naked if he was in the middle of a crisis.

Leaving the bedroom, the sound of Gray opening the front door made me pause. Voices travelled to me, and I frowned with confusion. Was that Angelo?

Hurrying downstairs, I gasped to see Angelo striding through the front door carrying a badly beaten woman whose long red hair trailed over his arm like blood.

"Vee?" I exclaimed, pressing a hand to my mouth to hold back my scream. "What happened?"

"That's what I was asking," Gray rumbled, closing the door, locking several deadbolts, and activating his alarm once more. "Take her to the couch."

Angelo said nothing, just strode through Grayson's house with the confidence of a man who knew where he was going. He lowered Vee carefully to the couch, and she whimpered in pain, tears rolling from her swollen, purple eyes.

"Shhh," Angelo hushed, ever so gently drying his wife's tears with a fabric handkerchief. "Sleep, *amore mio*. You're safe now." He sat on the carpet beside the couch, his concern etched all over his face as he whispered to Vee in Italian, soothing her back to sleep.

I shook my head in disbelief, looking up at Grayson. "She needs to go to the hospital." I said it quietly, not wanting to wake her, but Angelo's head snapped around in response.

"No," he snapped. "No hospitals. Not here or in Siena or anywhere in between."

I swallowed hard, understanding exactly what he meant: This was done by mafia, and if she showed up at a hospital, they'd likely finish the job.

"I know someone," Gray rumbled. "She can help. Discretely."

Angelo jerked a nod, rising to his feet. "Good. Call her." He stalked out of the living room and headed to the kitchen, going straight to Grayson's liquor cabinet. He'd definitely been here before.

Grayson didn't even bat an eyelid at Angelo making

himself at home, just scrolled through his phone to find the contact he was looking for.

"Angel, *what happened?*" I asked, panicked and desperate to help, somehow. I'd followed him into the kitchen where we could speak louder than whispers, but my concern was so thick I was shaking.

Angelo poured a small glass of whiskey and downed it in one gulp before answering. "We happened, Bella. You and me."

My jaw dropped at the implication that I was responsible for the horrific injuries his wife was currently sporting. "*What?* No, because *we* haven't happened, remember? It was all bullshit. Fuck, Angel, we haven't *happened* since before the fire." And by that, I meant *fucked.* Despite the picture of domestic bliss we'd been playing at, Angelo had only kissed me that one time.

"Whether we were actually screwing or not, it's irrelevant, Bella. We wanted people to think we were and had been for some time. They believed it. And now Vee is paying the price." He scowled at me, shaking his head. "No good deed goes unpunished, I guess."

"Don't you *dare* blame me for this, Angelo Ricci. The entire plan was *your* idea, remember? It wasn't so long ago that I was in the exact same position as her. Remember? Tell me, Angel, why didn't you just fake a pregnancy with Vee to appease your parents, huh? Why not give her the fake belly and pretend to lose it in order to buy more time? Why *me*, Angel?"

He stared at me for a long moment, his expression utterly blank. Then he dropped his eyes to the empty glass in his hand. "I don't know, Bella. But I'm asking myself the same thing right now."

Furious and disgusted—with myself just as much as him—I threw up my hands and stormed back to the living room where Vee's broken body lay on the huge sofa. She seemed like such a nice woman; she didn't deserve this. No one deserved this.

Sniffing back my own guilty tears, I fetched a blanket from the recliner and spread it out over her gently. She didn't stir, but her breathing was a soft rasp that reassured me she was still alive. Fucking hell, she must be in *so* much pain. I remembered how it felt to be in that position and wouldn't wish it on anyone.

"My friend will be here in half an hour." Gray's low voice made me flinch, not having heard him enter the room again. "She suggested getting ice onto her face in the meantime. I'll grab some."

I just nodded. What else was there to say?

He returned a minute later and handed me a frozen gel pack wrapped in a tea towel. As gently as I could, I brushed Vee's hair back from her damaged face. The strands snagged on my fingers, and I winced at the crust of blood. Slowly, lightly, I applied the ice to her more swollen, purple eye.

She inhaled sharply in her sleep, giving a shiver, but I kept the ice in place. Anything had to be better than nothing, until Gray's friend arrived.

"Take a shower," Gray rumbled a couple of minutes later. I blinked up at him in confusion, then realized he was addressing Angelo, who'd returned to the living room with a fresh glass of whiskey in hand. "You're covered in blood."

Angelo glanced down at his shirt. I imagine it used to be white, but now it was red-brown with dried blood. Vee's blood. Maybe someone else's too, depending on how he'd found her. Did he kill the ones who'd done this to her?

I desperately hoped he had, but my gut said it wasn't so black and white. Vee was a mafia princess, and if this was on the Riccis' say so...

Bile burned in my throat, but I choked it back. Vee needed the focus on her right now. I could be strong for her, couldn't I? She didn't need to die, like Flo.

Angelo said something to Gray, but it was too quiet for me to make out. My focus was back on Vee and making sure I wasn't pressing too hard with the ice on her bruised face.

I zoned out while sitting there, mentally chatting to Angelo's wife, who I really knew very little about. I knew that she and Angelo weren't *lovers,* even if they clearly loved each other, and that Vee had a secret girlfriend that she'd been hiding from her family. What was her name? Had she told me?

Looking up, I searched the room to find Angelo had returned and was sitting in the armchair, wearing one of Grayson's black t-shirts and gray sweatpants. His feet were bare, and his jaw set in fury as he stared silently back at me.

"Vee's girlfriend..." I started, feeling like I was hugely overstepping, "is she... okay? Were they together?"

Angelo arched a brow. "She told you about Giana?"

I nodded. "At the party thing. She cornered me in the bathroom, and I thought she was going to claw my eyes out or something. But she just wanted to reassure me that she wasn't *threatened*... that you two weren't..." I trailed off, my voice breaking.

"That we weren't fucking?" Angelo finished for me, his tone harsh. "How nice of my wife to offer her blessing to my pregnant mistress."

I bit my tongue to hold back the desire to yell at him. This wasn't the time or the place. "Is Giana okay?" I asked instead.

Angelo stared at me a moment longer, then sighed. "She's fine. I called her while driving over here; she isn't even in Siena right now and had no clue about this."

I nodded slowly. "Good. That's good. I thought maybe..."

"That Vee's family found out she's gay and tried to kill her?" He gave a cold laugh. "No, Bella, this is all about politics. They must have decided that with our history, I was at risk of divorcing Vee to marry you." He scoffed like it was the most preposterous thing he'd ever heard.

I frowned. "Wait. *Must have*? You don't *know* that's what happened?"

His dark eyes narrowed. "I know enough."

"Bullshit," I snapped back. "You assume you know, but what if this was something else entirely? God, you can be so fucking pig-headed sometimes, Angelo. You can't just—"

"Ahem," Grayson cleared his throat, cutting off my quickly escalating rant. He'd just returned with an elderly woman a step behind him. "This is Morgana." He gave no further explanation, and I quickly clambered up from my seat on the carpet to let her closer to Vee.

"Thank you, dear," she said to me softly with a smile as Gray dropped her huge medical bag on the coffee table, then fetched a chair from the dining room so she could sit beside the couch without being on the floor. "I appreciate your concern, but I'd like some privacy while I examine Valentina, please."

She gave a pointed look between Angelo and me. He looked like he wanted to tell her where to shove her polite request, so I marched over and grabbed his hand to pull him up out of the chair.

"Come on," I ordered him, yanking him out of the living room, "let her work."

"I'm not just going to trust—" he started in protest, but Gray had followed us and now blocked the doorway to the living room with nothing more than his bulk, his thick arms folded over his chest.

The level glare he gave Angelo was patient but didn't offer any wiggle room. "Last I checked, Angelo, you don't have a medical degree. Nor have you trained as a paramedic or as a trauma surgeon or even as a psychologist. You have *zero* useful skills here, and no one in this house needs to be shot. So take your bad-tempered, tattoo-covered ass to the kitchen and wait patiently."

Angelo was never one to accept intimidation, so it was no shock when he just raised his chin and met Gray's glare with his own. "Or what?"

I needed to intervene before things turned violent.

"Or I'll search Google for a late-night clown-o-gram to come over and make balloon animals."

Both men, with their badass attitudes, inked muscles, and deadly stares, turned to look at me. Gray, with pure confusion, Angelo with a twitch of horror in his gaze.

"You wouldn't," he whispered, shaking his head. Angelo wasn't scared of anything... except clowns. Particularly clowns that made balloon animals. That was a story from our childhood for another day.

I folded my arms and matched his stubborn energy. "Try me."

Angelo's glare narrowed like he was so damn tempted to call my bluff. But then he swallowed hard and stalked into the kitchen without another word.

Gray's eyes widened with admiration. "I don't understand it, but I like it. You're a badass, Prickles. Yet another thing I like about you."

I flashed him a grin. "Another?"

His smile turned sultry. "Alongside the sweet taste of your cunt and the glorious way you moan my name while you come."

Oh. Good answer.

thirty-eight

RHETT

Nearly a week passed between Grayson rescuing us from the wilderness and Flo's funeral. All the while, we were under strict instructions to stay in our homes. Don't leave, not even for groceries. We had people deliver everything we needed to avoid offering any ammunition to *Dirty Truths*.

Not that it made any difference. Almost daily there was a new post about us. About Bellerose. Speculation over who would replace Flo in the band were the hottest discussion threads right now. Somehow, Angelo and Jace's connection was revealed, and the fans were losing their minds wondering if Angelo Ricci, mafia bad boy and panty-dropper extraordinaire, would be joining the band.

Already, the press was having a field day with those rumors, calling us the *boys of Bellerose*. Like Flo had never even existed.

My phone rang as I stood in front of my mirror, attempting to get my tie to sit flat. A glance at the caller ID eased some tightness in my chest, and I answered it on speaker.

"Thorny babe," I greeted Billie. "How's Vee this morning?"

Angelo's wife had been heavily drugged with painkillers since her vicious beating a week ago. She wasn't in a coma, but she also wasn't conscious. Each passing day seemed more hopeless than the one before, but Gray's medical friend assured them it was just her body healing in its own time.

"No change," Billie replied with a sigh. "Her bruises look so much better, but she's still way out of it. Morgs thinks it was a nasty concussion that her brain is slowly recovering from."

I winced. I'd never met Valentina, but Billie had assured me she was a good person. The kind of person deserving of her care and stress, I hoped.

"Well, she's the expert," I murmured, referring to Morgana. She'd always been cagey about her qualifications, but from what Gray had said, she was more than experienced enough to help Valentina. The only thing better would have been a hospital. Angelo wouldn't entertain that idea, no matter how badly she'd needed it.

"Yeah, she's been great. We have her staying here to keep an eye on Vee today," Billie said, then yawned. "Crap, sorry. I didn't sleep well last night."

Jealousy sparked through me. "Uh-huh, do I need to have words with Gray?"

Billie's laugh was low and throaty, making my dick twitch. "I wish. Man, do I wish. Unfortunately, nothing so fun. With Vee and Angelo both staying here, the mood isn't amazing for, uh, quality time."

That made me smirk. As shitty as the situation with Vee was, at least Gray wasn't just fucking Billie all over his house twenty-four seven and erasing little old Rhett from her head and heart. I still had a chance to win her over.

"Do... um, do you think something will happen today?" she asked cautiously, sounding like she was hiding out in a bathroom by how her voice echoed. "Like another attack?"

I gave up on my tie and grabbed my blazer from the hanger. "I have no idea, Thorn. Part of me thinks it's inevitable, with us all being in the same place, in public, for the first time since..." Since Flo's death. "But then I really hope there was another reason for it all. Maybe, I dunno... What if the farmhouse attack was all just a big mistake? What if Brenda's godparents were the target and we were just in the wrong place at the wrong time?"

Billie gave a sad laugh. "Imagine that. Someone puts out a hit on an anonymous old couple and instead finds a mafia prince, his pregnant mistress, an ex-gang enforcer, a badass guitarist with a fake name and mysterious past, a girl with mountains of bad debt, and... Jace Adams."

"Yeah," I agreed with a chuckle. "Some things are too coincidental."

She sighed. "You never know. Nothing is impossible."

Jace rapped his knuckles on my door, then let himself into the room without waiting for a response. "You ready to go? Brenda said our car will be here in five."

I snatched up my phone, quickly switching it from speaker to handset before Billie spoke, but his expression darkened faster than a thunderstorm rolling in. He knew who I was talking to.

"Thorny Rose, I've got to go," I told my girl. "I'll see you there?"

"Of course," she replied. "I... um, yeah. See you soon, Zepp."

I smiled at the nickname, then ended the call before shooting Jace an accusing glare. "Just because you're refusing to forgive her doesn't mean I'm going to freeze her out. I care about her, Jace. A lot."

He grimaced. "I can see that. But remember how it felt when she walked away last time? You'd only been fucking for, like, two weeks then. Imagine how you'll feel when she does it again, if you don't cut her out of your life soon."

I shoved past him, heading for the door. Flo's funeral was in an hour, and Jace was still attempting to drive a wedge between me and Billie, same as he'd been doing all fucking week since we got home.

"That drug spiral wasn't about Billie," I muttered as Jace caught up before I got into the elevator. We lived on the penthouse floor; no one else had access to our level. So the car was empty when we stepped in. "Not *just* about her," I amended.

Jace shrugged. "I know. I'm just saying..."

I shook my head. "You're jealous. You just can't admit it to yourself, let alone anyone else. So you think that if you can't have her, no one can. It's fucking messed up, Jace, and you need therapy."

The words were harsh, but it wasn't *news* to him. I'd

already told him the same thing a hundred times over the last week. He didn't actually hate Billie; he hated himself for not hating her enough, particularly after her revelation in the forest that day.

As badly as Jace was hurting, he was also a decent enough human that he *had* to have some empathy for the position she'd been in all those years ago. She'd been a child making adult decisions, and she got it wrong. But she was the one who'd lived with the consequences while Jace went on an eight-year temper tantrum, turning their story into platinum records and rubbing her face in it.

Wisely, Jace shut the fuck up after that.

As Brenda had said, there was a town car waiting out the front of the building, but there were also several photographers lurking like vultures, waiting to snap pictures of the grieving *boys of Bellerose*. Soulless bastards, the lot of them.

We rode in silence across the city to the massive cathedral where Flo's funeral was being held. She hadn't been a religious person at all, but Brenda had informed us that with the impact Flo's death was having on our fans, this was the type of *grand* location they expected. Anything less might be seen as us disrespecting or diminishing how important she was to our band, neither of which was true.

The plan was to arrive well in advance of the ceremony, but as our car drew closer, we saw how badly we'd misjudged how the day would go. People were crammed along the street, all in black, with thousands of placard signs with heartfelt messages to Flo or to the rest of the band.

It shook me, and I found myself choking back tears as I saw someone holding a huge poster of Flo's smiling face. It was a picture taken on tour, the night before I'd met Billie. It seemed like we'd lived whole lifetimes since that night.

"This is bullshit," Jace muttered as fans knocked on our blacked-out car windows, trying to see through the privacy glass. "This feels like a publicity stunt from Big Dick."

I swallowed the hard lump of emotion in my throat. "It is," I agreed. "But it's also the sort of farewell Flo deserved. Especially seeing as..." *Especially seeing as we'd covered up what really happened to her, and those responsible were still out there, walking free.*

Jace blew out a breath, scrubbing his hands over his face. "You're right. She'd love this, too."

I nodded, staring out the window as our driver edged forward, waiting for fans to move aside as even our police escort was having trouble clearing the road. "Flo always thought she was the least popular member of Bellerose, you know? Like she was just a backup musician. She never thought of herself as famous like the rest of us."

"She was, though." Jace fidgeted with his cufflinks, his expression pinched like he was holding back tears. I knew the feeling all too well.

A few minutes later, our driver got us through the secured gates of the cathedral, and we both pulled on our brave faces as we got out of the car. Actually, fuck that. I pulled a pair of sunglasses from my pocket and slid them onto my face instead.

"Good idea," Jace commented, following suit. We were still rock stars, after all.

An usher directed us up the main steps, and we didn't hesitate to get out of sight of the screaming, sobbing fans. I loved that they were showing their grief for Flo—she deserved it—but I could have done without the attention, myself.

Brenda was further into the enormous cathedral, handing her baby off to her husband, Humphrey, and loading him down with an enormous diaper bag.

"Boys, you're on time," she greeted us with a sigh of relief. "Thank fuck for that."

Humphrey scowled and covered the baby's ears, like the kid could understand cursing already. "I thought you were supposed to have another six months of leave," he told Brenda in a pissy tone, barely even glancing at Jace and I. He was firmly not a fan of our music, more of a classical *jazz* fan. Weirdo.

"Yes, well, that was before someone murdered one of my artists, Daniel," she replied. She always called him by his surname because she said Humphrey was an old man's name. "Take care of our little monster; I'll be home as soon as I can." She showered kisses on her baby, then smacked a quick one on her husband's lips before effectively dismissing him and turning to us with her manager face firmly in place. "Where's Gray?"

"On his way," I said before Jace could be an asshole. "Should be arriving any minute."

Her gaze shifted over my shoulder, and her lips tipped up in an affectionate smile. Gray had always been her favorite. "Speak of the devil. Right on time."

"She shouldn't fucking be here," Jace snarled as Billie walked in with Grayson holding her hand firmly. She was a vision in her simple black dress, her golden-blonde hair sleeked back into a low bun. Gray said something to her, and she tilted her head to look up at him with the sweetest look on her face...

Maybe he'd already won.

But then she searched the room until her eyes met mine, and her lips curved in a smile of pure joy. I was back in the game. *Thank fuck.*

"Save it," I snapped to Jace, "you know why she's here. Same reason as *he* is." Angelo had just stepped through the front door, unwinding his charcoal scarf like he had every right to be here at our sister's funeral.

He didn't even try to hide his gun as his coat billowed open, and a jolt of fear ran through me. It was Flo's day, her final farewell... and yet we were all armed and ready for an attack.

Would we all leave this cathedral alive? I wasn't so sure.

I barely got even a moment to hug Billie before we were being ushered to our seats, and the rest of the invited guests—celebrities, influencers, corporate assholes—were all allowed to enter. I had no interest in playing nice, so I just slouched low in my seat between Jace and Billie with my fingers tightly entwined with hers.

Most of the ceremony bypassed me like a haze of white noise. I had to block it all out because every kind word about Flo made me want to cry. Fuck, she hadn't deserved this.

When a montage of photos started playing on the huge projector screen, I lost my fight. Tears rolled silently down my face, and I fought the urge to pull my sunglasses back down. I could hardly believe she was gone. Really gone. No more tours, no more song collaboration...

It'd been so easy to convince myself over the last week and a half that she was just away, just off doing her own thing, and we'd see her again in the studio. But that wasn't the case, and the reality was finally setting in.

Jace nudged me as the photo montage ended. "You're up, bro. You got this?"

I'd foolishly volunteered to read a eulogy, written on behalf of all of us. I felt guilty about how I'd treated her in the last few months, and that guilt pushed me to take on this responsibility. Now, though, I was second guessing myself.

"You've got this," Billie whispered, squeezing my fingers. "Speak from the heart."

Fuck. I really did not have this, but I couldn't let Flo down now.

Choking back my tears, I stood and slowly made my way up to the podium. Before I got there, though, a loud crack rang out through the cavernous cathedral, and something hard smacked into me, sending me crashing to the ground in pain.

thirty-nine

ANGELO

Everyone had been so sure that Florence's funeral would be the target of another attack, whether on Billie—as I expected—or on the rest of Bellerose. As such, the security was *thick* to ensure whoever made a move would be apprehended *alive* and delivered to my warehouse for questioning.

When a shot rang out through the cathedral and Rhett disappeared out of sight, all I felt was surprise. Of everyone involved in the farmhouse attack, Rhett Silver —or Ryan Gold—was probably the least likely target. Okay, not true. Jace was the least likely. Smug fuck that he was literally had no ties to crime, no skeletons in his closet, no debts... he was the epitome of squeaky clean.

Still, I was more than taken aback to see Rhett targeted... only to realize that it wasn't an attack at all. Thanks to the heavy security protocols we'd put in place, within just a minute of chaos, we'd worked out what had happened.

Some grief-stricken—or celebrity obsessed— members of the public outside the cathedral had scaled the fences and tried to force their way into the cathedral to see Bellerose *in the flesh*. Our trigger-happy security had seen this person as a threat, mistaking the drink bottle in their hand for a grenade. And shot them.

Another member of security had reacted to the sound, diving on Rhett to protect him.

How utterly anticlimactic.

Of course, a Bellerose fan was dead, and that cut the remainder of the ceremony shorter than anticipated. Celebs and cashed-up assholes were all ushered, crying, from the cathedral by various bodyguards and private security, but my focus was entirely locked on Billie. Her safety was my primary objective. The dress she wore was cinched under her breasts but loose around her midsection to hide the lack of residual baby bump. So far, she'd garnered *plenty* of curious looks, but most of those were about her relationship with Bellerose, not her connection to the Ricci family.

"Holy fuck, that guy was heavy," Rhett grumbled,

rubbing his shoulder where he'd struck the stone steps when he'd been shoved to the ground. "I can already feel the bruise coming up."

"Better than being shot," Grayson commented, and I smirked my agreement. Rhett was just being a little bitch to gain sympathy from nurse Billie. Sly bastard. "I wonder what this is about." Gray was looking over my shoulder, and I turned to find a harried Brenda striding toward us through the remaining mourners. We'd been waiting until our car was ready to take us to Florence's wake; the front of the cathedral was already roped off in a crime scene. Now, though, it seemed like something else was going on.

Brenda's lips were pursed tight, her brow tight with frustration. "Don't make things difficult. You lot have already caused enough of a headache as it is."

Jace bristled, his bad mood darkening with every passing moment. "What the fuck is that supposed to mean?"

Brenda drew a breath, presumably to explain, but before she could get a word out, Big Dick Hamilton— Big Noise Records CEO and my father's newest lapdog —slithered over to us.

"Angelo," he greeted me with a frozen smile. "I wasn't aware you'd be attending. Did you know Florence?"

I leveled him a hard glare. "What can we help you with, Dick? The band are in mourning, as I'm sure you can appreciate. All business matters can go through their manager." I gestured to Brenda, who nodded her agreement.

Big Dick's complexion blanched somewhat. "Actually, this is a matter that requires urgent attention from the band directly. It's with regards to Florence's estate and her named *beneficiary*."

This couldn't be good. More money games?

"Flo didn't have an estate," Rhett rasped, red around the eyes. "And she had no family. So what—"

"Ah, see, that's the problem. Someone has come forward claiming to be her legal spouse and, therefore, the sole beneficiary of Miss Foster's estate, which, incidentally..." He trailed off, glancing around. "This isn't the time or place. I'd, of course, like to save this for another day, but with Florence's spouse pushing the matter through legal channels, it really can't wait."

Jace was two seconds away from losing his shit; I could see it all over his drawn features. "What the fuck are you trying to say, Big Dick?"

The designer-suited CEO sighed. "Miss Foster's spouse is demanding a meeting with the remaining members of Bellerose to discuss future royalties and remuneration for the canceled portion of the recent tour."

Jace squinted at the businessman a moment, then just shrugged. "So? I assume this is Tom *Fucker* we're talking about. Tell him to get fucked or to deal with Brenda. That shit doesn't need our personal attention. They weren't married, so he can't—"

"He says they were," Dick disagreed. "And apparently has proof."

"What?" Gray snarled. "Since when?"

One of the event staff came over then to let us know our cars were ready, and Big Dick scowled daggers at us all. "Just head over to Big Noise's Riverside office; the lawyers will all meet you there."

"Now?" Jace exclaimed, horrified.

"Yes," Dick snapped. "Now. Christ, as if I don't have anything better to do than deliver messages for some spoiled musicians." He started to walk away, then hesitated and glanced back awkwardly. "Uh, sorry for your loss, also. We will wait a week before auditioning replacement bass guitarists. Out of respect."

That man wouldn't know respect if it came up and bit his shriveled balls off. I didn't know Florence, aside from our brief interaction before she'd been killed, but even I was insulted by the lack of sensitivity for the band who'd lost a family member.

"Fuck him," Jace spat, raging as we exited the cathedral through the back door. "I'm not fucking dealing with lawyers. Not today."

Rhett shook his head, agitated and visibly pissed off. "I will. I'm not letting that lying snake get away with taking anything from Flo, even if it's just her legacy. Regardless of what she had in the bank when she died, she's still entitled royalties from future sales, and that slippery shit isn't going to touch one fucking cent of it." He stormed over to the first town car and gestured to Jace. "You go on to the wake. I'll deal with Tom."

"I'll go with him," I said quietly. "And keep him out of jail."

Rhett was likely to pitchfork someone in his current mood, and while I'd thoroughly enjoy watching that happen, he was too high profile to commit murder like that without repercussions.

Jace shot me a hard look, then sighed. "We'll all go. Bellerose is a family, no matter what. We can't let Tom weasel his way into that. You can take Billie to—"

"She's coming with us," Grayson snapped, grabbing Billie's hand and dragging her into the second town car without waiting for a response.

Flames shot out of Jace's ears, and I bit back a smirk as I clapped him on the shoulder. "Looks like we're all going." I didn't wait for him to argue either, sliding into the first town car with him following a moment later. Rhett had switched to the second car with Gray and Billie, and it didn't escape my notice that I was alone with my old best friend again.

"Don't," he said in a cold voice when I started to speak. "Just *don't*. She told me everything. The baby..." He trailed off as his voice broke, and it made me feel like the lowest of scumbags. Jace had been my best friend, closer than a brother, and I'd screwed him over hard.

"She told me," I murmured, acknowledging the fact that I knew he knew. "You're understandably pissed at both of us, but one day you'll see that we both made choices out of love for *you*. Even back then, you were the most important person in the world. Nothing mattered more than Jace Adams's future, Jace's happiness and success. Everyone else? Fuck them. Who cares, right? So long as Jace Adams becomes a superstar."

Stunned silence met my bitter statement. Of course he hadn't seen it like that, he never did. Selfish prick.

"You have no idea what Bella went through back then, Jace. Your bruised pride was more important than *anything* or *anyone,* so you never looked back. Maybe if you had, you'd have seen the destruction and anguish happening behind your fat head." I drew a breath, trying hard to clarify the eight and a half years of resentment and hate that I'd built toward Jace.

He stared at me in bewilderment. "Angel, you can't just—"

"Blame you? Guess what, Jace, I do. If she hadn't loved you so much, she never would have lied. She never would have come crying, begging for my help when she found out she was pregnant at *sixteen*, Jace. Sixteen. She was a *child* making decisions no adult should even have to suffer, yet she loved *you* so much she was willing to break all our hearts. And it worked. Look at you now." I gestured out the window as our car passed under an enormous billboard promoting Bellerose's recent tour, with Jace Adams front and center, glaring at the camera like the world owed him a debt.

"Your entire career was built off of pain, Jace. Hers and mine. And you have the utter audacity to play the victim? Pull your head out of your fucking ass and look around. You were spared, but us? We weren't so lucky. She lost *her* baby. Penelope, by the way, because I bet you never even thought to ask."

He reared back like I'd slapped him, and I was glad. At least *that* had an impact, hearing that Billie had named her baby after his grandmother.

"I didn't..." He frowned, shaking his head. Denial.

What a shocker. "No, that doesn't excuse you both lying to me all these years. I had a right to know, Angel."

I scoffed. "No, Jace, you didn't. And right now, you're just acting like a spoiled little brat. It's not cute, and it's sure as fuck not doing you any favors in winning her back."

His jaw dropped. "I'm not *trying* to win her back. That's the last thing I want."

"Sure, bro." More denial. "Well, that's probably for the best. Compared to Rhett and Grayson, you're just a whiny little bitch with nothing to offer. If I were her, I wouldn't come back to you either."

I saw the punch coming well before it landed but didn't move out of the way. He needed to vent, and honestly... I needed to feel something. Even if that something was his fist in my face.

"Child," I spat, batting away his second attempt before it could land. Otherwise, I'd get angry and then accidentally kill him. Bellerose had lost enough members for one month. "Nice work proving my point."

Thankfully, we arrived at the Big Noise recording studio before our little chat could get any further out of hand. Jace pushed open the door before the car fully stopped, storming up the entry path to the glass monstrosity without looking back. Classic Jace.

"Thanks," I said to the driver, who was—quietly—

on my payroll. Lots of the Bellerose staff were and had been for years. No one else needed to know that, though. They weren't Ricci employees, but *mine*. "We'll try to keep this quick."

The driver nodded silently, indicating that he'd wait right there until we were done. The second car pulled up behind as I stepped out, and I waited for the three of them to get out.

"Brenda is on her way," Gray told me, his expression dark. "She's having a disagreement with Humphrey."

Again? Her husband was a twat. She should have left him two years ago when she discovered he was cheating. Instead, she went and got knocked up.

"Jace is inside," I said, nodding to the front door of the building. This wasn't Big Noise Records's head office, which was a high rise over in the business district. This was their *creation space,* which was a sprawling glass building on the side of the river, fully decked out with state-of-the-art recording studios and countless songwriting rooms. "He's in a mood."

Gray arched a brow, catching on immediately. I might have made a few pointed comments over the last week that gave him an idea what I thought of my former best friend.

Rhett just slouched his way up the path, his shoulders hunched and his hands stuffed in the pockets of his coat. Gray wrapped an arm around Billie, tucking her small body against his broad frame, and a pang of regret snapped inside my chest.

She'd always have a piece of my heart, but I'd accepted a long time ago that we didn't work together. There was too much *history*... and pain. For now, I'd be content to just see her happy with her new future, free of my messy family politics.

"Where is everyone?" Billie asked as we entered the main foyer. There were a few decorated Christmas trees scattered around, along with an enormous contemporary, bronze sculpture suspended over the space, seemingly hanging in thin air. Creepy. Her voice echoed, and it filled me with unease. "Is it usually this quiet in here?"

Rhett glanced around and shrugged. "Everyone is on vacation already. Even the wankers who release Christmas albums have had them out for weeks already, so this place is probably only open for our meeting with Fucker."

It made sense, but I couldn't convince my instincts to calm down.

Gray exchanged a knowing look with me, then smoothly transferred Billie into Rhett's care without her even sensing anything was wrong. "You two go on;

they're probably in the conference room," he told Rhett. "I'm going to hit the restroom."

"Aye, aye, Captain," Rhett drawled, and I briefly wondered if he'd been drinking in the car. His drug dependency was a concern, for sure. But he protectively wrapped an arm around Billie and continued past the vacant reception desk.

We waited until they'd rounded the corner, then without a word, Grayson and I both pulled our weapons.

"I'll take the ground floor," I murmured. "You check the upper level."

He jerked a nod, already moving toward the stairs on silent feet. Impressive, considering his size, the dress shoes he wore, and the marble floors.

Systematically, I checked room by room through the entire ground floor, trusting Grayson was doing the same on the upper level. When I returned to the foyer—bypassing the conference room where Billie, Rhett, and Jace were making uncomfortable conversation with a handful of corporate lawyers—Grayson was on his way back down the stairs.

"Anything?" I asked, already knowing his answer.

"Nothing," he confirmed. "Maybe we're just paranoid."

I frowned, glancing back out to where the cars were waiting. "Maybe."

Satisfied—for now—that there was no ambush waiting within the building, I followed Grayson to the conference room.

"Where's Tucker?" Gray asked, scowling around the room.

"Great question," Jace replied, his lip curling in a sneer. "We were just asking the same thing. He's the one who called this fucking meeting while we're supposed to be at Flo's wake. Is this all just a bullshit game to make us look like we don't care enough to attend her farewell?"

One of the corporate lawyers sighed, checking his watch. "If we knew..."

"Yeah, yeah, save it," Jace snapped back. "Five more minutes, then we're out of here. Understood?"

Grayson reached into his coat pocket and pulled out his phone, answering a call that must have vibrated since I hadn't heard anything ring.

"What's happened?" he asked, his tone sharp. He locked eyes with me, then he jerked his head toward the hallway. Without question, I stepped outside after him as he spoke again. "Slow down. How? She couldn't have—"

"Morgana?" I asked, and he nodded. I held out my

hand. "Give it to me." With a brief frown, he handed the phone over. "Is Vee okay?"

"I don't know, *Angelo*," Morgana snapped back with scathing-level sarcasm. "That's why I called Grayson. She woke up earlier and was rambling nonsense, asking where you all were. I gave her a sedative because she was going to hurt herself and put her back to bed. Now I've checked, and she's *gone*. Bed empty, nowhere to be seen. She's on so many drugs right now she could be in danger or—"

"Is my car still there?" I cut her off. Vee was drugged, but not dead. She could hotwire a car. "In the garage, is it there?"

Morgana paused, and her footsteps sounded through the phone. "No. No, it's gone; the garage door is open."

That was all I needed to hear. Tossing the phone back to Grayson, I pulled out my own and brought up the tracking app attached to all my favorite cars. Right at that moment, my Charger was—

"Here?" I said aloud, reading the map in confusion as I strode toward the front entrance. "What the fuck?"

Two seconds later, my battered, bruised, and delirious wife staggered through the glass doors screaming my name.

"Angelo!" she cried out as I ran to catch her before

she fell. "You have to get them out. Everyone needs to get out! They want you dead; they all want you dead!" She was rambling, panicked and unfocused as I picked her up, then her eyes rolled into her head, and she sagged with unconsciousness.

"Bad reaction to the drugs, maybe?" Grayson suggested, frowning hard at my beautiful, broken wife. "I didn't find anything suspicious on my sweep."

"Me neither," I agreed. Holding Vee close, I looked around the foyer. She needed to rest. Ideally, I needed to take her back to Grayson's house, but I was reluctant to leave Billie.

Gray held out his arms. "I'll take her out to the car," he offered. "Maybe just grab Billie to come back with us. Vee would like it if she was there when she woke, I think."

Good excuse. Yes. That.

I gratefully handed my wife over, knowing that he would take care of her, then kissed Valentina's head. "It'll be okay, *amore mio*; we'll take you home."

She moaned and mumbled something about Tom, and I sighed as I made my way back toward the conference room. *How did Vee know we were waiting for Tom?* Just before I got there, though, my wandering gaze snagged on a sign attached to a door.

B1 Fire Access.

Then Valentina's mumble clicked in my brain. She'd said *bomb*, not *Tom*. A cold thread of panic wove through me as I yanked the door open and hurried down the stairs with my gun drawn.

The basement was dark and silent, though. I found the light switch, flicking it on and waiting a moment while the space filled with light. Then I systematically made my way through a basement level full of janitor's closets, electrical supplies, spare furniture, all kinds of crap.

Then I found it.

Tucked in behind the fire extinguisher—like someone with a sick sense of humor had set it—a heavily wired plastic explosive with a rapidly declining digital display.

Adrenaline and fear filled me so fast I nearly choked on it as I ran full speed back to the stairwell. "Get out!" I bellowed even before I got to the top of the stairs. "Everyone get the fuck out!"

My shouting drew a quick enough response that Jace, Rhett, and Billie were already out of the conference room when I burst through the stairwell door. I dove at my Bella, sweeping her up as I screamed for Jace and Rhett to *run!*

Fuck the lawyers; they were dead already. But I could save Bella. I could save *Jace.*

The bomb detonated just as we reached the foyer. The sound deafened me, knocking me from my feet, and I rolled before landing to keep Billie safe. She was all that mattered.

Jace and Rhett were ahead of us, Rhett almost out the door already when he fell. I screamed at them to get up and *run*, but I couldn't even hear myself. Had I lost my voice, or had I lost my hearing?

Scrambling to my knees, I rolled Billie over. A small cut on her eyebrow leaked blood, but otherwise she seemed okay. Dazed, but okay.

I patted her cheek, probably harder than necessary, and pointed frantically at the exit. Behind us, fire had begun raging, and broken glass lay fucking *everywhere* in huge, jagged shards.

She nodded at me, using my grip to get back to her feet, then gasped in pain. She'd lost a shoe somewhere and stood right on broken glass. I didn't even hesitate before sweeping her up in my arms again and staggering for the exit. My left leg wasn't working properly, pain radiating from my knee, but it was unimportant.

Jace was on all fours, shaking his head with a hand pressed to his bleeding ear. Fuck. Had he burst an eardrum?

"Get up!" I snarled, this time hearing myself from

the end of a distant tunnel. I shifted Billie in my grip to hold her one-handed, then gripped the back of Jace's collar to literally drag him to his feet.

He staggered, wobbling dangerously, but I kept my grip on his shirt to pull him through the debris. We were getting out, all of us, if it was the last thing I did.

Billie was quivering against me, her whole body wracked with uncontrollable tremors of fear, and one glance over my shoulder told me why. The building was on fire, and she was locked in a memory of losing her parents.

When we reached the exit, I shoved Jace through so hard he collided with Grayson, who'd been running back in.

"Get him safe!" I shouted to Gray.

"Billie!" Jace exclaimed, his dazed expression clearing. Seeing him coherent, I forcefully peeled Billie from my arms and handed her fragile body to him.

"Take her," I barked. "Don't fucking leave her for even a second, am I clear?"

He nodded sharply, not hesitating to rush away from the cracked glass entry. Gray had run back in, and I joined him a second later to lift Rhett's dead weight between us and get him out.

"Where's Vee?" I asked, once Rhett was safely clear of the building.

Gray's eyes widened. "She ran back in. I held onto her as long as possible, but—" That explained the scratches all over his face and arms. I'd assumed they were from shattering glass, but no. Those were my wife's claw marks.

I nodded, swallowing hard. "Look after her for me, Gray. Keep her safe. Keep *them* safe."

Not waiting for his response, I sucked in a deep breath and ran headlong back into the burning building. Vee was in here somewhere, come to save us all, and I couldn't let her die for us.

"Vee!" I shouted, blinking through the smoke already billowing from recording studios. "Valentina! Where are you?"

In the distance I spotted a shadowy figure running toward me, and I ran straight for her. Thank *fuck* it was Vee and not one of the lawyers. She was coughing hard, her t-shirt over her mouth and nose as her eyes cast around in utter terror.

"Vee!" I exclaimed again, grabbing her around the waist. Another sharp lance of pain shot through my leg, and I nearly collapsed. "Vee, you *idiot*, we need to go!"

"I had to," she babbled back, her gaze unfocused, "I had to, A, my family set this all up. That's why they beat me, because they found me listening in and thought I would tell you. They set it all up with the Wilsons; it's all part of their—"

She cut off with a scream as a huge chunk of burning plaster broke from the ceiling and crashed to the floor of the hallway we stood in, cutting us off from the foyer.

No. Fuck that. We would not die like this. Not when it was all a setup from our mafia families.

"Come on," I grunted. "We need to go."

Gritting my teeth against the pain in my leg, I lifted Vee into my arms, holding her as close and tight as possible... then leapt directly over the flames of the burning plaster board. She screamed in terror as I ran a few steps to get her into the foyer, then had to drop her as the flames grabbed my pants.

"Get out!" I roared, pointing at the exit where Gray was already running back to collect her.

I dropped to the ground, rolling to put out the flames because they were already eating into my flesh and my survival instinct demanded I deal with it *right fucking now*. What a shame that instinct couldn't have waited just a few more moments.

As I flopped around like a fish, desperate to stop the agonizing pain of fire melting my flesh, my gaze caught on that fucking suspended sculpture. And on the single remaining cable holding it in the air directly above me.

Then it snapped, and a woman's bloodcurdling scream echoed through my head as the whole world went black.

To Be Continued in...

SHATTERED DREAMS

March, 2023

also by tate james

#3 TBC (TBC)

Undercover Sinners

#1 Altered By Fire

#2 Altered by Lead

#3 Altered by Pain (TBC)

also by jaymin eve

Boys of Bellerose (Dark, RH rock star romance 18+)

Book One: Poison Roses (Release Jan 2023)

Book Two: Dirty Truths (Release Feb 2023)

Book Three: Shattered Dreams (Release March 2023)

Book Four: Beautiful Thorns (Release April 2023)

Demon Pack (Complete PNR/Urban Fantasy 18+)

Book One: Demon Pack

Book Two: Demon Pack Elimination

Book Three: Demon Pack Eternal

Shadow Beast Shifters (Complete PNR/Urban Fantasy 18+)

Book One: Rejected

Book Two: Reclaimed

Book Three: Reborn

Book Four: Deserted

Book Five: Compelled

Book Six: Glamoured

Supernatural Prison Trilogy (Complete UF series 17+)

Book One: Dragon Marked

Book Two: Dragon Mystics

Book Three: Dragon Mated

Book Four: Broken Compass

Book Five: Magical Compass

Book Six: Louis

Book Seven: Elemental Compass

Supernatural Academy (Complete Urban Fantasy/PNR 18+)

Year One

Year Two

Year Three

Royals of Arbon Academy (Complete Dark Contemporary Romance 18+)

Book One: Princess Ballot

Book Two: Playboy Princes

Book Three: Poison Throne

Titan's Saga (Complete PNR/UF. Sexy and humorous 18+)

Book One: Releasing the Gods

Book Two: Wrath of the Gods

Book Three: Revenge of the Gods

Dark Legacy (Complete Dark Contemporary high school romance 18+)

Book One: Broken Wings

Book Two: Broken Trust

Book Three: Broken Legacy

Secret Keepers Series (Complete PNR/Urban Fantasy)

Book One: House of Darken

Book Two: House of Imperial

Book Three: House of Leights

Book Four: House of Royale

Storm Princess Saga (Complete High Fantasy)

Book One: The Princess Must Die

Book Two: The Princess Must Strike

Book Three: The Princess Must Reign

Curse of the Gods Series (Complete Reverse Harem Fantasy 18+)

Book One: Trickery

Book Two: Persuasion

Book Three: Seduction

Book Four: Strength

Novella: Neutral

Book Five: Pain

Printed in Great Britain
by Amazon

20581164R10251